Bones of the
Black Warrior

Bones of the Black Warrior
By Doug White

Published by Creative Texts Publishers, LLC
PO Box 50
Barto, PA 19504
www.creativetexts.com
ISBN: 978-1-64738-110-3

Bones of the Black Warrior

by

Doug White

Table of Contents

Chapter 1
The Runners

October 15, 1540
Southwest corner of present Alabama

Nitakechi and his twin brother, Apuksunnubbee, whom he simply called Bee, emerged from the shadows of the tall pines into the clearing of a green, grassy meadow. Immediately, without any urging or words, the two broke into a run back towards the village of Corn Town, their home. Normally, Bee would win easily, being somewhat lighter and with slightly longer legs than his fraternal twin, affectionately referred to as Nita. Today it was Nita who ran faster and at the halfway mark passed his thinner brother.

"Hey Nita, not fair. Slow down. You carry my otter and I'll carry your five squirrels and we'll see who is faster then," Bee yelled between gasps for breath.

"Bee, you will long remember this day, the first time I beat you in a race," the slightly taller sibling taunted as he pulled ahead. Just as he finished his sentence, a brown blur passed his peripheral vision. His brother had dropped the otter and spear and was sprinting the last thirty paces to the finish line of the twin cypress trees. "Bee you're cheating!"

"Brother, we are both members of the Deer Clan, as Mother has told us our whole lives," Bee said as he stopped running just past the parallel trees and whirled around to go back and pick up his otter prize.

"And what do the deer, the Kinta, do so well? Run! Run fast! Ha!"

"But I made it across with my kill for the evening meal. That should count for something, brother," pleaded Nita.

"Indeed, quite indeed Nita. I will tell all our friends and Uncle Mataha that there was a race today. You didn't win, but you did come in second place," teased Bee as he retrieved his spear, the dead otter and slung them both over his shoulder. His eyes grew wide as a rock about the size of his thumb went whizzing past his ear. The offended brother had heard enough.

"I could have hit you if I wanted, but Mother would scold me and likely not feed me dinner if you'd shown up with a bruise on your chest. Just know I can as I've been practicing with my sling. You never even asked how I killed these squirrels? With my sling, my rocks flew straight, hard and true to stun all five. Then I finished them off with my bone knife. So, watch your tongue."

Bee warily strode past his brother who stood firmly on his ground and fiddled with another rock between his thumb and forefinger. "So, you've practiced your sling? Very good Nita, very good. Let's go home and show Mother our kills for the cooking fire. I'm hungry." Bee said respectfully as they continued their walk towards Corn Town and their family lodge.

"I too am hungry, but Uncle Mataha will not hear of our footrace today. Right?" Nita said as he tossed his rock up and caught it, making sure his brother saw he still had another available.

"Uncle Mataha will only hear of your talent that's so effective as to empty the forests of all the squirrels," Bee now said in a less condescending tone and a slight dose of humor.

With that Nita pointed to a pine, made sure his brother was watching and swung his slingshot, the rock missile, hitting it squarely about five feet above the ground. Bee nodded in approval, reaching out his free hand to rub his strong-arm brother on the head. Rivals yes and always competitive, but also best friends and fiery defenders of each other. True brothers.

Apuksunnubbee and Nitakechi were enjoying their day off from the tribal work detail. Tomorrow they would be hauling dirt from the pit to continue the mound of the eagle, a talako, that was taking shape. The brothers belonged to a community of about 450 members. Their community was one of six towns, spread out evenly around the neighboring countryside, collectively known as the Yowani sub-tribe of the greater Choctaw Nation. For protection purposes, the six towns encircled the Yowani capital town of Mabila.

"I already dread tomorrow. Carrying basket after basket of dirt is so boring. I hate it," Nita said before they reached the village, where words like that would mean not only a painful punishment, but dishonor the lodge of his Mother. "Mico had us finish the burial mound less than one full moon ago and now we're beginning a new mound. I mean are we really sure the Great Spirit even really exists?"

Bones of the Black Warrior

"Shh, brother. Don't say that!" admonished Bee, who also added a quick jab from the blunt end of his spear into his brother's backside. "Understand this, the land, the water, the food is all because of the Great Spirit Nanapesa, Nita. For our mother's sake, please never utter those blasphemous words about our duty to build a great mound for the blessings of our Great Spirit. Nanapesa. Promise me!"

"Gosh, Bee, I didn't know you were so, so religious. When did this come about?"

"When Uncle Mataha took me to meet his friend, Roniaba, when he moved his family to Corn Town, this was when you were sick with the sweats, twice ago, when the last moon was round.

Uncle took me to meet his new friend saying he is a great and talented man, who happens to be Cantea's father and one day hopefully, my father-in-law. Roniaba, has great knowledge of Nanapesa and even speaks to him directly."

"Impossible brother, that's not true; no one has that power," protested Nita, who then realized his brother's other bold statement of marrying Cantea, the most beautiful maiden in Corn Town, but chose not to respond to such a boastful wish as a union with Cantea, who was well-known and admired from afar by the young men and boys of their village.

"I too did not believe it, but after a demonstration by Roniaba, I changed my mind... He told us that the spirit predicted a great flock of ducks would fly by just after sunrise and with our arrows we could knock down a great number, if we were ready. And it happened like that, just as he predicted. The sun was completely shadowed by the huge number of birds. Roniaba said the Great Spirit had come and alerted him to the ducks. It was proven true. I ate duck at the morning, midday and evening meals. You were ill, but a grand feast we had, little brother."

"I still don't know. Bee, you seem easily convinced sometimes."

"Uncle Mataha said Roniaba has done similar things for years and holds great power in all the Yowani towns. No chief will commit to an important action without first consulting Roniaba. He's not only a true prophet, but has great worth as an interpreter. Uncle says he knows the tongue of the Cherokee, Coosa, Osochee, and the Apalachee."

"I can see that. If he has the ability to talk to other tribes, that is useful, but still?"

3

"Uncle told me to keep my mouth closed about Roniaba. He's afraid another tribe will come to capture him and enslave him for his powers and connection to Nanapesa. You must promise to never reveal what I have just said, Nita. Especially the part about Cantea. I am not sure she even knows who I am, but she will soon."

"Sure brother, if you ask, I will do it," Nita said as he punched his twin's upper arm to retaliate for being jabbed in the backside and laughed a quick chuckle at the admission that the beautiful Cantea was hardly ready to be his bride. He'd grown a more aggressive streak lately and wanted to make sure his brother knew he wasn't going to allow any disrespect.

Showing up at the family wigwam, or atepa, with five squirrels would not draw anyone's attention or envy, but a plump otter was another issue. Bee hung back and instructed his brother to procure a buffalo robe and bring it back as a covering for the otter. Like all the other six towns of the Yowani Choctaw, theirs was plagued by the unfortunate inhabitants known as the female witches and conjure men, who provided no real everyday value to the village, in Nita's opinion. He believed they only persuaded those of a weaker mind about the spirit's coming and going and how to care for the ancestral bones. Nita was not spiritual, knew his uncle and mother disapproved, nor did he see any power in the bones of someone who died long ago. If Bee walked in with a fat otter the witches and conjurers could be all over their lodge proclaiming great insights into the future in exchange for a delicious, meaty meal. Nita had to admire his brother's ability to think ahead like he'd just shown.

That night, Uncle Mataha, Mother, Bee and himself enjoyed a fine dinner of squirrel, otter and ahe, or sweet potatoes. Nita was briefly tempted to bring up the subject of the prophet, Roniaba, but was quickly reminded he'd promised his brother to forget the subject. It would greatly shame Bee if he knew he'd been promised by his uncle to keep a secret and could not do so. Nevertheless, Nita wanted to bring up the possibility that Roniaba had just made a lucky guess about the ducks. After all, anyone old enough to notice knew the birds flew over in great flocks as the weather turned colder. Could not anyone make a lucky guess that one morning ducks will fly over the village? To Nita, yes, the easy answer was of course.

The next day the twins worked. Nita paused for a break from hauling dirt up the side of a manufactured hill to build the mound of the eagle on this glorious day. A new burial mound was needed as the old one, commonly called Foni Laua, which was their native tongue for 'many bones' could not hold more of their deceased ancestors. The sacred bones provided a physical link to their collective pasts. All members of the tribe were taught from a young age to attend to them with reverence.

A bright blue, cloudless sky, a mild breeze was blowing and the usual thick air from the heat of the sun was not beating them down. As Bee was talking to Cantea at the far edge of the dirt pit and Nita was positioned squarely in the center of the growing mound of soil, drinking water, when Uncle Mataha came up, running at full speed. He came upon Nita first.

"Young nephews, do not question me, only do as I say. Run to your lodge, grab your arrows and war club. Word has come that we have invaders, and all warriors are needed in Mabila for battle. Then, place yourselves at the far end of the circle of pines, underneath the twin trees in the Sacred Meadow with the other braves and await further orders. Go now!"

Nita's excitement was unbounded. This is what he'd practiced the last two years for, battle with another tribe, likely the Coosa, to the direction of the sun's rising. Heeding his uncle's instructions, Nita also packed up a deerskin bag of rocks and his slingshot. He and Bee flew to the meadow and awaited the others in the cool shade of the cypress trees. After only being there a moment, they were joined by four dozen or so other males from their village. Waiting in the Sacred Meadow, a rumor went about the men that these invaders were not hostile Coosas, but men of an unknown kind, never before seen by any Yowani Choctaw.

Nita and Bee studied the others gathered as entire male populations of Corn Town, except for the very young and very old, sat on the shaded grass. Off alone were Uncle Mataha, Roniaba, the village mico and a representative from the capital of Mabila, talking in hushed whispers while the Choctaw gathered in the Sacred Meadow watched intently. Eventually three of the four were shaking their collective heads in disbelief and finally, in a mocking manner at whatever the representative from Mabila had said. Surely, the words that had just reached their ears had to be some elaborate joke?

Doug White

(Nita and Bee, of course, had no concept of longitude and latitude, unknown to the New World, but their Sacred Meadow outside Corn Town and twin cypress trees, revered by their residents, were located at latitude 31 north, longitude 87 west. Or, in present day southwest Alabama, 23 miles east of the Mississippi border, 46 miles north of the Gulf of Mexico.)

Chapter 2
The Don

October 17, 1540

Diego was happy just trying to take it all in. So far, in the past year and now in his sixteenth year, 1540, he'd seen a vast array of God's handiwork in the New World. Having landed in Florida with their expedition leader in May of 1539, Diego was amazed at all he'd seen and encountered. Just a year earlier he was a meager son of a cattle shepherd and altar boy at the Church of San Miguel in Jerez de Los Caballeros, Spain where his priest introduced him to this famous man who was looking for men and capable teenage boys to accompany him on his upcoming journey of exploration to the New World. Diego, following his fraternal twin brother, Vasco's lead, had forged their father's signature to the expedition's secretary for the family patriarch's permission. Under the cover of night, the two Etchevarria brothers ran away and joined the troupe for a chance of enrichment.

Luckily, Diego and Vasco both easily looked the part of the expedition's minimum seventeen years of age when they'd joined, what to them and hoped to be, not only just a great adventure, but one that would enrich both their purses. Vasco, the older by one hour, looked more like father with darker skin, brown eyes and brown hair, while Diego favored mother, a native of the Galicia region, with green eyes, a lighter complexion and sandy brownish-blond hair. After landing in Florida a year ago, Diego recalled the expedition with 700 men, 250 horses, 200 pigs, 50 war dogs and 75 cattle for which he, Vasco, and one other teenage boy were responsible.

All the way back in Spain and on their sea voyage, they'd heard rumors of fabulous gold for the taking in the New World. The Spaniards, led by the experienced soldier and negotiator, had previously traveled up a long, low range of mountains called the Appalachians by the native savages, but so far, the rumor of gold had been just that, rumors. The land was quite different from their native southwest Spain of Extremadura. Here, there were many more rivers and the unimaginable, lushly great, expansive forests of the New World that stretched as far as the Old-World eyes could see, along with the good fortune that these mountains were considerably easier to cross. By late spring of 1540, the intrepid leader had given up his northern treks into the Appalachians and had turned south and west.

Once out of the ever-decreasing mountains and finally low strings of hills, the expedition leader had found a large expansive grass plain with many a small clear-running stream through its heart. He proclaimed it a fine place to set up camp, rest the men, graze their horses and fatten the pigs and cattle. Diego and Vasco knew the drill without being told. The three cattle shepherds took their valuable beef towards the center of the expedition's camp line, where protection could be offered from thieving Indios and the big cats and bears occasionally encountered. The third shepherd and now good friend of Vasco and Diego was Pablo, who immediately assisted the brothers in roping off a perimeter for the cattle to graze.

Making small talk as they set their rope lines, Vasco volunteered what he'd overheard their superior talking to the quartermaster of the gunpowder supplies. He recounted that the quartermaster knew some of the contents of the expedition leader's last will and testament. Their rich leader wanted to be known as more than Pizarro's first lieutenant in the conquest of Peru. He wanted the entire world to know, after his death, that he was not just a man of courage, but also one of charity and considerable wealth.

The expedition leader's wealth was so vast that before making preparations for the New World, he had prepaid for a chapel to be erected in his hometown. Also, once completed the priest would hold five masses a week specifically for his immediate family. In addition, separate masses would be held daily for the Virgin Mary, another for the Holy Ghost, and another just for the lost souls in Purgatory. Lastly there would be an annual sum awarded to the town's three poorest damsels of marrying age to assist their monetary needs to establish a dowry and eventually acquire husbands.

Diego and Vasco knew their leader was affluent, however, this new information implied he was obviously not far from being as rich as King Carlos. The brothers marveled that such a fortune could have been gained in a short period of time and by one not of the noble class. Their leader had made quite the impression on Francisco Pizzaro and had accompanied his troops to Peru. His brave leadership in battle with the Inca Indians, superb horsemanship and unwavering loyalty to Pizzaro made him the right man at the right time to reap the lavish rewards graciously given by God from the pagans of the Inca Empire.

Vasco and Diego, like the expedition leader, were not first-born sons and thus not in line to inherit the family farm. Thus, gambling on a career in soldiering and exploration made sense for both of them. The twins could only pray that their leap of faith might reap a portion of the profits their courageous leader had strongly suggested his followers could find.

After Diego, Pablo and Vasco herded the livestock into the roped-off pen, another teen boy brought them over half a loaf of bread, a thick slice of pork, and each a goblet of wine. They welcomed the food and drink as they walked the perimeter of the improvised corral. In between bites, Pablo offered up the latest camp gossip, "the Don is requiring every man, except the priests, be trained to protect themselves should the Indio attack. He added that one of our native interpreters, one they call the Cherokee prophet, had predicted an attack any day now."

"I don't mind learning to fight, in fact, I love holding a sword in my hand. Wielding one gives me a desire to one day be a soldier," Vasco volunteered without anyone asking.

"I agree," echoed Diego. "The feeling is all-powerful. I'm holding life or death in my hand.

Someday I hope to own one of the finest swords ever made; Toledo steel."

"Perfectly stated brother," said Vasco. "It is a grand feeling. The might rises from your hand, up your elbow, into your shoulder and finally into your mind. The same strength and powerful swords of our great countryman, Hernan Cortes, conquered the pagan Aztecas."

It went unsaid and as soon as the meal was consumed, the three teen boys found appropriate sticks and began sparring with their practice swords. Another teen male, Alberto, came over and hailed Pablo, Vasco and Diego. Alberto said he was about to feed the seven war dogs that were his responsibility and asked his fellow teens if they'd like to come and watch. After they cast dice for arrangements for who would remain behind, Pablo lost and stayed behind.

On the walk over to the designated area where the dogs were, Alberto, in somewhat of a braggadocious manner, told them about his dogs. "I have three male sons of the famous war dog Leoncico. Leoncico was sired by the even more famous Becerrillo who was the greatest of war dogs. Six years ago, on an island called Bimini where Don Ponce de Leon was in the process of conquering, alone, the great war dog was set loose on a group of about fifty Indios who were fleeing the conquistadors' approach. The Indios had been ordered not to flee, so when they did, had to be punished. All by himself, Becerrillo intercepted the fleeing group and in less than one quarter of an hour's time, he had killed twenty-three pagans and on verbal orders from his handler, herded the remaining back to the village to serve the needs of the Governor de Leon's conquistadors."

At the same time, Alberto, Vasco and Diego, somewhat excited, broke into a run. Then, they cleared a small creek and were at the dog encampment. One of the other dog handlers yelled a few obscenities at Alberto for walking away at feeding time, but he shrugged it off and went to his seven dogs. The animals were tremendous. All were fully grown, male Spanish mastiffs. There were also a dozen Irish Wolfhounds under the harness of three handlers; the powerfully built canines prized for their speed, sense of smell and keen eyesight. The huge Spanish mastiffs, each wearing a thick leather apron protecting internal organs, a small metal cap with two sharpened steel horns, a collar of long, sharp spikes and a woven vest for protecting the chest area.

Then, before Vasco and Diego had much time to think about what was happening, a young Coosa Indio girl, probably about eight years of age, was brought into the midst of the seven mastiffs. Something had badly injured the girl's leg and she no longer had any value to the expedition's wants and needs. Alberto ordered Vasco and Diego back about twenty feet, for their protection, dropped the individual leashes of each dog and then gave the order.

"Sic 'em!" ordered Alberto in a masterful tone.

With that, the beasts jumped on the girl, who immediately began to scream. Their massive weight of 200 pounds per dog easily dropped her to the ground. With hissing and growling one dog ended it quickly with a decisive bite to her throat and there was no more screaming. The ravenous dogs attacked her midsection, ripped her torso open and began devouring the internal organs in great gulps.

Bones of the Black Warrior

Alberto, with a huge grin on his face, looked over in the direction of Diego and Vasco, who were speechless, but watched nonetheless. The dogs, so vital to the expedition, had to be fed. Soon, the animals finished eating, there was little meat left on her bones; a little on her hands, feet and scalp as it was covered by her long black hair. Suddenly sorry to have witnessed the site, Diego and Vasco headed back to their area of the camp, before their meal of pork and bread reappeared.

Halfway back to camp the twins were alerted to a loud series of noises. A nearby cursing soldier immediately recognized the sounds of two swords being beaten against the other in anger. He broke into a run towards the source, hidden behind a green wall of shrubs. Vasco and Diego took one look at each other and began to follow. Coming into a clearing, a circle of soldiers were loudly cheering and placing bets continuously with one another. Two soldiers, one in his late forties, the other in his early twenties were fiercely battling it out in the center of the circle. They wore no armor on their respective heads or legs. This was not battle practice; this was a real fight.

"Why are they doing this?" Diego asked another teenage boy in the line of the circle.

"Senor Ruiz, the older gentleman, is angry with Senor Mendez. Ruiz had taken a beautiful young Indio woman to share his blanket each night. Captain Gallegos had sent Ruiz out on a mission today and Mendez used his absence to advance on the woman. She resisted and Mendez cut off her ears and her nose, disfiguring her," the other teen explained.

"I shall be for the old man then," declared Diego. "There are plenty of women here so Mendez deserves whatever wound he receives."

Clang-bang, clang-bang. The steel swords manufactured in central Spain met with a violent crash and the ringing echo bounded off the trees and back to the men and boys gathered. Diego glanced to the side to see Vasco mimicking the motions of the fighters, slashing and thrusting with an imaginary sword. Diego could not resist the opportunity, left the circle and placed himself in front of Vasco and he too wielded an imaginary sword.

They were too involved in their play fight to notice a priest, one of the twelve on the expedition, running through the circle of onlookers. Surprised by their sudden interruption, the fighting men stopped. The lone priest tried to reason with Ruiz and Mendez to settle their differences, stating the health and welfare of both were paramount to the mission. It didn't work and Mendez once more slashed at Ruiz who responded and deflected the blow before raring back to deliver his own mighty slash. It was after a few more clang-bangs of the fight that it happened. Four more priests pushed through the crowd and this time came prepared. Two of the priests carried a life-size wooden statue of Christ on the Cross. Immediately, everyone knelt, dropped their heads in reverence and crossed themselves. The other two priests got between Ruiz and Mendez and after a few words encouraged them to rise and leave the circle in opposite directions. The priests then began a chorus from a solemn chant as they formed together, walked away and the excitement was over.

(Life returned to normal in the camp of the great Spanish explorer and conqueror, the Adelantado of Florida and Governor Cuba, Hernando de Soto, located at latitude 31.20 north, longitude 87.50 west.)

Chapter 3
The Black Warrior

Mid-morning
October 19, 1540

Bee and Nita, if they had not heard it with their own ears, would not have believed the words of Roniaba. After the assembled Corn Town warriors marched toward the rising sun and arrived in Mabila, the word passed they would be addressed by none other than their supreme chief. Six thousand braves, including Bee and Nita, in hushed reverence, sat among the assembled warriors inside a grand log-walled palisade awaiting an address from their levithan chief of all the Choctaw Nation, Tuskaluca.

(The grand chief had inherited a rare and great gift of physical stature. Oral accounts passed down generations described the chief as seven feet tall in a time when most adult men, Old World and New, were typically five-foot-four.)

The mood inside the huge Choctaw fortress of logs was not lost on Chief Tuskaluca as he took to the earthen mound, usually reserved for the most holy of days, in the center of the compound to address his anxious warriors. He saw his duty, hushed the throng of gathered warriors, and addressed them with his booming and forceful voice. Chief Tuskaluca recalled a story from his youth. He told of a trip downriver, when he was yet to become a man, to the great sea of salty water on which he accompanied four uncles to gather fish.

Fearing ridicule when they returned to the tribe, for such a ridiculous story, the uncles and he had all sworn secrecy and to this day, he'd honored their wish, but now it was time to reveal what his eyes had seen. His fishing party had witnessed a gigantic canoe approach the land, halt and spit out a small dugout filled with a handful of men. The small vessel beached nearby as they hid in the reeds and in awe saw the hairy-faced white-skinned men come ashore. On this long-ago afternoon, the snowy men split up in pairs and began to scour the nearby land. The chief recounted how he and his uncles eventually retreated, but not until the strange men had walked by close enough for their inspection. Yes, they looked different, had hair on their face and spoke an odd language, but they were just men.

Chief Tuskaluca continued his speech, stating now the white-skinned invaders had returned, but were now far more numerous. He'd heard the rumors and said likely some assembled here also had heard. The invaders with no skin coloring and hair about their faces were approaching Mabila and would soon be among them. Another difference from the first time Tuskaluca had seen the invaders was that they possessed dogs of gigantic proportions, could straddle their animals' bodies and swiftly ride upon its back!

Rumor ran roughshod through the gigantic fort at Mabila. Were they here to battle? Why are the invaders here? Chief Tuskaluca sensed the apprehension and once more spoke. Despite the rumors, the invaders were not gods or immune to death. They and their giant dogs were mortal and could be killed by Choctaw spears and arrows, he assured his warriors. That was why they were assembled here today. Calmed by their leader's showing of himself and his words, the 6000 warriors let loose a mighty war whoop.

Still too far away to have heard the warriors' hearty cry and making considerably better progress now on the flat plains, the always bold Spanish marched directly towards the Indio capital of Mabila. De Soto had been warned by the Cherokee tribe that to the direction of the sea breeze and of the setting sun, lived a great tribe, the Choctaw, led by a formidable chief, taller by three heads than any normal warrior. His name was Tuskaluca and could be easily recognized by two identifiers; he always painted his entire body black as readied for battle and his extraordinary height. The Cherokee warned de Soto not to enter the land of the Choctaw and raise the ire of the fierce Black Warrior chief.

Governor de Soto had heard this ploy before; scare tactics were usually employed for a reason. These heathen savage Choctaw must possess something of great value to have another tribe issue this warning. To the great explorer this meant only one thing: gold! At long last, after more than a year and a half of wandering with nothing to show, the governor felt his reward of treasure was near. His fifty advance scouts, all on horseback, returned to the main fold. The leader verbalized these thoughts to any within earshot. Just as the Choctaw chief's enthusiasm was contagious, so was that of de Soto to his troops. Then, the leader paused to think, yes, if his dozen priests could convert some of the Indios to Christianity, that would bode well for his legacy, too.

The Spanish governor of Florida called his number one lieutenant, Commander Luis de Moscoso, who had been one of the fifty who'd gone ahead, to his side for his opinion and subsequent instructions. Neither man was going to waste this golden chance for an opportunity if it presented itself on this flat, treeless plain before them. If the hostiles made the mistake of leaving their fortress, their two men of Spain knew their experienced, vaunted and deadly effective calvary would be the deciding factor in a victory.

Further behind the two leaders, Vasco and Diego paused from the march for a minute and respectively wiped the sweat from their brows as they cast their gaze skyward to the mid-morning sun as their thoughts wistfully dreamed of home. "Think of it Vasco, this same sun we are now seeing on this day is also being seen by our family back in Extremadura."

"You're right Diego. They are probably sitting down to a nice hot bowl of cocido extremeno. Oh, what I'd give for a meal from Mama's cooking pot."

"The days are getting shorter, and the nights are cooler. Back home they will have finished the fattening of the hogs under the spread of the oaks and acorns aplenty. The slaughter is beginning," waxed Diego.

"Papa would bring the meat to Mama, and she would do her magic; jamon iberico. Oh, so good."

"The finest of all hams, so tender no knife is necessary, it melts like butter on a hot day," Vasco added. He then joined Diego in the shallow puddle of water and like his twin cupped up water to splash on his face and wet his long hair. Movement to their left caused a pause in their morning baths. Out of the long cast shadows from slightly ahead, in the only stand of pines in sight, moved the nearly naked, light-brown skinned porters following the priests who led them to a shaded rest before preparing the midday daily Mass. There were a few dozen Coosa women, tall and strong, hand-picked to accompany the priests and their luggage, belongings and religious paraphernalia. The Indio porters moved in complete silence. The

15

priests, as usual, were singing hymns as they marched, low, solemn in their bearing of indiscernible words.

As was their normal marching order, Vasco, Diego and the other herders of the cattle, pigs and a few spare war horses were bringing up the rear. After they passed the copse of tall trees the priests, the Coosa porters and the rest climbed a slight rise in the land. There Vasco and Diego viewed Mabila. Spying on an Indio village usually was no cause for excitement, however, this was a different scene. Mabila was no circle of small log huts; it was a gigantic wooden palisade of pine tree trunks rising fifteen or more feet above the ground, raising the question of why the elaborate effort? Were they protecting something of value? Maybe these savages did possess gold and silver?

Chief Tuskaluca's troops were in a fevered, frenzied pitch, but this was not to his liking or goal. His plan called to lay a trap so the chief summoned his hand-picked dozen leaders to the base of the holy platform and instructed them to settle the men. His battle plan was to disperse all but a quarter of his forces for show; then half of that remainder would hide inside the grand ceremonial lodges on the far side of the compound and lull the hairy-faced-dog-riders into a false security while the last quarter would exit the fort's rear gate and sneak around behind the approaching invaders. At the appropriate time, they would all burst forth and surround the invaders before bludgeoning them with war clubs and firing thousands of arrows, as per his carefully designed plan.

After his twelve sub-chiefs moved to their appointed duties, Tuskaluca called in his personal guard which were his ten best fighters. He instructed them to escort his gifts outside the walls to the hairy-faced invaders and to leave their bows and arrows behind. They would present a submissive, peaceful scenario. Next, he summoned a small number of the drum and flute musicians, along with fourteen beautiful maidens. The maidens already were prepared with fresh chestnut bread and brewed holly leaf tea and lastly, Roniaba, the prophet and interpreter from Corn Town.

Uncle Mataha had been busily biding Chief Tuskaluca's orders since they arrived in Mabila and had seen little of his nephews. Now he and Cantea accompanied Roniaba out from the holy platform towards the main gate. Nita and Bee had no idea Cantea had come to Mabila, but there she was, among the fourteen young maidens, bearing gifts of food. The fort's entrance opened and the three joined the select warriors, other maidens and musicians to go meet the hairy faces.

The flutes and drums began a lively, happy song as they marched out on the flat plain.

This planned and noisy distraction from Tuskaluca would, he hoped, cover his 1,500 warriors' exit from the rear of his grand stockade. Nita and Bee felt lucky as they would be among those who were to run directly away into the nearest wooded area. From there they would trek around and to the rear of the invaders, all the while covered by the trees and bushy undergrowth. Included in this number. Nita couldn't believe his good fortune and took immense pride in the fact that Uncle Mataha had lent him his personal war club for the upcoming battle. Their uncle had told Bee and Nita to stay close to one another and that Chief Tuskaluca was the greatest of all chiefs and had never lost a battle. Also, to remain confident as their sheer numbers were ten-fold those of the hairy-faces.

Across the plain, Captain Gallegos rode up to the outer edge of the group where Vasco and Diego stood and dismounted his horse, both he and the horse already in full armor. "I have an important job and it can only be handled by someone out of the fight. You there, young man, what is your name?" the soldier said directly to Diego. After he answered, Deigo did as he was told and followed the cavalry captain. The two moved over and away from all the others and knelt down as if in prayer.

The soldier questioned him if he was literate, to which Diego gave an affirmative response. "You will not be expected to fight. In fact, obey me and do not enter the fight. Am I clear? I have a sacred duty, given to me before each battle, directly from the governor. Here." Captain Gallegos reached beneath his breastplate armor and produced a small leather pouch and then another rectangular leather bag. He instructed the teenage boy not to open the pouch of Governor de Soto's gold coins, that he'd already counted them and recorded their value.

Handing the boy a carbon stick and a scrap of parchment paper, Diego was to record details: the larger purse held the Governor's gold, the smaller his own. He would also put to paper where they were now, how he came to possess them, the date and that he was instructed to hold the two on his person. Both coin purses should remain tied shut at all times. Capt. Gallegos also gave strict instructions that their leader should, God forbid,

17

die in battle, and the money should be returned to his home church back in Jerez de Los Caballeros, Spain. Capt. Gallegos explained normally he had the duty of guarding the Don's personal bank, but a spy had let on that inside the Indio palisade were over 7000 warriors. Today, he feared might be his last day on God's earth and someone not involved in battle should hold the important purse of their leader. As an afterthought, should he die, his own modest purse of fifty silver quarter reals should also go to benefit the Don's chapel. Gallegos also ordered Diego to keep his purse contents separate.

Diego was astonished. He had just been handed a tremendous responsibility. Sensing the captain was in no mood to tarry or any further discussion, Diego did as instructed and secreted the small, but heavy pouch, along with the small one, into a goat skin bag he always carried over his shoulder. "Go with God young one and most importantly protect our leader's money," the burly captain stated as he moved back to his war horse.

At the same time, from a distance at the head of the column, de Soto ordered de Moscoso, Mendez, Rangel, Captain Ruiz and ten infantry to cinch up their armor, batten down their helmets, and mount up for the short ride out to meet the Indios marching out from their protective palisade. Walking with them was their own Indio, Oncona, a Cherokee interpreter who'd been with them almost a year and well-versed in Spanish now. As they slowly made their way, de Soto instructed Ruiz to have Oncona immediately relay his demand for the surrender of the fort and that the chief of the Choctaw must come out and submit. He would be held hostage to ensure no harm would befall the Spaniards and Tuskaluca should also make the necessary arrangements to feed de Soto's army who planned to camp here and rest for three days.

Ruiz, de Moscoso, nor de Soto verbalized that once the Choctaw chief was their hostage, there would be a demand for ransom in the form of gold and silver. This method had proven extremely successful, right before de Soto's eyes, in the Inca Campaign with Francisco Pizarro. Holding their leader, Atahualpa, captive in 1532 had produced an entire room of gold as plunder. The gold's total weight was an incomprehensible fifteen cartas.

(Present equivalent 5000 pounds)

Bones of the Black Warrior

Oncona did not show any surprise at Ruiz's words as he'd repeated the same to twenty other chiefs encountered on their journey so far. The two parties of emissaries marched closer, halted and each side sized up the other. The musicians ceased playing as Governor de Soto's eyes immediately inspected the Indio's wrists, necks, ears and ankles for gold or silver ornamentation, but sadly found none, even on the fourteen young women, one of which was extraordinarily beautiful. This one could likely start trouble between Ruiz and Mendez, the governor silently thought for a brief moment before returning his attention to Oncona who was engaging the opposite Indio spokesman now. The two ceased talking, de Soto watched and listened. Why were these Indios not taking action? Were they now silently inspecting the Spaniards' fighting ability?

Dismounting, Ruiz approached de Soto,"Governor sir we have an issue. Oncona tells me…"

"I heard his words, captain. The chief's message is defiant and says he serves no man; that others serve him, and we should not tarry but immediately remove ourselves from his territory. Correct?" de Soto said, his voice growing into a guttural growl as he spoke.

Then, to the Spaniard's surprise, their interpreter began speaking on his own accord to the visitors in their midst. That action prompted the expedition's second in command, de Moscoso, to also dismount and approach the natives. Just as de Soto had expected, Ruiz singled out the prettiest Indio girl and took her by the arm to escort her back to his tent. It was Cantea and her father, Roniaba, who moved over to prevent what he saw as an abduction and spoke in Cherokee to Oncona, "These hair-faces must be taught a harsh lesson."

"You are correct, my Choctaw brother," Oncona answered in his language as Roniaba shook his deerskin cloak free of his shoulders, revealing two ochre-stained war clubs. The Choctaw interpreter, incorrectly identifying Captain Ruiz as the invader soldier in charge, moved toward the Spaniard with the intent of rescuing his daughter. Mendez, even though Ruiz's recent disfigurement of his Indio girl had angered him, quickly decided deterrence was necessary. In a flash, the angry soldier of fortune drew his sword and moved in on the arrogant Indio with two, heavy, red sticks.

(Hernando de Soto, his expedition, including Vasco and Diego, Chief Tuskaluca and his 6000 warriors, including Bee and Nita, had no clue that their collective feet were planted on latitude 31.5 north, longitude 87.2 west; on the cusp of an event of world-changing magnitude only moments away.)

Chapter 4
Born Under Fire

August 29, 1813
4:30 p.m.

A scorching hot day had just become significantly hotter. August was always insufferable in this portion of the Mississippi Territory of the young United States. However, these were days of war. Hostilities had begun between the U.S. and Great Britain in June of 1812. Both sides of the conflict were spread thin and as the theater of war shifted to the American South, proxies were imposed on both sides. For the British, setting a $5 bounty (equalling $150 today) for the scalps of any American settler, man, woman or child, was eagerly accepted by the restless Creek Indian tribe. Already prompted to eradicate the white invaders by the Prophet Tecumseh the prior year; a monetary bounty was an extra incentive, while the American southern forces relied on militia, volunteers and Indians friendly to the whites.

Recent American immigrant, Wyatt Douglass, a native of Scotland, was learning just how hot his August afternoon had become when two flaming arrows, fired by Creek Indian braves, came through his open front window. After using the last of his savings, Wyatt had purchased twenty-two acres of virgin timberland on the eastern shore of the Alabama River near the confluence with the Tombigbee. He, along with his very pregnant wife Abby, had only completed their small, crude log cabin three weeks before today's attack. A pair of U.S. Army riders had come by three days prior, warning of a possible Creek attack and urged the Douglass' to seek refuge in nearby Fort Mims, two and a half miles due east. It had been their intention to do just that in the morning, after he and his team of oxen finished clearing their land on the riverbank, but the situation had completely changed. First, Abby had gone into labor just after the noon hour and eight Creek Indian warriors had set up camp outside their homestead. One of the Creek, a half-breed, spoke English and hurled threats, oaths and curse words their way for the past ten minutes. Finally, when Wyatt refused to surrender, the two flaming arrows were fired.

Wyatt had also wisely purchased two long guns: a Springfield Model 1795 musket and the more updated rifled-barrel Harper's Ferry Model 1803. Abby, with practice, had become a fast reloader and had the tedious task down to just over one-half minute. Wyatt, after retrieving the two fiery arrows and tossing them outside, immediately answered the Creeks with his own audacity and flying splinters from a near miss sent wood shards into one Creeks' face with his first shot. His howls of pain caused his fellow braves to pause and when Wyatt quickly fired again, they believed there were two white men, not one, holed inside the stout cabin. This meant a change in the attack plan. The Creeks split up, four on the north side and four on the south, covering any escape route.

Wyatt, now with Abby in full-blown labor and contractions every five minutes, couldn't leave anyway. Another arrow, the flame extinguished by the flight this time, came into the cabin and struck the wall less than a foot over Abby's head. The close call had Wyatt order his wife to make a pallet of quilt blankets and find refuge on the cabin's hard dirt floor. She complied in silence as she reloaded the musket.

The Creeks continued their waiting game, but with still three hours left until sundown, were now reduced to throwing rocks at the cabin as an annoyance as much as anything. In a lull, Wyatt had finished the last touches of his cabin window's sliding barrier. Once it was done, he placed the wooden guard over the front window, stuck his musket barrel out and fired once, putting the Indians on notice his cabin's defenses were now more formidable. To keep up his ruse, Wyatt immediately ran to the opposite rear window and fired his 1803 rifle once, almost hitting the half-breed in the knee and keeping up the appearance of two men inside the cabin. He even yelled across the cabin and changed his voice to make believe two men were there. Abby, huffing and puffing air, quickly reloaded.

Around 6:30 p.m. a small passing shower drenched the waiting Creeks, but more. The rain had aroused a bed of deer flies, the summer afternoon bane of Indians and settlers alike. The fast-flying black pests smelled blood and attacked, stinging and biting the Creeks. As they slapped their bare skin, the noise gave away their hidden positions and Wyatt was ready. He fired at the half-breed again and sent a .69 caliber lead bullet into his torso, just above his loincloth line.

As he doubled over in pain, a fellow Creek moved to assist his wounded comrade and presented a target for Wyatt's rifle. His .58 caliber slug entered the Creek's left cheek, took out four teeth on that side, half his tongue and three opposite molars before exiting the right cheek.

The Creek leader, attempting a rally, let loose a long, loud war whoop and rushed the cabin door. Despite a great effort, the door was secure and when the musket barrel once more presented, the leader quickly ran. Seeing that, the remaining five Creeks also decided it was time to retire.

Just before the Indians fled, Abby gave a great push and into the world at 6:45 p.m. came a healthy 6 lb. boy, already adorned with a surprising head of reddish-blonde hair. The name, already chosen, was announced by the proud father; John Knox Douglass was born near Tensaw, Mississippi Territory and was an American citizen, during a hostile Indian raid in a minute portion of The War of 1812.

A few hours later, the excitement had waned and as newborn John Knox and mother, Abby slept, Wyatt took the family Bible down from the mantle over their fireplace. By the light of the fire with quill and ink, he turned to the last page and recorded his son's full name, settlement nearest his place of birth, date and time of day, also the circumstances and that the cabin, having held up to Indian attack, was now deemed Fort Douglass.

(If Wyatt had possessed the knowledge, he could have also recorded his cabin was affixed at latitude 30.75 north, longitude 87.79 west.)

Chapter 5
Two-Faced

August 30, 1813
11:15 a.m.

"Lt. Burns, sir, theys be everywhere 'round the fort. I means everywhere," said his twenty-two-year old slave, Morial.

"Calm yourself down, Mory," the lieutenant of the Mississippi State militia said as he lit his pipe, seated in his officer's chair inside the confines of Fort Mims. "McNally told us they'd be gathering up. It's their corn harvest time and all those Indians that don't live in Tensaw village come to town to help pick corn. It's of no concern, Morial, none," he nonchalantly dismissed the slave's fear.

"But, master Burns, sir, I don't think that Mr. McNally be tellin' truths. I seen with my own eyes. These Creeks all got war paint out in little bowls, just ready to smear on and, Lordy, lot of 'em drinkin' whiskey and theys all carryin' dem clubs and I seen him, the man hisself. McNally even gotta a pistol."

"Morial, how do you know which one is Stewart McNally?"

"Staley and me was lookin' for drinkin' water and we heard someone a-comin' up, so we's hid in bushes. You can ask Staley, we heard him to tell two or three other Creek halfbreeds he'd done changed his name. He ain't a Stewart McNally no more, callin' hissself Burnt Hawk now. He be wearin' a white man suit of clothes, but a headdress of big ol' hawk feathers, too."

"So, you've deduced that an educated man, like Stewart McNally, changes his name to a Creek one, automatically loses all his gentlemanly traits and becomes an outright savage liar? Is that what you and Staley expect me to believe? Hmm." Burns finished with a long exhale of gray-blue pipe smoke in the slave's direction.

"All I knows is what I know. Thems Creeks is fixin' to be in here. I can feel it. Please, sir close them gates and run them Creeks already in here out. We gots to get 'em out now, before-n it's too late. Please, sir."

Bones of the Black Warrior

The normally silent and shy Staley interjected, "He a two-faced rascal."

"I can see you are terribly worked up over this. So, let me do this, hopefully you and Staley will calm down and get back to making bricks for my quarters. Winter will be on us before you know it. I'll mention what you said to the major and get his opinion. Will that suffice?"

"Lawdy, Master Burns, I don't knows. That major, beg pardon, sir, but he don't know nothing about fightin' Indians. I heard tell he ain't nuthin' but a fancy-dan, New Orleans lawyer and that he's just here for looks because-n-one day he wants to make a run to the governor's chair," pleaded the slave as he anxiously looked about the compound.

The army's cook appeared and with an iron rod clanged the metal triangle which was the mess call for all the enlisted men and officer's noon-time meal. After resting to digest his dinner, Lt. Burns walked outside of the gates of Fort Mims and upon spying on Stewart McNally, approached the half-Creek-half-white, motioning him over for a private meeting. After a fiveminute conversation, the Indian chief mounted his horse and took the northwest trail off in the direction of Old Mabila. The lieutenant returned to Mims with important information to pass along to the major. Before reporting to his superior officer, stopped to engage his two slaves: Staley and Morial.

"Sure hope you two kept your lips sealed tightly. You're both aware of the penalty for spreading false alarms? Whippings. Ten lashes apiece, I believe the normal punishment for slaves that..." Burns saw it unnecessary to finish the thought.

With an air of self-importance and with much pleasure at his newly acquired news, the lieutenant told the major that the Creeks had indeed gathered for more than picking corn. To their west, approximately seventy-five renegade Creeks were massed at the confluence of the two major rivers nearby, the Tombigbee and the Alabama. Their intent was to threaten an attack on the outpost settlement and trading post at the village of Mt. Vernon. Around a dozen white settler families had interloped on this land sacred to the Creeks as it was dotted with massive burial grounds. The whites had already begun to build cabins, work the land and in two instances, destroyed mounds for dam building on a major stream. This strip of land had been granted to them under the terms of the Sintee Creek Treaty, signed less than four months ago, and had already been violated.

McNally told Burns had just heard the news himself and was riding with instructions for the angry Creeks not to attack the white settlement; to return to the negotiation table for a resolution. McNally explained the feather headdress was to convince his people outside Mt. Vernon of his sympathy and even though half white, he represented the Creek Nation.

The militia major paced the dirt floor of his rustic cabin headquarters inside the log palisade of the fort. He too lit his pipe and exhaled a stream of smoke before announcing that Lieutenant Burns should begin with plans for one-half of the total militia stationed at Mims, eighty men, to leave at dawn should McNally's peace efforts fail. Also, the lieutenant should take a wagon of small gifts, things such as pots, kettles and woolen blankets as a gift to McNally to distribute to his people for keeping the peace.

Same Day
12:25 p.m.

Chief Burnt Hawk did not even approach Old Mabila, or Mt. Vernon. Once he'd left the visual range of Ft. Mims, riding north and west, he wheeled his horse to an about face. Using the thickets and overgrown flora, he discreetly made his way back to his 900 warriors awaiting orders half a mile south of Ft. Mims. Burnt Hawk gathered his top aides, Paddy Wetlich, also a half-Creek-half-white man and a full-bloodied Creek by the name of Wayward Warrior.

Wayward was all for a full-frontal assault this very moment, while Wetlich deferred to Burnt Hawk's wishes. Wayward teenage boy spies had recently counted approximately 150 soldiers, around 100 other white males at the fort and another 300 women and children.

Burnt Hawk's plans had called to slowly, during the past two hours, have unarmed braves infiltrate the inner confines of Ft. Mims. Then, at his signal of a loud war whoop and two gunshots; one from his musket, one from his pistol the attack would commence. Pre-teen boys, too young to join the fight, would rush in with war clubs, bows and arrows to arm what Burnt Hawk hoped would be two hundred or so braves already inside Mims. Also, at that time his remaining 700 warriors would rush through the open gates to fight. One argument Wayward Warrior had successfully pressed was that of total annihilation; no whites, no soldiers, civilian males, woman or child, or half-breed in league with the settlers, would be left alive. As the prophet Tecumseh had said on his visit two years before, the greatest weapon the rightful owners of the land, the Indians, had was fear. The great Shawnee chief and warrior stressed that instilling panic in the whites was their best chance to halt the invaders' westward march.

Another Wayward Warrior's idea used to disguise a hundred or so braves under deerskins and to have them approach through the thickets on their hands and knees. The white soldier guards may not believe they were deer, but all knew of the Creek hunting method of disguise to gain a closer arrow shot at their game. It would not arouse suspicion. So, the Creek plan went into effect, knowing that after their midday meal, the white soldiers usually relaxed and many would retire to nap. This was the opportune time.

(Stewart McNally, a.k.a. Burnt Hawk, confident leader of the Creek warriors, wholly cooperating with the British Army to not just fight, but obliterate the Americans, gazed out at the fort and its unsuspecting inhabitants. He readied his guns to signal the attack. All concerned players unaware of its precise location of latitude 31.10, longitude 87.30)

Chapter 6
La Catastrophe

May 13, 1817
Philadelphia, Pennsylvania

Henri Tombes was incredulous. By fleeing France, with his family and 300 others less than a year ago, he presumed his troubles with the Bourbon Monarchy were in their collective pasts. King Louis 18th had different ideas. Using his influence and even reminding Governor Snyder of Pennsylvania of the loyalty, heritage, and monetary assistance of the French Crown during the American Revolution, the French king was asking for a not-so-subtle favor.

So deep was Louis' fear and hatred of the supporters of Napoleon Bonaparte, currently exiled on the remote island of St. Helena, the king wasn't content to only remove the supporters from France, he wished to imprison them. The copy of the letter in Henri Tombes' possession was proof. Even Bonaparte supporters who had fled the country were now being rounded up abroad and being returned to Parisian prisons. Henri Tombes had no intention of ever returning to Paris, even if it required leaving Philadelphia, so be it. Many of the refugees were unhappy there anyway and Henri had little doubt his group would almost unanimously agree to move away.

Henri sent word about for the menfolk to secretly meet quickly as time was crucial.

June 21, 1817
Southeast quadrant - Alabama Territory

And so it was, at mid-year 1817, Henri and 206 other supporters of Bonaparte found themselves disembarking from a series of hired barges on the eastern side of the Tombigbee River, five miles north of its confluence with the Alabama River. Here was their new home. Connections in the U.S. Congress had pushed through a land deal where the Bonapartists purchased land in the newly formed Alabama Territory, 436 acres at $2.00 per, with half of which were purchased on credit. The leaders, wary of King Louis, so decided their new home would be far from civilization, courts and governors friendly to any French monarch. The refugees from King Louis also had to bear the stipulation that the land would not be resold for a period of not less than twelve months, physical improvements had to be added in the form of barns, wells, fences and of course homes and as soon as weather permitted, crops would be sown.

The western side of the Tombigbee River was in possession of the peaceful Choctaw Nation. The eastern side, just a scant three years prior, was occupied by Creek Indians. Once utterly defeated by General Andrew Jackson, forced into treaty, their land was confiscated by the United States. The virgin land was ripe for white settlement. As by far the largest contingent of the 207 new settlers to the land were former officers and soldiers previously serving the Emperor, the lines of authority and standing also fell along their previous lines of rank, with civilians below.

Colonel Ruul, as the former leader of a cavalry regiment, assumed control of the Bonapartists in their new home. The colonel had the foresight to bring surplus tents of the Grand Armie when fleeing France. Although never used in Pennsylvania, the 207 found immediate use of them in Alabama. A grid was set up, tents erected, and work began on a dock on the eastern shore of the Tombigbee. Another flotilla of barges was expected in less than ten days bearing the vital agricultural seedlings of the newly formed French-speaking conclave. Also, the arrival in the same flotilla was the lifeblood of every Frenchman, an entire barge devoted to wine. The energetic Colonel Ruul, at the same time, expressed wishes for a ferry to be constructed across the river, linking his settlement for trade with the Choctaws, widely known for having a surplus for the trade of corn, peas, squash, venison and for the past few hundred years, ever since the Spanish conquistadors traveled through, domesticated pigs.

September 30, 1817
7:00 p.m.

Colonel Ruul fired his pistol into the air at the town center, without a bullet of course. It was his usual call to a meeting as this was a deadline day. The last log cabin was to have been finished on this date, meaning every Bonapartist should have a solid roof overhead and no longer rely on the drafty, holey, moth-eaten tents to serve as their protection from the elements. After experiencing their first American winter, a year prior in Philadelphia, the displaced French were wary of the weather, not completely convinced that their southerly move would entirely remove the threat of ice and snow from their calendar. As the days had gotten shorter, Col. Ruul had been afraid of the possibility and here on the last day of September, their lack of progress was palpable.

While the majority of settlers knew their way around a sword, musket and cannon, few were good with their hands especially in woodworking. The dock they'd planned ready as of July 1, did not get completed until July 22. The ferry barge was still under construction and of the sixty-eight log cabins needed for housing, only twenty-one were complete. Another five were about halfway done, while the logs were felled for another dozen, but that was all they had to show in four and one-half months.

The whole purpose of the colony's existence was also far behind schedule. The primary aim of the Alabama colonists was to grow the two crops of which they actually did have some rudimentary knowledge: grapes for wine and olives for their prized oil. Also hampering them was their lack of training with four draft horses and eight oxen. The cavalrymen and their horsemanship talents were geared for awe-inspiring charges, not for plowing. Three weeks later, the first frost came to the southern Alabama Territory. Only supplied with two moldboard plows, less than fifteen acres had been turned for their immature olive trees and grape vines. It wasn't until the second night's freeze that they built numerous all-night fires among the plants to ward off the cold. By then half the plants were severely damaged.

Compounding their agricultural issues were their deteriorating relations with the Choctaw. A series of misunderstandings had resulted in the cessation of trade. It was a widely accepted native practice, that if someone possessed something you needed, if you could, you borrowed it and did so without asking permission. This, to the whites, was sinful, outright theft was generally punished severely. The Choctaw regularly canoed the river at night to pilfer the settler's iron tools, further hampering their cabin and other necessary construction. To the Indians, it was not their responsibility to return the tools, in their world, logically the whites should have come over the following night and taken them back.

Finally, when the last of the big whipsaws turned up missing, the colonel and nine other ex-soldiers used flat sticks to paddle three logs across the river to the Choctaw village. Accustomed to going up, or down, a chain of command, Ruul, was surprised when the village chief refused to meet with him and his entourage and instead, saw their arrival as an excellent opportunity to cross the river and rummage the white men's construction sites for more metal tools. Thoroughly angered upon returning to the eastern side of the river, Ruul and the men confronted four Choctaws as they wandered among the standing Grand Armie tents. The differences in language and culture were on full display as one burly, ex-sergeant, fed up with the Indians' thievery, retrieved his horsewhip and began his own punishment on a young male.

Only the thought of future white American soldiers' retribution kept the village chief from agreeing to a council of war and instead issued a no trade edict. Not blind to the French's plight, the chief convinced his people the coming cold and hunger would substitute for war to punish the strange white invaders. Colonel Ruul and his now 199 numbering Bonapartists would face the coming days alone, without any assistance from the Choctaw.

By February 1818, the largest construction project completed by the settlers was the ever-expanding community graveyard. So far, forty-six forever rested in Alabama soil. The overcrowded, now twenty-six cabins, were bursting at the seams and frustration. Luckily, spring came early that year and by mid-March, many settlers had returned to life in the tents rather than live in the cramped proximity and growing animosity inside the small cabins.

Compounding the myriad of problems Col. Ruul faced was thievery among his own people.

When the ferry barge was finally complete, a secret group of twenty, crept away under the cover of night to the vessel and floated downstream to reach Mobile, safety, skip out on the dangers, and the accrued debt, of what was now called the Olive and Vine Experiment.

Wear and tear and lack of protective shelter proved too much for the two mold plows in their possession and by mid-April, both had broken into unrepairable splinters. The settlers were reduced to furrowing the field with sticks and their hands. Nevertheless, Ruul saw to it that the remaining seedling olive trees and grapevines were planted. The weather cooperated for a few weeks until a storm, unknown to the former Europeans, tore through the main field. Terror dropped down from the sky in the form of a tornado. Damage was extensive and deadly for three residents, also.

Weakened by lack of food, a fever made a run among the French, taking out sixteen more, by the middle of May, they numbered just 122 souls. Within the week, another dozen, even without a barge, stole out at night, headed south for Mobile and gave up the experiment. Then, the wife of Col. Ruul died during childbirth, his fighter's spirit left him for a month and little was done around the settlement as apathy and doom weakened the survivors' will.

Finally, as the olive trees and vineyard showed signs of healthy growth the colonel and the Bonapartists' collective enthusiasm returned. It was short-lived as the July and August heat combined with a short drought killed the tender plants. They were wiped out. Pleas to the Choctaw went unanswered and they possessed nothing of value now to even barter. Henri Tombes, Col. Ruul and five other men in leadership openly discussed their options; stay put and continue to starve or go back to Philadelphia where the seven, plus the thirty-five other surviving men who'd signed promissory notes, would be thrown into debtor's prison, leaving their families wanting and vulnerable.

The final straw was when another strain of feverish disease claimed nine more souls, including their leader, Colonel Ruul. Henri Tombes was elected as his replacement. After a week of sleepless nights, Henri decided, one way or another, the survivors deserved some options. He called the entire group together and announced the Olive and Vine Experiment was over. Each family was to decide on their own accord what direction to go. Was debtor's prison a better option than probable starvation in the wilderness? Moving to Mobile or New Orleans was a cheaper possibility. But for some without financial resources, staying put was the only option. Then, over the course of the crucial next few days when decisions were imminent, a blind stroke of fortune rode into their midst. Henri was approached by a traveling sutler and budding entrepreneur, who saw their pitiful shape, listened to their problems and stated that he could supply a remedy for the Europeans' difficulties.

The bold traveler, originally from South Carolina, arrived with a promising idea and told the Bonapartists that he, Benjamin Travers, would buy 426 acres for the same $2 per as the disgruntled setters had paid, thus making the survivors whole. Henri and the humbled French jumped at the chance opportunity to return to civilization and salvation from their doomed experiment that never produced an ounce of wine or olive oil.

(The failed Frenchmen abandoned the settlement with only two pieces of real tangible evidence; one, the seventy-six graves left behind, bodies moldering in the soil, the other being the crude, small twenty-six log cabins at 31.4 latitude north, 87.6 longitude west.)

Chapter 7
The Bounty

January 1, 1822

Annual flooding every spring of the Tombigbee and Alabama Rivers had laid down rich, fertile alluvial soil, perfect for growing crops; the kind suited to these weather patterns. This ground, known for being porous and therefore thirsty for rain, retained moisture to nourish crops, even during dry spells. This layered, floodplain dirt was also known for being soft and without rocks, easy for working and on a well-made plow.

A few years earlier, Ben Travers had placed his trust in a chance meeting with a gentleman from Natchez, who by trade was a breeder of racehorses, but dabbled in botany. The man from Natchez claimed he'd developed a strain of cotton, interbred with what was being grown in Mexico, that could survive the hot, humid summers of the Deep South. Previously, American cotton growers were limited to the temperate coastal regions. The Natchez fellow was quite the braggart, claiming his hybrid strain was capable of producing a quality fiber suitable for high fashion. He'd named his creation Lower Black Seed, happily telling all who'd listen that it would source the new El Dorado of the South and planters could quickly create vast fortunes.

Back in 1819, Travers bought enough of the new seed to experiment with one of a few, vacant acres he owned north of Mobile. At this same time, during a Mardi Gras social, he met two former French soldiers, now residents of Mobile, describing how they'd come to live there, the prior year having fled the disastrous farming experiment upriver. Travers' acre of the new cotton strain was extremely promising, so he begged and borrowed all the money he could and sensing a good deal could be found forty miles to the north, he'd trekked upriver, met Henri Tombes and bought out the desperate Napoleonic transplants.

So, it came to be on this first day of the new year, 1822, Ben Travers' gamble of betting everything he had on a cotton crop, and a new, somewhat unproven variety at that, rode mainly on the fickle whims of the weather.

He wouldn't know the results until late September when the bolls were mature and ready for harvest.

Besides his aspirations to become a cotton grower, Benjamin Travers was ready to christen another new, prized possession. Two years prior, having purchased an additional hundred acres along the river adjacent to the old Wine and Olive land he'd acquired in 1818, along with another fifty acres due south, Travers laid out his plans for a grand home and now with his new wife, the former Eliza Delchamp, only daughter of a prominent Mobile physician; the Delchamps also having been among the original French settlers in Mobile's early history, who once owned substantial downtown real estate.

New Year's Day and his home was complete. Having been married all of two weeks, he and Eliza were moving in, but the home, yes the entire place, needed a name. Dr. Delchamp, a wealthy and generous man, had funded the building of their home as a wedding present for his daughter, Eliza.

In the three years of owning the land, having turned thousands of spadefuls of dirt and discovering hundreds of arrowheads, Ben Travers decided a local Indian title was fitting. Some research talking to a few of the local elders supplied his answer: Alabimo. Eliza liked the name, saying it was close to their new state's moniker, but different enough to lend character. The Alabimo had been a sub-tribe of Choctaw who'd lived along these two riverbanks that framed Ben Travers' land up until the mid-1700s. Ben's shovel and plow had also uncovered hundreds of human bones; some whole, but most in pieces. Knowing some people were squeamish about human remains, he never mentioned them and if another spied them, he always remarked that they were animal.

Dr. Delchamp had also lent his good name by co-signing a working capital note for Ben through the Bank of Mobile. Travers had used the funds to purchase the required Lower Black Seed, two of Eli Whitney's cotton gins and ten, young male slaves to work the land. Taking his father-in-law's advice, even though he was priced over his budget, Ben took an older slave from Virginia, named Theo, who had extensive experience growing cotton. Although Theo's best years physically were behind him, he possessed invaluable knowledge for Alabimo to succeed. After all, Ben

Travers had indeed gambled everything and if his investment in cotton failed, so would his financial credibility, likely his marriage and his future.

Chapter 8
The Plunge

May 14, 1836
Mid-day

Colonel Yancey Grace, inside a stifling hot, airless army tent, poured from a pitcher of cool spring water into three glasses. One was for the Indian agent, appointed by the U.S. government, a Mr. Wallace McMullen, and the other for the local Creek Indian chief, Yahola. It was a scorching day, without any cloud cover, outside of Fort Stephens, Alabama. The three men thirstily drank the refreshing water and the major quickly gave refills as he spoke.

"I met with the largest landowner in these parts, Ben Travers, last night. He not only produces more cotton than any other planter in the southern half of the state, but he also carries significant influence in the state capital, Tuscaloosa. Which, of course, implies he also has ears in Washington, too."

The Indian leader and the agent both nodded; they already knew these items. Yahola extended his empty glass for the third time, which earned a harsh glance from McMullen, knowing having a white man serve him was considered a subservient act. The Creek smiled in return at McMullen's sour face. It was not a smile that would last as the military officer continued.

"Travers didn't push the fact he knew the president, only if he wrote Washington, Andy Jackson would read it personally. Plus, Travers knows his local history. Old Hickory made a name for himself, right here, twenty years ago."

That erased Yahola's grin. He, too, knew the history of General Andrew Jackson's complete defeat and utter humiliation of his tribe during the War of 1812. The mere mention of Jackson's name anywhere in the southern United States, to any Indian, would shiver their spine. The general had shown no mercy to the warring Creeks and took no quarter against men, women or children. The village elders had retold the brutal stories to a young Yahola. Respect for the white man's military prowess and sheer numbers were the main reasons Yahola had chosen to live his adult life as he did.

Yahola's ancestors became tribal chiefs due to their hunting and fighting ability. In today's world of 1836, one became chief by owning possessions, just like the whites, such as a home, land, horses, slaves and political clout.

"I'm not telling you anything you haven't already suspected out of Washington. The president, given urging from the governors of Georgia, Tennessee, Alabama and Mississippi, who in turn owe their respective political posts to the big cotton planters, made his executive decision. The Five Civilized Tribes must vacate and move west," the colonel said matter-of-factly.

Agent McMullen saw a chance to speak, and cut a glance to the Indian, "I'd prayed this day would never come and now you just made it official."

"My people have feared these words," Yahola added. "We already are hearing aggressive words from the young braves. They won't listen to the lessons from the old ones about the white army soldiers and believe they must fight."

"Precisely the reasoning from Washington and Tuscaloosa, chief," the colonel said emphatically. "This is no longer a single family of white settlers on five acres in a log cabin. There's big money coming into the South now, Yahola, and large investments require protection."

Once again, McMullen saw his opportunity to engage, "Yahola, you own quite the mansion yourself."

"The mere threat of rampaging Creek Indians, looting, burning and stealing is too much for men like Travers. The South has a lot of catching up to do with the North. They had a big headstart and one of the main reasons for their advantage is there weren't Indian wars or raids since before the Revolutionary days."

"Yahola will do what he sees necessary," said the Creek chief. "I'm not here to drink cool water. I presume you have a message for my people, colonel?"

"Jackson seeks a different solution than what we have in the Florida Territory and the pesky Seminoles. There is unsettled, free land west of the Mississippi River. In repayment for a peaceful migration there, by the five tribes, Jackson will compensate the chiefs and make land grants to those willing to move. It behooves men like Travers to contribute cash for these chiefs to lead a peaceful migration. In return, he'll likely buy the former Creek lands for more cotton production."

McMullen again added his opinion, "We all know that's the real reason, just can't say it aloud. Mainly because of the Northern press. They're organizing up there. I've read it myself. There's a growing movement of men and women calling themselves abolitionists, meaning they want to abolish slavery, with the exception of cotton which benefits their giant textile industry and many the Yankee pocket."

"I know well of the abolishers," said Yahola. "I've even received mail from a group in Boston and Philadelphia, critical of my owning slaves, that I should be sympathetic to their plight. Bah!"

"It's a free country, Yahola," said the colonel with pride. "You own whatever you feel is right and don't let anyone tell you otherwise."

"You called us here because," McMullen said, directly to the officer, "you desire Yahola and me to convince these hotheads to peacefully relocate out west, giving up their ancestral hunting grounds and leaving behind the revered bones of their ancestors?"

"Treaties are cheaper than bullets and gunpowder, but the president will, and has the power at the ready to, do it either way. We're certain of that," Col. Grace replied, again stressing the armed forces strength.

Indian agent McMullen and the Creek leader, both knew the military man's description of Jackson, although callous, was correct. The Creek had previously nicknamed the general, "Sharp Knife."

They were free to object, but it was a fruitless cause. The dye for the natives' future had been cast; the men with money and power wanted these lands. Knowing that, the two silently decided to make the best of their current situation. Soon, it would be too late.

July 29, 1836
3:15 p.m.
Front grounds of Alabimo plantation

Of all things, a court case had changed Creek Chief Yahola's entire mindset. Six weeks earlier, while visiting the agent, McMullen showed him an article in the leading newspaper in Alabama, *The Mobile Commercial*

Register. The paper recounted the decision from the U.S. Supreme Court, on appeal from the state's highest court. Two years prior, a white man unquestionably murdered a Creek man and woman on indisputably Indian-owned land. The defense claimed the arrest by Alabama law enforcement was invalid as the land was administered by federal jurisdiction. Alabama's court system agreed, and the man was freed from jail. The state's other Indian agent, Wm. Bailey, from the northern portion of the state, used his New York connections to fund the appeal to Washington. Once more, the white man's court system failed the native's rights and refused to hear the matter, so the murderer went completely unpunished.

Yahola saw this treatment of his people and was rightfully angered, but more. He came to understand the matter personally. No matter what he did, the power accrued or the credibility he garnered in the white world, he'd always be judged by his ancestry and skin color. It was also accurate; it just is a matter of time and circumstance before some white man realized Yahola's worldly possessions were actually unprotected by current law and could be stolen without recourse. His own murder a probable avenue for some man to grab his holdings. Instead of meeting with the young warriors to discourage them from attacking the white settlers, he volunteered to lead them into battle. Remembering his meeting in May, Yahola decided to make the first strike of the new war against the powerful man with money and intentions on tribal land, Ben Travers.

So, it came to pass in the afternoon of July 29, ten armed Creek warriors confidently veered off the Federal Postal Road connecting Athens, Georgia to Mobile, Alabama to the short walk to Alabimo plantation. Yahola was immediately impressed by Travers' holding and improvements to the land. He'd hunted this area as a youth and remembered there was little here save scrub bushes, a creek and the occasional stand of cypress trees. Travers not only had a huge mansion, but two large barns, great fields of cotton, a fine stable, a protected well and assorted sheds for storage, plus what appeared to be two dozen log cabins, homes for Travers slaves.

Yahola's envy was that of a white man's view of the world, something he'd recently reversed.

Besides the court case, spending a few days around the old warrior, Burnt Hawk or Stewart McNally, had cemented his cause to fight the whites. Both leaders knew this would be the last chance to reclaim their land. Burnt Hawk's impassioned plea had touched Yahola. He said he had one real regret in all of his sixty-two years; not killing General Andrew Jackson in 1814, just after the hostilities of the Creek War had ended.

Yahola was enthralled at Burnt Hawk's memory of the tragic, final battle in their war. It was called the Battle of Horseshoe Bend, for a turn in the Tallapoosa River, north of their location. In a world not known for generations, Burnt Hawk said the Creek fortifications reminded the elders of the tales from old about the great palisade at Old Mabila, constructed by the legendary Chief Tuskaluca, long ago. And like before, it was a one-sided slaughter. Bows and arrows were no match for guns and cannons. Burnt Hawk said of the 1000 warriors in the Creek fort, only one hundred survived the onslaught of Jackson's army while the Creeks could only claim 125 white lives in the battle. Only by feigning his own death, as he was covered in blood for two head wounds, awaiting dark, and finding a buoyant log to rest upon and floating downriver before dawn, did Burnt Hawk escape. He continued stating when he'd recovered enough to travel, he sought out General Jackson and requested a meeting. To entice the army's top officer, he told the liaison he'd offer his life to the Americans in exchange for his role a few months prior at Fort Mims.

Jackson was impressed by his brave offer and allowed the meeting, alone with Burnt Hawk, in his tent. He was, of course, searched for weapons and had secreted a small knife inside a tucked cavity of the feathered headdress.

On this day, on the approach to the Travers' plantation, Yahola had listened to Burnt Hawk's statement of his life's biggest remorse. He didn't lack the courage, but instead was momentarily awe-struck by Jackon's physical bearing, manliness, confident manner and graciousness towards a sworn enemy. How could he have changed history, likely the fate of his people if he had retrieved the hidden knife and driven it into the cold heart of Andrew Jackson? The missed opportunity was the old chief's admitted biggest guilt.

All these thoughts ran through Yahola's mind as he approached Alabimo and an enemy he could kill, Ben Travers. A young teen boy, likely Travers' son, saw the war party coming up the drive and began sounding an alarm by ringing a large bell. Burnt Hawk took four warriors to the left of the house, leaving Yahola with four to make their way around the right, encircling the residence.

Besides the teenage boy, there were four white men for Yahola and his warriors to contend with. Ben Travers was not hard to identify as he was dressed in a suit, while the others were in work clothes. Travers also had taken the high ground on the second floor wrap around balcony and was trailed by two slaves, each holding long guns, ready to reload their master's shot. Burnt Hawk had a musket and a pistol, while Yahola only had a war club and an ancient pistol that was only accurate at point-blank range. The other eight Creek had knives, war clubs and bows and arrows plus an angry spirit of desperation.

Simultaneously, Burnt Hawk fired his musket at an armed white worker by the front steps, but missed. As he stopped to reload, his comrades also stopped. It proved to be a mistake as Travers got off three shots, and all three found their mark, killing two Creeks and incapacitating a third. The flurry of shooting gathered Yahola's attention and he left his group to assist the old chief. Together the two joined up, rushed the front door, and gained entrance, seeking their goal. As they made their way up the main staircase, the old slave, now over eighty, Theo, appeared at the head of the steps brandishing a sword. Burnt Hawk moved in and as Theo slashed the air, Yahola fired his pistol from six feet, the bullet found Theo's chest and he tumbled face down to the bottom of the blue-carpeted stairs.

Burnt Hawk and Yahola heard Travers' gun continuing to blast from the balcony and followed the sound down a hall and through a great bedroom. Bursting through a huge open window, large enough for a man to walk through the sudden arrival of the Creeks, panicked Travers' two slaves reloading as they both dropped their weapons and fled around the corner of the balcony, leaving Ben alone. Yahola swung his war club, but Ben's raised forearm took the brunt of the blow instead of his head. It gave Burnt Hawk his chance and bearing a huge knife, moved behind Ben, grabbed the white man's somewhat long hair and placed the blade at the top of his forehead.

He'd kill him later, first he was going to scalp the rich cotton planter.

Suddenly, from below came a series of musket fire. Burnt Hawk turned his attention from his grisly, yet satisfying task, just slightly away to see an explosion of gray matter and red blood splatter the exterior white wall of the mansion, right at eye level. It was Yahola's brains as a dozen uniformed white men, all on horseback, were just below the balcony. The county militia, led by Lt. John Knox Douglass, had arrived.

It briefly flashed to Burnt Hawk his old regret with General Jackson and undeterred returned to his bloody job as angrily, in English, he cursed the white man for invading his tribal land. As his knife was about a third of the way slicing towards the back of Travers' head, a bullet from Lt. Douglass pierced Burnt Hawk's arm. Winching in pain he dropped his knife and climbed back through the window. Again, in the gigantic bedroom, Burnt Hawk encountered a white woman in a fine dress, a slave woman and the same teenage boy who'd rung the bell, but was now seeking an escape, ran by them, down the stairs and out of the back of the main hall. He exited the house, spied a horse tied to a column on the back veranda and quickly mounted the animal to flee.

After a few seconds Burnt Hawk had the horse heading across the plantation's vegetable garden behind the house. He half-turned in his saddle and saw the militia had rounded up the remaining Creeks in the side yard, but that one soldier was giving chase. Burnt Hawk dug his heels into the animal's flanks and tried to increase his speed, but the horse was an older animal mostly used for Mrs. Travers' carriage. The garden clearing ran out and he saw two dirt paths through the woods, both headed in the direction of the Tombigbee River. He briefly reigned up and turned again to see the soldier was now much closer. With no time to waste, he chose the southernmost of the two and continued to ride at full speed. Tree branches, and limbs of bushes slapped his body and face as the trail narrowed, he heard a pistol fire from close behind, but it missed. Taking another glance, he saw the soldier, not knowing it was the same infant who'd been born in a Creek raid, that he'd orchestrated, on the Douglass family cabin back in 1813. Twenty-three years later and now a grown man was bearing down on him with a cavalry sword and blood in his eyes. The trail was almost obliterated by undergrowth now and Burnt Hawk could barely see through the green wall ahead, but he rode on. The narrow path briefly opened up as, closing in, he heard the soldier's curse words shouted.

Then, his escape line abruptly just stopped However, Burnt Hawk's horse did not. Still in his saddle, the Creek held on as the horse's momentum carried them off the bluff of the river's eastern shore, through the air, over the water before falling forty feet, jumping off the animal just before splashing in the green water. Above, Lt. Douglass, familiar with this path, reigned up his horse and quickly reloaded his pistol as he kept an eye down below on his target; Burnt Hawk's bobbing head, having survived the plunge, was now swimming toward the west bank. The militia officer knew it would be a miracle shot, but had to try, took aim and squeezed the trigger, but fired high as the renegade chief continued to swim away out of range.

A disgusted John Knox Douglass waited and watched as Burnt Hawk exited the river, turned and looked back his way briefly before walking up the red clay bank and disappearing into the thick woods. The militia man squinted hard in an attempt to discern any possible features of the gray-haired Creek, vowing if he ever saw him again, he would not miss again, as he'd done at latitude 31.15, longitude 87.79.

Chapter 9
Retribution

December 20, 1836
Alabimo Plantation

Eliza Travers was finally at ease with her new horse. Ulysses, who'd transplanted Theo as the leader among the family slaves, had broken one of Ben's riders for her carriage replacement. Her previous animal had not survived the mighty fall off the bluff, six months earlier and drowned in the Tombigbee River. Surviving was a keyword around the plantation.

The cotton gamble had paid off royally and the new strain had out-performed Ben's highest expectations. Travers had survived the July raid and although he'd likely never regrow hair on his frontal scalp and he'd have a serious scar, he was back to good health, otherwise. There was local peace, too. The uprising, now being called The Second Creek War, had shifted to the north and east, into more central Alabama and closer to the Georgia line. The occasional article in the Mobile newspaper kept the Travers informed, after President Jackson had ordered regular Army troops to mobilize and assume the majority of the fighting, it was only a matter of time until any further threats of Creek Indian trouble would be extinguished for good.

On this afternoon, just four days before Christmas Eve, Eliza directed her carriage north and east up the Federal Postal Road, toward home and away from Ft. Stoddert, the closest hub of civilization. She was accompanied by Ulysses who led the way on his mule, and she had a passenger; a small four-year-old boy.

The little boy was full-blooded Indian, or so the official census and county records stated. Eliza had just left the courthouse and completed the adoption papers. The boy had been the lone survivor of 1834 murders on Indian land about a mile south of the Ben Travers' southernmost landholdings. The crime had been the basis for the monumental case that the U.S. Supreme Court had refused to hear regarding the legality of Alabama law enforcement's authority on federal land. The boy, just an infant at that time, had been spared having been hidden by his Choctaw mother under the dried husks in the corn crib under the cabin. The child had later been discovered and been in county care as a ward of the state until being put up for adoption just three months prior. He likely had an Indian name, but with both parents murdered by the Irish immigrant named Stockton, no one knew it and so simply was known as Ward.

Ward, just an hour earlier, had rewarded the last name of Travers. Eleven years earlier, Eliza's birth of their only child, Benjie, had rendered her barren. Loneliness and an urge to care for a poor child who'd been unjustly orphaned had been calling and Ben agreed to the adoption. To everyone in Ft. Stoddert's surprise, as little Ward grew, he became quite the talk of the little village of 400 people. There was no doubt about Ward's heritage; his father was fully Creek, his mother a full Choctaw, but Ward only bore a little too typical physical Indian characteristics. Ward's skin was olive tone, not half as dark as most and instead of deep brown eyes, his were of a greenish tint, but the major difference was his blonde locks, not bright yellow, a darker version, nonetheless plainly a blonde.

It was upon hearing of the strange child that perked Eliza's interest as Benjie also had green eyes and blonde hair. But the brutal murder of the parents had bothered her, too. Everyone in her circle knew it was a heinous and unpunished crime. The poor Creek man had just been following Agent McMullen's urges of quitting tribal life, adopting the ways of the whites, trying to assimilate into the new order of farming and settled home life. He'd purchased a small acreage to grow corn, indigo and tobacco for resale in Mobile. He'd married one of his own race, they both had accepted Christianity and joined a local Baptist church specifically for Indians. The man was a great example in McMullen's plan to save the local Indians from destruction, but the greed of an evil white man had wiped them out. The murderer was well aware that the court system was stacked against the Indian. It was state and federal law, at the time, that no Indian testimony was allowed in court. So, Stockton saw a situation he liked, murdered the two and using the possession of nine-tenths of the law theory, moved in, survived the court case and took over the farm without any consequences.

The callus murder had bothered Ben, too. While it was true that he saw the Indian way of subsistence survival as wasting prime farmland, he drew the line at violence. Once Eliza had completed the adoption process, Ben formulated a plan. First, he'd use his and his father-in-law's Mobile connections to have the merchants boycott Stockton's goods for sale. This would bankrupt the Irishman and engage part two of Ben's scheme to swoop in and acquire Stockton's land cheap at a tax foreclosure sale and expand his adjoining acreage.

Chapter 10
The Slides

September 1846

The past eight years had been good for the Travers. Earlier, he'd successfully put the murderer Stockton out of business, but Ben Travers had a near brush with bankruptcy the next year. It was known as the Panic of 1837 and U.S. banking concerns, inflation and low cotton prices triggered the national financial demise. Locally, more cotton growers had crowded into the area and Ben's local monopoly no longer existed. Some had even acquired more land than Ben, but none had the advantage of his super rich, alluvial soil.

　　The years have seen family changes at Alabimo, too. Ben was just fine; looked even better now that his hair had naturally started to fall out and his strange frontal bald spot wasn't so conspicuous. Eliza was also well and had even become wealthy from her father's recent death, will and inheritance. Son Benjie had been doing great until late in the year 1845 when he'd been kicked in the head attempting to assist in shoeing a horse. His Mobile doctors advised more healing time should be allowed before declaring permanent brain damage. However, since the mishap, Benjie's mental capabilities were just not right. His memory and ability to keep his thoughts straight were wildly inconsistent. Little Ward, now a healthy, intelligent sixteen-year-old, spent much of his time at the exclusive private boys school in Mobile, St. Mark's, where he excelled in every subject and made his parents proud.

　　However, there was an intriguing amount of speculation going in and around Alabimo for Ben, but this was atop the soil. Blessed with a mind for business, Ben was not just satisfied with growing and ginning the cotton. He had yearned for more control and despised paying others to transport his crop to market. So, as his fortune and number of slaves increased, he built docks; one on the eastern shore of the Tombigbee, his land and another on the western banks of the Alabama River, also his. Although, sadly, Theo never lived long enough to see his vision come to fruition, it was the brainchild of the transplanted Virginia slave.

Theo had seen them back home, just on smaller scales, but with the same principle of gravity as the power source. After the ginned cotton was baled, it was transported on flatbed wagons to the riverside bluffs. Alabimo was blessed in that her major east and west cotton operations had their separate points of shipping instead of one central location, should any calamity befall. Theo had drawn plans for Ben to build slides from an unloading point, high upon the bluffs. These 500 lb. bales would then use a slide of smooth half-logs laid down like a road, leading right to the wharf. Gravity supplied the force to move the cumbersome bales while, under Theo's system of strategically placed guiding rope pulleys, only two slaves were needed to safely control the steep downward slide from the high bluffs down to the river-level piers.

The intensity of labor to construct the two slides had been great; Ben saw another way to save money, too. Generally, a steamboat would be hired to come to one's riverside plantation and for a fee, generally of fifteen percent of the gross sale at market, the boat would haul the cotton down to the Mobile market. It hurt Ben's pride to give up such a significant percentage for what he saw was only two days of the relatively effortless job by the boatmen.

Harking back to his sutler days of travel, Ben had seen Kentucky riverboat men haul goods on major rivers using long poles on their rafts. From a distance it seemed fairly simple, especially in his case, going the easy way, downstream. So, pulling Ward from school, back when he was fourteen, he gave the boy supervisory powers to lead a team of male slaves, hand-picked by Ulysses, to build the two cotton slides, the pulley-counterweight system and the minimum number of barges to float the white gold every October and November.

Ward understood the responsibility and devoted his unswerving attention. After a few weeks, he reported to his father, Ben, that one slave had shown extreme promise in the woodworking and engineering required for the three jobs. His given name was Isham, but generally was called Ike and had been in the second round of slave purchases by Ben back in 1824. Actually, Ben had obtained a young female for cooking duties, but after a month at the plantation, discovered he'd made a two-for-one bargain.

Ward noted that Ike, after the workday's end and on Sunday when there was no work, did not stay in the company of his age group. Ike was always with two middle-aged slaves, Wash and Deely. The threes' companionship struck Ward as odd. Even though away at school half the year, he was around enough to observe Wash and Deely. the two most troublesome of his father's slaves. No, they didn't run off or start fights with the two overseers, they just never went along easily with the flow and were always the most vocal, constantly complaining.

And so it was on the last day of September, 1846, when the cotton harvest was complete and the product was ginned, the first bale headed from the Tombigbee gin baler to the river bluffs for their first trial. Nothing on the plantation, nor anything produced by the plantation was cheap. An average acre of bottomland, replacing the plows and digging two new wells would have cost Mr. Travers a total of seventy-five dollars. A broker in Mobile would pay him the same amount per bale. Meaning, if the cotton slides didn't work and a single one tumbled into the river and sank, it was the equivalent of losing funds for those essential items at Alabimo.

By the two weeks of the next year the ninety-day collection period for his cotton sales was all realized, Ben felt very proud and also indebted to ole Theo. With great weather, a pair of good, seasoned overseers and enough field hands plus, in addition to saving fifteen percent of his profit, by using his own slides and barges, made wonderful improvements to the bottom line. Ben's proceeds for his 1846 crop doubled his previous best year and something happened to him that he'd never dreamed: he was a millionaire.

He didn't have to, and no one would have known if he hadn't, but that cool night of January 16, 1847, after doing his financial books and seeing that wonderful eleven-letter word, alone, Ben took a stroll after dinner, out past his stables to the slave graveyard. There was enough moonlight to see Theo's resting place, Ben went over and stood next to his tombstone.

"Thank you, Theo. Thanks for everything. Not just the slide plans or your guidance my first-year planting or your bravery in standing up to fight the Indians that cost your life," Ben said as a tear welled up, slowly trekking down his cheek before he gave a hard sniff and wiped it away.

"For all you did for me and my family, Theo, rest well in Heaven, old friend."

Chapter 11
Ambush

August 10, 1847

It had been a day of firsts as Ward and the slave Ike sat on a wooden bench in the Pensacola, Florida train depot for their return to Mobile. The distance was fifty-five miles, the train averaged fifteen miles per hour and with stops for wood and water, would take five hours. Ward had been hearing about the new invention of the steam locomotive train and was eager to try the experience. Ike, eight years senior, was along for company and any necessary assistance. Father Ben had ordered the trip. Other local men of the planter class had been discussing obtaining a spur from the Mobile to Chicago railroad to be built connecting Jackson, Alabama to the main line. Jackson was the new county seat at the intersection of two major roads and useful as a cotton export station. Ben was happy with his current slide and barge setup, but surmised this method should at least be looked into. So, he sent Ward down to experience a train ride for firsthand insight and then decide afterward.

Being sent on an out-of-town mission alone was a first for Ward as was the train ride. As Ike and Ward explored Garden Street between train trips, another first was the item Ike purchased at a general store run by a Free Black man. Upon entering the store, Ike's demeanor changed as he soured on Ward and intentionally kept his distance.

It wasn't until hours later and relentless pressure from Ward to show him what was in the bag, did the slave relent. It, too, was quite a first. Ward held the human scalp in his hands. There was some age to it, but it was in decent shape. The hair was that of a brunette man and upon turning it over and inspecting the scalp, Ward read two permanent inscriptions on cloth sewn into the leathered skin. Nearest the forehead it stated, "Taken Aug. 1813 Ft. Mims, Ala." an inch below, "From Lt. Burns by Wayward Warrior sold to British Army."

Ward was in shock at the scalp's purchase, then by the effect it had on Ike. The slave, formerly amiable, now seemed filled with hate. Ward immediately recalled the extensive time spent with Wash and Deely. They were certainly behind this dark change. He'd have to report this to his father and that they should do something. The once bright promise for Ike seemed to have vanished as Ward could not help thinking. The unspoken message was that Ike wanted Ward to also hate all whites, like Lt. Burns and Ben Travers, as did the subservient people, Creeks such as Wayward Warrior and slaves, as Ike did.

The train slowed down for water at a little burg called Williamsburg. Most everyone smelled the wonderful fresh bread and coffee for sale at the depot and departed to partake, but Ward remained on the bench seat. Was that the message Ike was trying to tell him? Which world did he belong to? Was he in the white world like Benjie, or the Indian, once he'd learned his true lineage? Was Ike now dangerous? Further, why did life raise such tough questions?

Alabimo Slave Quarters
Five Days Later

Ike had come to admire Deely's long-range thinking and hoped he could emulate it, too. His comrade Wash had been placed in charge of deciding which of Ben Travers' now twenty-nine adult male slaves could be trusted and asked to join them. Deely, due to past bad behavior, was never allowed to leave Alabimo, but young Ike could and had. Deely had placed himself in charge of equipment in addition to the plan itself.

The event would happen on a Sunday, like this day, and during both church services held on the Alabimo grounds. There was a crude building behind the saw and grist mill buildings for the slaves there and those of the two neighboring plantations who voluntarily attended. Also, for the whites, Ben had a small, but tasteful chapel erected next to the big house kitchen. On occasion, a few neighboring whites would also come and attend.

And so it began. The signal was the ending of the hymn "Swing Low, Sweet Chariot." Ike had already left, riding to the neighboring Dunn plantation where their fourteen adult male slaves would be enlisted to help. Wash's job was to lead the seventeen slaves of Alabimo who'd sworn to help. Then, Wash was to get the others their equipment to fight: hoes, pitchforks and axes, strategically hidden in the vegetable garden. Deely's duty was to enter the big house, find the stash of pistols and rifles and then lead the men. The plan called for their group, after killing all the whites at Alabimo, to begin marching south and east on the Federal Post Road towards the stache of U.S. military guns at Ft. Stephens, so not only could all the slaves be armed, but deny the white volunteers firearms. Deely's plan had not accounted for one rare occurrence; Ward and Benjie skipping the church service.

Eliza Travers always had the minister preview the sermon and upon hearing that today's covered God's wonders and the magnificent creation of the human mind, she deemed it not suitable for poor Benjie's ears and for Ward to stay with him for company. Never one for idle hands, the brothers had decided to use this morning for cleaning Ben's collection of three pistols, two muskets and two rifles.

Tipped off to their hidden location in the armoire of the family dining room, Deely crept down the main hall and opened the door as he heard the last refrain of "Swing Low, Sweet Chariot." Benjie had been dismantling the firearms and Ward reassembling them. When Ward saw Deely and the fire in his eyes, he grabbed the only two weapons still fully intact, two of the pistols, the powder and lead shot bag.

For some strange reasons even the doctors did not understand, Benjie's kick in the head from the horse had given him twice the physical strength he'd had prior. Frustrated at his lot, Benjie enjoyed proving it. He rushed Deely, who was a well-portioned muscled man as the two began wrestling about on the table and then the floor. It gave Ward his chance. Deely's behavior indicated Eliza, Ben and others were in dire trouble. Ward bolted down the hall, jumped off the porch, burst open the church doors, slammed them shut, dropped the heavy wooden bar down to lock and secure them.

The Travers, the old preacher and their Sunday guests were safe as they began to listen. Wash had his group armed and they came to the church screaming death threats and vulgar obscenities. Ben now had one of the pistols and strived to keep the gathered worshippers calm. When he refused to open the door, Wash threatened to burn the church. It was then that Ward revealed to Ben that Deely had engaged Benjie inside the house. The fact tore at Ben, but he was powerless to assist his son's current predicament.

Things were eerily quiet in the church as Wash's group went silent and all listened to the wild yelling, the crashing sounds of glass breaking and bodies falling, emanating from inside the big house. Benjie and Deely were in a tremendous and literally the fight of their lives. Wash took four men, two with axes and two with pitchforks towards the frantic racket. A few moments later, the church group heard a blood-curdling scream from poor Benjie's mouth and then total silence.

With the realization his brother had been killed, Ward started to raise the locking bar and seek revenge, but Ben stopped him, stating the safety of the whole demanded the door to remain closed. Wash came back and began yelling orders for a fire to be built and it was quickly obeyed. Three small fires were lit at the base of the south, east and west walls. Wash made a statement they'd stay around long enough to see the fires kill the white devils. Deely overruled him and loudly demanded all to know the plan called for fast movement. There was no time to watch a church burn inhabited by the whites. They were off to murder the Dunn family, increase their number and move on to St.Stephen's armory.

Ben, Eliza and Ward went to the closed door. The renegade slaves were leaving down the drive and had broken into song.

After a moment, Eliza spoke softly, "They're singing 'Go Down Moses'. The hymn about the slaves in Israel where God told Moses to get Pharaoh to let his people go."

Ben had no time for Biblical music lessons and opened the door just enough for Ward and one of the overseers, McPhail, to slip out. Immediately, Ward took his place, now with both pistols, on the steps and kept an eye for any indignant slaves returning. The overseer and Ben dashed over to the well, drew water buckets, ran back and forth a total of ten times until all three blazes were extinguished with minimal damage.

"I'm going to check on Benjie," said Ward as soon as the fires were under control.

"No! Ward, take my horse and go alert the militia command of the situation. Don't forget to tell him about Deely and the armory. Go quickly!" yelled Ben.

McPhail placed himself in front of Ben for orders. He was told, although it might be too late, to take a horse, somehow get around the rebellious slaves and warn the Dunn family of the coming danger. He nodded and headed full speed to the stable, just as Ward was exiting. Out of the corner of his eye Ben saw Eliza moving towards the big house and her son, Benjie. He pointed to Jones, another overseer, to stop her as he placed himself between his wife and the house.

"Eliza, wait. I don't know what I'll find, but please let me go first for Benjie," Ben said, his voice cracking on the name of his firstborn as he mustered all the calm he could. They both knew.

Chapter 12
The Storm

August 16, 1847
South of Fort Douglass
Pre-Dawn

There was a thick, wet breeze blowing in the faces of Col. John Knox Douglass and Ward Travers as they rode at the head of a dozen volunteers. Their intentions were to gather more men and place themselves, somehow, on the road east of St. Stephens to block the slaves from the guns therein. The fierce storm's wind blew harder, but the good news was the road had been baked hard dry and the horses were not yet mired in mud. Time being of the essence, Douglass and his crew rode hard. When the news began to spread men were needed to quell a slave uprising, and volunteers increased their number. Ward took the lead briefly to a small ferry Ben Travers had built south of the old Vine and Olive Experiment location.

Angling south and east instead of due south towards St. Stephens would use a better, wider road. Col. Douglass had a combined force of forty militia and civilians by midday. As the wind continued and the rain returned, the militia officer's two main concerns were timing and how large his foe number was? Later, as they briefly rested their horses just beyond a no-name village that had just sprung up to work a salt mine recently discovered there, under a canopy of live oaks Douglass noticed an ominous sight. Below, there were wagon tracks, lots of them, almost about to disintegrate from the rain, but unmistakable. He called Ward over.

"This Dunn plantation, would you happen to know how they get their cotton to Mobile? Do they hire a riverboat?" the colonel inquired.

"No sir, Daddy always laughs saying the wind blows half of Mr. Dunn's pickings out of the wagons on the trip south, that's why he had so many, more than anybody else in the southern tip. Why?"

Col. Douglass pointed at the myriad of rutted tracks in the damp dirt. His opinion was once his quarry discovered the mules and wagons at Dunn's they'd be difficult to overtake. He decided to about face and use a narrow, discontinued path that headed due west towards St. Stephens in an effort to arrive before the slaves.

An hour after he'd decided to ride west, he and his men saw the dreaded sight of Deely, Wash, Ike and over 100 others piling out of the armory each one armed with a musket. The slaves saw the white militia at the same time and formed a line next to the building in an open pasture. Deely had chosen the fighting ground. Col. Douglass' men on horseback did the same and all immediately noted the difference in numbers, the white men were far less than half their opponents' number.

Then the wind howled as tree limbs began cracking, crashing and falling in the near distance. The rain which had briefly ceased came back again, too. Lifetime local resident Col. Douglass recognized the signs at this time of year; this was a hurricane, or the very least, the outer edge of one. Instead of postponing the fight, he saw an advantage. He knew the only arms left at St. Stephens were outdated Revolutionary War muskets. All the newer arms had been shipped to the now state capital of Montgomery. Douglass also knew the Army's western Indian-fighting forces had taken possession of the entire supply of edged weapons there, such as Bowie knives, tomahawks, swords and most importantly, bayonets.

Inclement weather would be his equalizer. The regulars and nearly all the volunteers carried tomahawks, swords and had bayonets fixed to their long guns. As gunpowder wouldn't flash fire in driving rain, the word went down the line to attack from horseback with such. His orders to the men were to take prisoners, if possible, for return to their owners, but victory was more important. Douglass feared losing might possibly affect the status quo on every plantation in the Southern United States.

Ward didn't have time to be afraid but did think briefly that if he could cut Ike out of the line and move him to safety, he would. The militia and volunteers, led by Douglass, proceeded at gallop speed towards the slaves, who, unfamiliar with firearms, did not realize the moisture problem, as they stood their ground, aimed and then pulled their respective triggers to a resounding 'click', as none fired. By the horsemen's third pass they'd cut down or stabbed the last rebel slave resistance and the remainder threw down their useless muskets and stopped fighting. Twenty-nine lay dead, a dozen more would soon die from severe wounds and the remaining fifty surrendered. Only four of the white were lost having been clubbed by the muskets and ten other whites bore minor wounds on that soggy afternoon.

The fight was over in five minutes, but now the men, slave and white, faced another survival obstacle. The raging storm. Multiple lightning bolts crashed all about the men, rendering the woods now too menacing as flying, splintered limbs and huge falling trees were no haven. Instinctively, the white men huddled their horses in the center of the pasture, dismounted with reins in hand and huddled under their animals, hoping it would soon pass. The surviving slaves, now with their hands and feet tied, just knelt in the open nearby and took it.

A rough half-hour later, the rain slackened to a light drizzle. Ward thought about Ike, back at Alabimo, he'd, of course, be punished, but afterward possibly they could return to their former friendship. Two minutes later, after Col. Douglass ordered all to mount and head toward town, Ward discovered he and Ike would never have that chance.

Ward reigned up next to three of the buck-skinned-attired volunteers as they spoke between laughs. One said he'd cornered one young slave and noticed a white man's scalp hanging from his belt. Another recounted to his comrades he'd seen the same and that the brazen insult overpowered the order to capture those who surrendered. In his fury, he killed this one. Not only had he stabbed and slashed him ten times with a sword, but after being joined by two friends they dismounted and beheaded the offender. The three were now in the process of mounting Ike's head on a pike, right on the roadside, so every traveler, free or slave, could see the morbid future of those that dared to challenge the mastery of the planters' system.

Ward seethed in anger inside. His once friend's head was on public display! That sounded like something Mother had read to him about the barbaric Romans of old. Ward was but a teen boy and these were heavily armed men, he could do nothing to stop them. Then, he recalled what had actually just happened to him personally of participating in an actual battle, a real fight with killings and he'd not just witnessed, but played a role by battering two rebel slaves' heads with a borrowed tomahawk. Before the troops trotted off, Ward turned in the saddle and took a long look at the pools of water mixed with blood about the pasture battleground. Then, a second realization, he'd been in the saddle for almost thirty straight hours. How could he be so thoroughly tired and exhilarated at the same time?

Bones of the Black Warrior

(No one, black or white, knew or cared that what was later called The Dunn Uprising and Hurricane of '47 had taken place at 31.5 latitude north and longitude 88.0 west.)

Chapter 13
At Peace

December 20, 1851
Alabimo Plantation

"We've fallen further behind, Eliza. That California coming into the union as a free state makes it sixteen of them against fourteen southern states, more importantly thirty-two senators to our twenty-eight. Those darned abolitionists are only going to feel more empowered to impose their will on us. Mark my words, Eliza, those blasted Yanks are coming for our way of life," Ben said as he paced the family dining room.

"Dear husband, remember today is about Ward," Eliza chided. "Please postpone your political talks for your after-dinner cigars and brandy conclave with your gentlemen friends."

Eliza wanted the attention to be on Ward. As no one knew his exact date of birth, the Travers had used his adoption date, December 20. And this was a big birthday and Ward would soon find out as he entered the room just before a young female slave with a birthday cake.

After she left and Eliza passed each a sliver of carrot cake on a Sterling silver plate, she spoke. "Ward, your generous father has a gift for you. Go ahead Ben."

On cue, Ben reached into his silk coat's inner pocket and retrieved a neatly creased official-looking document. Ward smiled as he unfolded the paper, and read it to himself, before placing the paper on the giant mahogany table and hugging first Eliza and then Ben. "Thank you, dear parents, thank you so much. Just as was stated a moment ago, Father, so generous, so very giving, Mother. I hope to repay you someday."

"Hold on son," said Ben. "This is a gift, not a loan. Look again at the deed. You own that land, there's nothing to repay, son. The old Dunn plantation was held up in probate court for over three years. There was no way I was going to let ole Angus McIntosh or Farro Randon come in and buy prime land next to Alabimo. You deserve and earned it, son."

Eliza saw a chance to speak. "And today's my boy's majority birthday. Of course, besides now being able to vote, you *can* legally become a landowner and now you do. Here's the best part; you'll be our nearest, dearest neighbor."

More hugs went around the room as Ward fought back tears of happiness. The thoughts he'd had years ago about whether he was a real white man no longer mattered. In secret, Ben had put that question to rest by two separate actions the past year. First, when the census taker came by the plantation and asked the standard questions, Ben answered all the Travers were white. Earlier, Ben had monetarily rewarded a county clerk to adjust the roll going back to Ward's adoption records and changing Indian to White.

Eliza, naturally, had a more stylish question, what would Ward rename the old Dunn place? When her son hesitated, she offered a weighted suggestion. "Ward what if, and this is your choice entirely, you own the land, but what if you reversed the letters in Alabimo to O-m-i-b-a-l-a? Does that sound intriguing?"

Ward's eyes lit up and revealed his affirmative answer before his mouth could. His plantation would be called 'Omibala' and there was significant meaning attached. Then, a touch of sadness hit. The only reason the 400-acre Dunn plantation was now his was the loss of seven lives, eight if one included McPhail, the Travers' overseer. The '47 uprising rumors still persisted that the bodies were also terrifically desecrated. Enough of that now, Ward reminded himself to make sure the Dunn family plot would always be well-cared for.

March 2, 1852
Omibala Plantation
Front porch

"Colonel Douglass, I hope you'll be well-pleased and sir, I'm privileged to have you as a neighbor," Ward said as he pushed a glass of tea across the small table to his guest.

"Thank you, Ward. I'm counting on your instincts about Ben. You've only been the owner here a few months and you've made a major decision about the land. Hope you're right," answered John Knox Douglass as he nodded and took a sip.

Colonel Douglass had been forced into a decision. If he wished to maintain a military life, he'd have to join the U.S. Regular Army and likely move out west to a post somewhere in west Texas. No. So, he resigned from the Alabama Militia and decided on a new career in farming. But, he wanted to stay close to home, yet didn't want to upset the more established planters by competing. More important to John Knox was his private reason, strictly he was raised on the Bible and personally saw slavery as an inherent evil. One passage, when forced to deal with the subject, was readily available in memory: Galatians 3:28, there is neither Jew nor Gentile, neither slave nor free, neither male nor female, for you are all one in Jesus Christ.

John Knox kept this unpopular opinion to himself and vowed to never own another human being. He'd talked Ward into selling fifteen acres of cleared, but otherwise unimproved land on the east side of the Travers holdings. There would be no special name for his property, and he wasn't going to grow cotton. A friend had recently attended a seminar at Howard College, a few miles north in Marion. A traveling professor had broken down, on a per acre cost, the expense of growing cotton. He'd listed every item from interest on the loan to purchase the land, to how much it cost for a slave to hoe and clear weeds from an individual acre, all the way to transport the cotton bale to market and its net profit, if any. Then, in comparison, the teacher did the same for a traditional, multi-faceted operation that raised fruit as the majority crop, without slaves and their ever-rising cost. The fruit farmer's profits per acre were double those of the large plantation owner. John Knox was of the belief there was a stigma attached to *not* owning slaves, the growing of cotton and no local man had the gumption, or guts, to buck the status quo.

When a staffer at Howard College later revealed the guest lecturer was actually married to a Boston abolitionist, it was decided all his fancy numbers, ideas were biased as anti-slavery propaganda and nothing more. However, the former militia colonel did not see it that way and after signing the papers on Ward's front porch, owned the land. Now he'd begin the endeavor for his fruit, hog, chicken and corn farming operation.

Bones of the Black Warrior

(The previous week, in an unsigned letter to Governor Collier, John Knox had written to argue the newly created state public school system should include free blacks, also. He did not advocate, of course, mixing the races in school, but that they should have their own. Having access to basic knowledge, and the ability to read and write would only make the state a better place to live for all, in his opinion. It was a private thought and would have completely ostracized him from the community if revealed. He'd also encountered numerous human bones when planting his fruit trees, and like Ben Travers, kept the fact to himself.)

He turned back to Ward who felt he hadn't fully addressed John Knox's concern. With confidence he first stated that it was his land, second, fifteen acres in Ben Travers' eyes was not much, thirdly, with the land having been neglected three years, this sale would help him save the expenses of returning the land to proper planting form and last, Mama was in his corner, and she wielded more power at Alabimo than the outside world knew. After Ward's little speech, John Knox felt completely at ease with his purchase.

Chapter 14
A Challenge

July 8, 1852
Douglass Farm

A great and unfortuitous circumstance had warranted his land purchase. The past spring, a flood staged Tombigbee River had shifted and entirely obliterated the family farm of his father. John Knox Douglass rolled the last log off his flatbed wagon. It was time to reassemble the cabin he'd been born in nearly forty years prior, outside the Tensaw community, at its new property at the fruit farm. The final log bore two faded injury holes from Creek arrowheads in the 1813 attack and caused a moment of reflection. What drastic changes had occurred in this area from the day his life began to the present. Civilization had formed a wild country into a modern world.

He'd heard soon the Mobile and Ohio Railroad would complete the short line to Jackson, Alabama. If that didn't scream modernity and civilization, nothing did.

With so much work ahead, John Knox could not allow himself the luxury of thinking about anything other than the immediate task at hand. He'd tried to pay close attention as he dismantled the old family cabin in hopes that would help during the rebuild. This would be a first-time experience.

John Knox was lucky in that the hard work of felling the trees, notching the corners, finding stones for the fireplace and removing the bark had already been done. He'd chosen a spot near, but not too near Randon's Creek, for his water supply and faced his front door to the south for better protection from the elements. Another key factor in his choice for placing the cabin was the expansive, cleared meadow that was ringed by an unnatural circle of huge pines. At least his humble cabin would have an impressive ride up.

One item he'd need to show immediate attention was to replace four leather straps, used as door hinges, for his front and back doors. All four had torn, removing the doors. John Knox, for a military man, was an excellent handyman, but fabricating those was beyond his ability and would require a general store trip in the morning.

John Knox was short on supplies now, too, as he'd not wanted foodstuffs to be part of his move. As much as he detested Stockton, the Irishman who'd murdered the Creeks, he'd have to trade with him. Time, rather the lack of it, prevented him from traveling north or west to other communities' general stores. He had to buy his food basics, leather hinges and complete his cabin as fast as humanly possible.

Ben Travers had bankrupted the man sixteen years prior, but he'd survived and now, even thrived. Thanks to marrying a homely, but wealthy widow, in 1840, Stockton now operated a grist mill, blacksmithing shop and general store. People had started coming in and settling, many because of the thriving salt mine and by 1844 enough white, male Alabamaians were local to petition the state legislature for township status. Never shy, Stockton persuaded the state to name the little burg after him.

John Knox was acquainted with Stockton, Alabama, but had always been able to avoid trading with the old scoundrel, until now. Swallowing his pride, Douglass went in for his hinges and foodstuff. His plan to despise every moment in the general store immediately vanished when a young lady, about thirty years in age, welcomed him in and assisted his restocking needs.

Her name was Matilda, and it was only the two of them in the building. Mr. Stockton was off tending to some business. Douglass learned she, once like her mother, was also a widow. Her husband, a sutler named Shivers, had been killed three years prior when a boiler exploded on a river steamboat plying up the Alabama River. In his thirty-nine years, John Knox had been too busy keeping the militia organized and trained to be anyone's husband, or that was his Sunday morning excuse to the interfering old biddies at church, the past twenty years.

Matilda Shivers and John Knox Douglass were hitting it off famously and even after purchasing his supplies, hinges and reloading his wagon, he'd not left. Matilda had invited him for a cup of cider in the back room. Thoroughly wrapped up in each other's company it took a mighty crash and the breaking of glass to bring them both out of the back. Someone, who'd fled now, had reached over the counter to reach the licorice jar, but instead had pushed it off and fled.

John Knox moved back and away to allow Matilda room to sweep when Mr. Stockton entered through the front door. Stockton looked about, then angrily moved and stood directly in John Knox's face.

"Mister, you will owe me for your clumsiness," Stockton roared with venom. "Twern't no ordinary jar you broke. No, that candy jar was custom-made for me in New Orleans. Had the glass blower engrave me dear ol' homeland map on both sides. No sir, twas one special to me and one I paid a dear price for."

"Look, Mr. Stockton, I'm sorry for your breakage, but I had no part in it," John Knox calmly replied.

"That's right, stepfather, sir, John Knox, I mean mister, I mean Colonel Douglass, had nothing to do with the candy jar breaking. We were in the back and…" a stammering Matilda let her word stream stop as she took a hard glare from her overbearing parental surrogate.

Stockton held his stern gaze on Matilda for nearly half a minute, before speaking to her male visitor. "Whoever you are, you shall pay $20 gold to replace me favorite jar in the whole entire store."

"Sir, I said I had nothing to do with your breakage," pleaded John Knox, maintaining his sensible tone.

"I said pay up," demanded Stockton as he inhaled and puffed his chest.

"Sir, if I was guilty, I would gladly pay for my error. Not your ridiculous $20 price, but fair market. As I had nothing to do…"

Angrily, Stockton interrupted, "So if'n you didn't, Matty girl, I'll take it first out of your wages and then your hide." Turning away from her, he again bellowed at John Knox, "Twenty, I said."

Matilda's face revealed fright, a fear of being beaten, like it was something she'd come to expect of the ill-tempered man. "Stepfather, if I'd broken the jar, I'd pay to replace it, however I was in the back when someone came in, likely tried to steal a licorice stick and accidentally pushed the jar off the counter. And besides, Mother and I were with you on that trip to New Orleans. I distinctly recall you paid $3.00 for that very jar and complained mightily that the Jew was a greedy man for gouging you with that price."

Stockton had now heard enough. He moved behind the counter and reared his right hand back to strike the young lady. As she cowered to accept the blow, Stockton threw his arm forward, but it did not reach its target. John Knox also moved behind the counter and stiffly blocked the arm's motion.

"Oh, mo dhia," spat Stockton in Gallic. "You didn't just meddle? You interfered with me punishment of me own daughter?" the store owner wailed incredulously.

"Stepdaughter," Matilda interjected with some force.

Once more it not only raised Stockton's ire, but his right arm. Douglass again used his ample muscle to make sure the arm did not move to strike the lady. "You cad, I don't even know your foul name, but you've dishonored me even more now, besides defiling me stepdaughter more than likely and causing me store damage to boot?"

"Stockton, I am a gentleman and, on my word, even though I was alone with Matilda…"

"I'll not hear more filthy lies from your filthy mouth, you son of an English dog," Stockton said with vim and hate. "I be challenging you here and now. To me, your name is of no importance. Somebody will tell it to the undertaker. I'm calling you to duel me at noon on the day after the Sabbath over to de Soto Island."

(De Soto Island was an anomaly; a small mound of dirt and mud located at the confluence of the Tombigbee and Alabama Rivers, over the years which had been the center of disputes. Going back years ago, both the Choctaw and Creeks had claimed ownership, later the Choctaws and developing American government had squabbled, most recently in 1819, as the new state of Alabama was being officially formed, two counties of Clark and Washington counties both claimed the ten acres and the lawsuits and appears were still unsettled. With no clear governing party, it remained a haven for those outside of the law. Although state law had outlawed dueling, de Soto Island, under no distinct jurisdiction, regularly hosted one-on-one battles.)

Chapter 15
Satisfaction

July 12, 1852
11:35 a.m.
De Soto Island

So popular was de Soto Island for settling disagreements, that one industrious soul had set up a side-line business there. For a fee, he'd rent two separate skiffs for the parties to paddle out with and also the use of either swords or dueling pistols for the squaring of differences. One could also purchase premade tourniquets, gauze, bandages and even the latest medical breakthrough for pain, ether. The ambitious man could also, for a higher fee, arrange for a physician to be on hand.

John Knox Douglass, on that morning, was accompanied by Ward and Ben Travers plus two of Travers' most loyal slaves. They were along to row the skiff and heaven forbid, if necessary, carry John Knox's body back to his little plot of land for burial. The angry Mr. Stockton was also accompanied by two slaves and his only friend in the world, H.T. Russell, a disliked local gambler, petty thief, drunk, rumored Mobile pimp and man widely known of low character. Residents of the area all agreed Stockton and Russell's friendship was tailor-made as no respectable person would give either the time of day.

Ben Travers would be serving as John Knox's second and had lent him his copy of *Irish Code Duello* on the carriage ride south. Ben, being older when dueling was legal, had always assumed some hothead would eventually challenge him, but it had never happened. John Knox, of course, knew the basics of dueling, but not the intricacies and so the book made him familiar. Both combatants showed up at the little shanty run by the man who rented the skiffs and other dueling essentials. Ben suggested they back off and let Stockton's group go in and paddle over first.

Upon arriving on de Soto Island, Ben approached Russell, the second for Stockton, and they reviewed the rules. Ben had his code book with him to settle any disagreements on said rules. Surprisingly to Ben, Ward and

John Knox, the rules were easily agreed upon. Stockton, having been born and raised in Ireland, had great respect for the Code Duello as it was almost a daily occurrence someplace in the Emerald Isle during the previous century. Pistols at twenty paces combined, a single shot and the outcome, be it a miss, a wounding or a deadly shot, will end the disagreement over the $20 once and forever future.

Finally, Stockton approached Douglass. "I'll be giving you your one chance right here, lieutenant," Stockton said, insulting Douglass' former militia rank, "you can back out, pay me the $20 gold and no one will ever hear of the settlement. Why, since you're a gentleman, I'd even take a promissory note for the money. So, would you be..."

Thoroughly insulted and now dead set on going on, John Knox interrupted his opponent, "Make ready to duel, sir," was his terse response. Stockton's eyes widened at the sharp retort and twisted his lips in amazement.

The others in attendance moved back away as Ward was given the duty of counting off the ten steps each to separate the combatants. Even though the day was hot, Douglass, on Ben's advice, had worn his heaviest topcoat to offer some protection. Stockton was in normal attire, except for green pants and his gold shirt, the colors of the Irish flag. The rules agreed upon allowed either man to turn and fire the instant the word "ten" was spoken. Douglass was a crack shot, and knew a rushed shot is generally a missed one and vowed to take careful aim. It began.

"Gentlemen, the noon hour is upon us," he began the count, "...eight, nine, ten," Ward said loudly and without hesitation, Stockton immediately spun on his boot heels, firing even before he'd stopped. A great cloud of white smoke spewed forth from the pistol barrel. All eyes locked on John Knox. Was he hit? Even he wasn't sure, and he inspected the front of his white shirt for blood, then he dropped his gaze to his gray pants and saw they, too, were clean.

John Knox Douglass allowed a smile, his first in three days, to crease his lips. He still had his shot to take. Now the attention shifted to Stockton. What would he do?

Under his breath, the cad Russell offered advice, "Run for the boat. I'm loaded for bear under my coat. I'll hold 'em off until you're back on dry land. Run Stockton."

But Stockton had the code rules drilled into him as a boy. He would not run. He would stand.

It did occur that he might try and reason with his opponent or blame his faulty aim on the pistol. Maybe they'd allow a reload? Then, Douglass took the questions out of his mind.

"Stockton, some part of me wishes to put this ball right between your eyes. However, I made a promise to Matilda and I'm a gentleman. You have her to thank. Here's the end," Douglass extended the gun and briefly pointed the pistol directly at his foe, before discharging the ball short, where a black streak of mud landed on Stockton's shirt.

Then, Ben spoke, "Mr. Russell, I believe that gives us the honor and priority of leaving the field first and we so choose. Good day." They took to the skiffs in silence and the slaves began rowing. They were halfway back to Alabimo before Ward broke the silence.

"A man was willing to give up his life or take another's for a mere $20. Tsk, tsk," he said as he shook his head. Ben and John Knox agreed in silence with a nod. Even the slaves knew it and also agreed. There wasn't a lot that could be said. None of the men had wanted to be involved in a duel. None had wanted to go to de Soto Island. Yet, they all knew they couldn't escape and were mostly using the time to themselves to thank the Lord that John Knox had not been killed or wounded.

(Meanwhile, still stunned and not wanting to accidentally overtake the Travers' entourage, Russell and Stockton, stayed put for while doing nothing with the two white men passing a bottle of rye whisky between them at 31.0 latitude, 88.0 longitude.)

Chapter 16
A Substitute

August 16, 1857
Alabimo Chapel

Eliza was beside herself. Exhausted, tired and worn out from grief, she stretched out, face down, on the first pew of the chapel and continued to cry. Dressed all in black, she, for a few more moments at least, was the only person in attendance at Ben's wake. Ben had died the previous day; ten years exactly on the death anniversary of their only biological son, Benjie.

Ward was outside of the chapel with the preacher who'd be presiding over the funeral in an hour. Their regular preacher, Reverend Forrest, had been lured away to preach in Memphis. Rev. Yarbrough, his replacement, was new to the area, had only met Ben Travers briefly twice, and Ward was supplying information crucial to the eulogy. Ward had already begged off. He was in equally as bad shape as Eliza as he had truly, deeply loved the man who'd adopted him and impossible for him to mutter the name, Ben, without breaking into a crying jag. John Knox Douglass would have been another logical choice, but he was unable to. Matilda begged him not to attend as he was very ill and off-and-on running a high fever, but although he did not have the strength to speak, nevertheless refused to miss the funeral.

No one knew the exact cause of Ben's death. He'd gone for his morning ride and never returned. A pod of young slave women at Alabimo, returning from the head of Randon Creek after doing wash, had discovered his horse, riderless by the stream. Looking further, one of the braver slave girls saw Mr. Travers face down on the side of the crude road sometimes called Burnt Hawk's Path. After his plantation was up and running, Ben had used his laborers to clean and widen the path the Creek leader had used to flee from Alabimo in 1836, while being chased by Col. Douglass, eventually tumbling off the bluff into the Tombigbee.

The somber procession made its way to the family plot, jointly chosen long ago by Ben and Eliza. A few years before Benjie's murder, they singled out a serene space, away from the common areas, for the Travers' family burial plot A shaded area between two towering twin cypress trees. Thirty minutes after it had started, the last shovel of dirt was scraped over the coffin of Ben Travers. Douglass wouldn't have said so even under torture, but the fact Eliza had allowed four of Ben's favorite slaves to carry his body, along with John Knox and Ward, to the grave in a show of white and black cooperation, had pleased him.

Another thought brought solace to him. The busiest time of the year, for the next ninety days, was upon Eliza, Ward and himself: the harvest. Fourteen or more hours, six days a week would totally be devoted to their respective crops and rain or shine, nothing would stop their work. It would be especially tolling on Eliza, now going it alone, but Douglass had come to know the lady and even though she'd been born in and always lived in luxury, she possessed the tough grit and necessary stamina for hard work.

By this time the importation of slaves from Africa had been outlawed for fifty years. In the states where more, not less, slaves were needed, such as Mississippi, Alabama, Louisiana and Texas, they were being bought in Virginia and the Carolinas. Before his untimely demise, Ben had chosen to increase his stake and imported another twenty workers. Next door, holdout John Knox, Matilda and little son Micah, remained steadfast, continuing to raise their pigs, fruit and other products alone.

And so it was as a typical busy day drew to an end, a hired cab dropped off a strange, unknown man, dressed all in black, on the front steps of Alabimo at sundown on August 28, 1857. Ronald, the lead house servant answered the door promptly and inquired politely who was calling. As the man answered as Ronald held his lantern up higher, the normally calm and reserved head house servant's eyes widened and bulged as if he'd seen the ghost of Ben Travers.

"Tell the widow Travers, her dear late husband's brother, Brett, is calling."

A curious Eliza had been halfway down the main stairs when she heard the door knock. She could not believe her ears. Did the caller say his name was Brett Travers? Not possible, but overwhelmed by her need to know, she quietly came the rest of the way down and stood behind the still opened door. She whispered, "Ronald, who is it?"

Bones of the Black Warrior

Before Ronald could answer, stepped in an almost exact physical replica of Ben. Eliza just barely made it to the nearest chair which she collapsed in and nearly fainted. Ronald, ever aware and prepared, knew exactly what to do. The writing desk drawer held Mrs. Travers' smelling saltshaker and soon Ronald held the strong ammonia-based cure under her nose.

It worked and Eliza was instantly fully awake and aware. However, to be safe and not fall, she remained in the chair as Brett approached with a broad smile on his tan face. Not waiting to be asked to be seated, he sat across from Eliza and gave a slight hand motion to dismiss Ronald from their midst. Laying his hat aside, Brett began explaining how he'd suddenly appeared at their door.

(Being from Beaufort, South Carolina generally meant the adult males would find some kind of employment in the line of seagoing vessels. Some men built them, others manned the sails, some owned them or like Brett, or Captain Travers as he was better known, some hired their talents out as ships' masters. Poor Ben had been cursed by a weak stomach, got seasick in even the slightest chop and so had chosen a land career as a traveling salesman or sutler.)

Two nights ago in Mobile, after his evening meal he retired to the Battle House Hotel lobby for his cigar. Perusing a copy of the *Mobile Daily Register*, Captain Travers had happened upon his brother's obituary and the information he was the owner of Alabimo Plantation, at the southern tip of Clark County. As captain and master of the clipper ship *Racehorse*, and on a run from Charleston to Galveston, he'd no intention of making any stops, but a broken mast from a high gale squall required immediate repair and luckily, he was due south of Mobile when he needed help.

Brett first apologized for not attending their wedding, but he believed he was in the western Pacific, on a whaling ship, when Ben and Eliza had been married. Ben had written home to Beaufort after Benjie's birth, so he knew of it and he'd also written about poor Benjie's tragic death, but that was the last communication with his brother. Sheer fate had brought him to Mobile and blind luck had him reading a newspaper, something he rarely had opportunity. Brett said he must travel, finally meet Eliza in person and pay his respects at Ben's gravesite.

By this time, Eliza was fully back in control of her faculties. She spied Ronald and motioned him to come back to the guest parlor. She told Ronald to bring a pitcher of tea, Brett interrupted and asked if he could, after his long, dry carriage ride, have something to better cut the dust, like a bourbon or rye? Ronald looked to the lady of the house before complying, saw her nod and moved off to complete his task. Old Ronald, who was probably in his mid-sixties, was the de facto leader of the house slaves and they dared not challenge his authority as many times they'd experienced Ben and Eliza's support of Ronald. While Ronald ruled the house, the grounds and the kitchen, Ulysses held the same power in the fields.

As Eliza told how they assumed something had spooked Ben's horse and his fall had broken his neck, Brett found it difficult to give his full attention. The home's expensive furnishings were hard to ignore; art, mirrors, rugs and all purchased from the finest London and Parisian import emporiums. Back in the hotel lobby, two nights ago, he'd asked a gentleman seated nearby the distance to the southern tip of Clark County and did he know of Alabimo Plantation? The stranger not only replied with forty miles, but he'd heard of Ben Travers' passing and the widow, the former belle of Mobile, Eliza Delchamp, already wealthy, should now be worth a few million dollars, in his estimation. That was all Brett needed to hear as he sent in his formal resignation papers as master of the *Racehorse,* and made arrangements to travel a very important, and hopefully lucrative one-way journey.

September 1, 1859

Two weeks and two years after Ben Travers' death Altar of the chapel at Alabimo, Reverend Yarbrough said the words, but was not happy. None, save the main two parties, were. "I now pronounce you man and wife. Captain Travers, you may kiss the bride."

He'd done the waiting game. Brett had held fast for two years since his brother's passing to make it official. Yes, they'd caused some talk when Eliza became engaged a mere ninety days prior, but her pause to marry was the accepted norm and no one could speak rudely of her.

Bones of the Black Warrior

Captain Travers had asked Eliza to loan him the money for their travel to and honeymoon in New Orleans, but he never intended on repaying her. In his mind, he too was now a millionaire and small money matters need not be repaid.

Ward was unhappiest of all at his mother's new spouse. While she went to her private boudoir before joining Brett for the carriage ride down to Mobile where they would board the schooner, *Dampier* to New Orleans, he approached her in private.

"Mama, you are going to think this is strange, but I had a very odd dream last night," Ward began. Searching for the correct angle, she was distracted, not paying full attention as last minute packing had her brain racing. Ward saw it and moved in closely, stating he had something of utmost importance. In his vivid dream, Father had come to him, clothed like an angel and directly said Brett was well-known around Beaufort as a known swindler. The angel told him to convince Eliza, no matter how much Brett protested not to add him to their bank accounts or to alter her will and testament. In his dream state, Ben adamantly warned adding Brett to her will would be the equal of signing her own death warrant. Poof, and the angel Ben disappeared.

Eliza stopped her actions of gathering perfumes and stared at Ward, long and hard. Had she just made the worst mistake of her life? Can you really trust a warning from a dream? Something made her flashback to the day of Ward's adoption. He looked, dressed, acted, sounded and on official paperwork, was white, but she knew the truth; Ward was full-blooded Indian. However, she didn't know what to do. Was that a common misconception that Indians had deeper insight into dreams than whites? Or do the more civilized whites and their pragmatic sensibility deem a dream about an angel to be just that? Make-believe. Confused, she nodded to Ward and agreed there'd be no harm in waiting to make changes to her will. Satisfied with his mother's answer, Ward hugged her and wished her a pleasant trip and to enjoy New Orleans.

Reverting back into her businesswoman mode, as Ward was leaving the room, she said, "We'll also be inquiring about purchasing a steam-powered cotton press. It was your father's intention to do so on his next New Orleans journey. Oh, and Brett has mentioned looking for a good deal at market. We're staying at the St. Louis Hotel, where they hold auctions once a week, so we shall look into that, too. Don't tell Ronald, you know he's going with us, but Brett's going to sell him there and find a younger replacement. You'll be in charge, so take good care of things in our absence, son."

Chapter 17
His Element

September 2, 1859
7:45 a.m.
Little Point Clear, Alabama

Captain Travers was well-versed with Mobile Bay's fickleness, known by old salts far and wide as a tricky body of water that changed depths with each daily cycle of the tides. Travers wasted no time in hiring a pilot at the mouth of the Dog River to ferry him and his new wife south to the anchorage of the schooner, *Dampier* and the tiny hamlet of Little Point Clear, the last vestige of civilization before the vast expanses of the Gulf of Mexico. Just back from the white sand and sheltered by scrub oaks, were a few shanties and shacks where passengers could buy a meal and drink while waiting to shove off.

The scene brought back bad memories to Captain Travers. He'd shipped out on an American freighter out of Wilmington in late summer of 1830. Seeking refuge from a probable hurricane as they trekked towards the tip of Florida to round and head west to Tampico, Mexico his captain sought shelter on Bimini Island. Unfamiliar with the island, the Wilmington master dropped anchor in a nest of pirates. After dark, the surrounding pirates boarded her, killed the captain and stole her cargo. One by one each crew member was given a life-or-death choice; join the captain at the bottom of the bay, or sign-on to crew the four pirate vessels. Brett, a mere lad of seventeen and a lot of life to live became an unwilling pirate.

The next morning his captors took him ashore to a string of crude shanties and shacks, lightly protected by a canopy of scrawny oaks. Each shack had a specific pirate trade going on inside.

At the first shanty, Brett quickly had his right ear pierced, and a cheap metal stud shoved in place. The next shack had a tattoo artist who inked the name of his new ship, the *Daybreak*, emblazoned on his left forearm. The third shack held armament for an individual pirate such as pistols, daggers or cutlasses Brett chose a cutlass and then was handed a note to sign for repayment to the ship's captain for credit to pay for all three of his newly acquired items. Of course, he'd never see the funds to have the option of paying the captain, it would just be withheld from his share of their next stock of stolen booty.

Unaccustomed to the hierarchy and pecking order on a pirate ship, Brett made a serious mistake on the first afternoon at sea aboard the *Daybreak*. A shipmate equal in age, approached and ordered Brett below to begin cooking their evening meal. Brett had thought he'd figured out the chain of command aboard and this fellow had no authority to order anyone to do anything. Brett punched the boy as hard as he could in the gut and when he keeled over in response, Brett added a swift kick to the ribs. Young Travers returned to his assigned duty of using a marlin spike to join two lines of medium length for a longer version.

The first mate saw the confrontation and with an assist from two other burly pirates came to Brett and after manhandling him, tore off his shirt and tied him face-first to the main mast. Before Brett knew what was going on, the captain and whole crew were gathered as the first mate announced punishment of five lashes with a cat-o-nine-tails whip for insubordination and refusal to obey orders. It began.

The initial swipe of the flail from the boatswain's hand shocked more than hurt. The next four made up for the initial lack of pain. Adding pirate insult to pirate injury, the fellow whom Brett had struck was given the honor of rubbing ash and mud into the fresh wounds, ensuring Brett would be left with noticeable permanent scars. The smelly mixture also drove home their pointed reaction of remembering his punishment. Later, the swelling would do so in a more prominent fashion and one more easily seen by the outside world.

Brett Travers' pirate life was a short career. Luckily for Brett a 74-gun ship of the line, pride of the U.S. Navy, The *Franklin,* ran down the *Daybreak,* forcing her to surrender off Great Abaco Island. Brett's youth helped convince the marines who boarded the pirate vessel that he'd been pressed into their illegal service. Also, his badly infected earlobe and forearm also helped sell his plea that he was not supposed to be on board and was, in fact, a prisoner. The ear was so far infected that *Franklin's* doctor half-amputated it, forevermore forcing Brett to always wear his hair longer than he actually wished.

Bones of the Black Warrior

Shaking the angry memories of that one terrible week from his head, Brett's thoughts shifted to the future and tonight, in the honeymoon suite at the St. Louis Hotel. He'd been careful in the past two years to always cover his left forearm tattoo and his mangled right ear lobe. His mantra was to wear a shirt under his daily dress shirt to help hide the scars on his back. All these things had the possibility of coming to the light of Eliza's eyes this very evening. Should he continue his physical deceptions? Or, should he openly display them, relate the story of their coming to be and hope she wouldn't be repulsed? It bothered him, not knowing what to do.

Back in the present, Brett kept Eliza firmly on his hip and glared at the three hungover sailors in the one shanty they dared enter for some coffee. Eliza did not care for the situation, feeling the lecherous stares and begged Brett to quickly exit, which they did. Just as they arrived at the westernmost pier, the *Dampier* threw her bow into the wind, slowed to a halt and luffed up beside the pier. Brett helped by grabbing her bowline as he recognized her skipper as an old mate from his whaling days.

It was an excellent day for sailing the Mississippi Sound on the twelve-hour trip to the Crescent City and Eliza thoroughly enjoyed her new experience at the bow watching the dolphins race and play as they accompanied the schooner. Seeing the flying fish flee the bottle-nosed mammals was a bonus. The salt air was lighter, cooler and carried a welcomed briskness that drove away the usual heaviness of summer humidity in the Deep South.

Brett was a different man, she quickly noted, once at sea. Here he was in his element and among those of his kind. She paused to wonder how Ben's brother would take to his new life as a cotton planter. Something told her it would not be easy for Brett, but she vowed to do her best to assist her new husband. Perhaps even, as she certainly had the funds, a cargo ship could be purchased in Mobile? After the cotton bales were barged downriver to be sold each October, could Brett master a family-owned vessel to move the cotton to the great textile mills of the Northeast? There might be money in that venture and one definitely deserving of discussion, on their two-week New Orleans honeymoon.

Breaking her thoughts about growing the family treasury, Eliza was drawn to the horrid sounds of a seasick Ronald, retching over the starboard rail. Poor, poor Ronald; seasick and the waves were only in a minor state.

It was only going to get worse for the clueless old slave upon their arrival at their New Orleans destination. Brett went to his rescue, produced a ginger cookie along with instructions to eat and swallow slowly, plus to keep his gaze up and fixed over the green lands at the northern horizon, find one lone cloud and stay focused on it alone. Brett's remedy worked and in about five minutes, Ronald was cured, no longer drawing raucous laughter and crude comments from the crew.

Glad to see old Ronald in better spirits, Eliza's brain returned to where she preferred; business. She reminded herself to make time while in New Orleans to tour not only the finest ladies boutiques, but the top men's haberdasheries as well. New Orleans was the most worldly and the nearest thing to a European city in the whole country. The Crescent City had the best connections to New York, London and Paris and the elite shops along Canal and Chartres Streets prided themselves by only displaying the latest sensations from those cosmopolitan centers. Eliza was interested in fashion, but more so, she wanted to check the fabric trends. What if wool was making a comeback? If so, they should reduce their acreage planted and number of working field hands. What if it was the opposite? What if cotton fabric was continuing to thoroughly and completely dominate the fashion industry? If so, it'd be a handy time to purchase more slaves while they were in the city and then, once home, look into increasing their acreage. There were many decisions to be made over the coming two weeks.

September 9, 1859
New Orleans, Louisiana
Rotunda - St. Louis Hotel and Exchange

Captain and the new Mrs. Travers stood alone inside the hotel's grand rotunda's outer edge as the scheduled events slacked off and the majority of the crowd noisily either left the hotel or moved to the lobby. The Travers stayed put and looked about the giant room. Just six hours earlier, how impressed they were at the lavish, decorative and even ostentatious designs. Now their impressions had flipped.

An arrogant gentleman from Baton Rouge, who'd stood next to Brett before the auction began, had predicted it. In idle small talk, he'd said the high-water mark for slave prices was nine months ago. The market was now all about cotton production and any slave not designated for sale as a field hand would be depreciated going forward. Brett, who'd noticed a strong smell of liquor on the man's breath, had decided if this man said it, the exact opposite was probably true.

Now at five-thirty in the afternoon, Brett wished he heeded the whiskey-laced warning and not wasted their time. One reason the auction was such a drawn-out affair was New Orleans itself; different auctioneers would repeat the same information three times on every item, once in English, once in Spanish and then in French. The weekly slave auction had ended. The lead auctioneer had pleaded for the remaining crowd not to leave, as next there'd be auctions for fine furniture and works of art.

Disgusted, Brett told Eliza to wait where she stood, he'd go behind the raised stage and find the unsold Ronald. Silently, she did not share his regret. Something had told him to take a straight razor to Ronald's bushy gray hair, that no hair at all would present a younger light. He'd also deferred to Eliza on the setting of his price. After all, the fact she'd not immediately added him to the bank account upon their marriage, hadn't been lost on Brett.

For her, selling Ronald was tough, but felt allowing Brett to win this and make a decision involving the plantation would help him in his transition from ordering men to sail a ship, to captaining growing the white gold. Eliza recalled Ben had traveled to Market St. in Mobile for his second round of slave purchases in 1824. There he had paid $350 for Ronald and immediately upon hearing him speak and noting his slight build, decided Ronald would never toil in the fields. Eliza's instructions said anything less than $700 was criminal today.

Ronald had appeared on the auction block about halfway through the experience. Brett immediately saw it was not going well when no one in attendance spoke at the $700 asking price. Brett, being Capt. Brett Travers, had gone behind Eliza's back and told the assistant to the main auctioneer that there was leeway to drop down as far as $550. Still there were no takers at that discount, either. After feigning shock at the auctioneer's audacity to drop Ronald's price, Brett declared no harm had been done as nothing had changed.

After Ronald's exit from the block came the field hands. Again, using Eliza's expertise and experience, Brett was prepared to go as high as $1500 for a prime example, but none of the first dozen sold for less than $2000. Using a tone that the gentleman from Baton Rouge was sure to hear, Brett declared these auctioneers were no better than the infamous local highwaymen of recent times, such as Big and Little Harpe or Sam Mason.

With a slight head nod, the gentleman from Baton Rouge said nothing in response, but slipped his sterling silver flask from the inner pocket of his linen frock. Again smiling, this time directly at Brett, he was offering the first sip. Brett declined and the man shrugged and took a deep pull of fine Kentucky bourbon.

Much to the new groom's surprise, Eliza leaned in and nodded at the stranger, "kind sir, don't mind if I do," she coyly said, surprising both of the men before taking a dainty sip, screwing the top back on, saying thank you and handing the flask back.

She gave no reason for her actions. They were her own. She severely dreaded having to be confronted with her old friend, Ronald, in a matter of minutes. How was she going to explain this to Ronald? The trusting and loyal servant had to feel betrayed, and she was angry at herself for allowing Brett to convince her that he'd needed to go. Maybe it wasn't Ronald who should go? After all, Ward, in all his years, had never revealed he was capable of such dreams, one that also carried a warning.

Same day
Downtown Mobile

John Knox Douglass' good mood was shattered after reading one particular obituary in the *Mobile Daily Register* paper. Exactly what was this writer stating? Did some people have no memory? Reading the write up of the death of Stewart McNally, also known as Burnt Hawk, was maddening. All right, yes, since the Second Creek War, Burnt Hawk had repented and preached peace. But after all who was he preaching to? Ninety percent of all the Creeks inside the borders of Alabama had been forcefully deported to the Indian Territory. There probably weren't 1000 local Creeks left. Subtract the women, children and aged and that might leave 150 males of age to wage war? What damage could that size of Creek warriors do against a half a million Alabamaians? Burnt Hawk's preaching peace since 1847 was worthless propaganda.

The controversial man was dead, passing away quietly in his sleep. Stewart McNally was certainly a man of his times and like the land he loved, as it changed, he transformed. Born from a union of a Scottish immigrant and Native woman, the area that would come to be known as the Southwest, was also a blend of red and white. Strongly attached to his mother, when Stewart saw her widowed and her wall of marital protection disappear, the abuse began. It did not matter that she could read, write, had converted to Christianity, dressed as a white and in actions acted like one, the simple fact she had been born Creek overruled all. When Stewart saw her abused; he began to seethe. Finally, after the broken promises, a never ending flood of settlers and acquiescence proved fruitless, he had donned the buckskins, moccasins, tomahawk, feather headdress and joined the people of his Mother. The angry and disillusioned Creeks quickly discovered his instinctive talent for fighting and leading men.

Then, after their defeat in the Second Creek War, Burnt Hawk reverted back to his white roots, clothing, name and lifestyle. In his last dozen years McNally ran a small farm, saved his money, increased his holdings, switched to cotton, and ironically, became a slave owner. He lived quietly and out of the public eye for those years, a mere twelve miles west of the great massacre he'd planned, led and carried out in 1813 at Ft. Mims. Why wouldn't he have preached peace? The tranquil life as a gentleman farmer had been good to him.

Where in the obituary was the mention of 1813 and Fort Mims? Five hundred and fifty white lives were lost in that one afternoon, suffering a most brutal, cruel and painful death. Burnt Hawk, on that fateful day had also sent out roaming small bands of warriors to individually kill and burn settlers' homesteads, such as Mr. and Mrs. Wyatt Douglass and the newborn John Knox. And what of Burnt Hawk's devious plan that sent small Creek boys into Fort Mims, pretending to play in the loose dirt, piling up an impediment, to prevent the gates from closing? Where was that remorse? Skip forward to 1836 and Burnt Hawk incites a new generation to wage war. Until his fiery speeches and rabble-rousing, the Creeks had been peaceful and were, with the help of the agents, acclimated to their new roles. Why did the writer not mention the 700 Creeks and 150 white settlers and soldiers that needlessly were killed in a pointless show of stubborn rebellion, orchestrated by and primarily instigated by Burnt Hawk or Stewart McNally?

John Knox, thoroughly disgusted, crumpled up the paper and threw the despised broadsheet down at his feet. Immediately, he chided himself for bringing on possible attention. He was in Mobile for a secret meeting with a representative from the hotbed of abolitionism, Boston. That exact moment was when their representative walked into the lobby.

The man from the North believed it was time for local, sympathetic whites to rally under their banner. John Knox was once leery, and now had a strong opinion. While his inner soul had recently quietly supported the abolitionists but acted non-committal. Over the past year, a string of letters to-and-fro between Douglass and Boston had produced many kindred thoughts and words on paper. Now, the abolition leaders wanted more than thoughts. A former militia colonel, who could train slaves for battle and then lead men into a pitched battle would be invaluable.

Uninvited, the representative wrote announcing pants to travel here for a meeting. Quickly, John Knox responded and cautioned if so, theirs must be a clandestine conclave. He agreed to meet one representative in a public setting.

Frustrated with the federal government's continued appeasement policy toward southern states, this abolition faction decided the only solution lay in supplying the enslaved with fighting equipment and battlefield leadership. Recruiting men such as John Knox Douglass was imperative. There was also the recent example from eleven months prior. John Brown's failed uprising of capturing the Harpers Ferry, Virginia armory was fresh in their collective minds. Those slaves, armed only with clubs, met failure when discovered by government troops before they realized a single gun.

John Knox was of the belief slavery's expenses were no longer sustainable. The prices involved had become prohibitive. In private, the majority of local planters agreed, but what could they do? Given time, the institution would devour itself and just peacefully die. Time. Just time. However, this traveling abolitionist had come south that day for one man to become a vital cog in their idea to solve this issue tearing the country apart.

Bones of the Black Warrior

John Knox's last letter instructed their representative when and where to quietly arrive.

Furthermore, he'd be in a black suit with a peculiar boutonniere; a beheaded daisy, with only the green stem pinned to the lapel. In response, the Yankee lawyer stated his signal would be a brass eagle pinned upside down to his right lapel.

After arriving, John arranged for privacy by quietly telling the Northern sympathizer to exit onto Royal Street, walk west until the sign stating, 'Spring Hill seven miles', and wait.

It went against John Knox's manners, but wasting time at the Spring Hill sign was dangerous. He interrupted the fellow, who was likely a serious and Godly man, but it was time for him to listen. Begging his pardon, John Knox stated slavery's cost would soon consume itself, to let it just fade out and the stack of $100 bills the man was offering wouldn't be accepted. He ended by adding that the abolitionists should redirect their efforts. They should start petitioning their contacts in national office to prepare for the coming large numbers of blacks, soon needing schoolrooms. With his point made, he exited the city, making north and east for home to Matilda and little Micah.

Chapter 18
Burned

May 18, 1865
Front drive of Alabimo Plantation

Mrs. Eliza Travers stood at the end of her crushed oyster shell drive, a quarter of a mile south of her mansion. She finally gathered the gumption to turn around and look back. The black smoke was smoldering up to the heavens as far as the eye could see. Her knees grew weak and to keep from keeling over, she dropped to the ground and just stared as best she could through tears.

Why? Especially now, three weeks after the end?

A post rider had come to the mansion yesterday at noon and given her two letters. One was from her spouse, Brett. He explained he was an officer with Captain. Raphael Semmes was aboard a Confederate raider and allowed he was in good health and presently anchored in a small harbor of a neutral European country. At least he was safe when he wrote the letter back on December 31, 1864. By comparison, the second letter was even older.

Ward's letter was dated June 9, 1864, and directly stated he'd been wounded three weeks before in the Battle of Resaca, Georgia. As he wrote, he was in a Union prison and specifically in the hospital ward; both of his eyes had received wounds when an overheated cannon exploded during the skirmish battle at Dug Gap. Ward quickly noted in his letter the Yankee doctor expected a full recovery of his vision. Ward revealed he was being held at Ft. Delaware on a small island in the Delaware River. The remainder of his letter inquired about her, Alabimo and Omibala.

As if that wasn't enough news for Eliza, the post rider, trying to make a little side money, had sold her the latest broadsheet published by the now combined Mobile newspapers.

It was worth the $2.50 gold piece as in big bold letters the headline read, "Gen.Taylor surrenders. War over!"

Bones of the Black Warrior

Trying to of course sell papers and push the local angle, the article stated the Confederate general surrendered all Rebel forces under his command in the Louisiana, Mississippi and Alabama theaters. Taylor surrendered to Union General Canby at the home of a friend of the Travers, Jacob Magee whose farm was approximately twenty miles south and west of Alabimo. To Eliza, the real news was the war was over. Ward and Brett were alive! This four-year nightmare was finally over. But those were yesterday's feelings.

Today the nightmare had only reached its most horrible and terrible conclusion when Union cavalry troops attached to General James Wilson's brigade came calling. Eliza met their captain here, right where she was in a crumpled mess, late afternoon of May 17. Her first instinct was to welcome them and let them know, since the hostilities were now over, it was time to be friends and Americans again. She offered them fresh water and bread, and volunteered to slaughter one sheep and however many chickens it took to feed the three dozen blue-clad horsemen. She presented the Mobile newspaper as evidence that peace now existed between the North and the South.

The cavalry captain just laughed, declared it a rebel trick and he appreciated her offer to feed his men infected chicken meat, but he'd pick and choose his own animals to slaughter and eat. Water? He could find water at any creek. They desired whisky, bourbon and wine. Twenty minutes later it started. After confiscating the last four healthy hogs and discovering Brett's extensive wine collection, the captain sarcastically thanked Eliza for her hospitality and that they'd be leaving. However, first his men were cold. He suggested a nice cozy fire and sent ten men to fire the cotton fields. Second, since the lady of the manor had been greedy and not offered up her best food and drink, he'd return the favor and poison both of the wells. The last gesture was for scheming to try and trick her Northern superiors with the false newspaper article of the war being over. The punishment for that must be severe. The house must feel the wrath and the might of the Union Army. Burn it!

After a sleepless night on a hard pew in the chapel, Eliza thought about Ben and how lucky it was he wasn't around to see his beloved home reduced to a pile of blackened wood and brick. She watched as a twenty-five foot front porch column, weakened from the intense blaze, decided it had enough and ever-so-slowly toppled over backwards into the mound of debris that was formerly her lovely home. Yes, it was better that Ben wasn't around to see this awful sight. It struck her as odd that seeing the last remaining column fall didn't make her cry, but then again, there were no more tears to flow.

Standing up and gathering herself, Eliza then saw an unusual sight. Almost silently, eyes front, humming a gospel tune, were all the Alabimo slaves, walking by her to the Federal Post Road. They carried bed rolls, boxes and all their worldly belongings inside of folded blankets.

She knew from memory that counting all the workers and children there were sixty-three slaves. It looked as if they were all leaving. None spoke and Eliza was entirely speechless. There was nothing to say. After the last few passed by, a ray of hope sparked; she'd not seen Ronald or Ulysses, nor their wives. Maybe all was not lost?

Chapter 19
Prison

July 12, 1868
Omibala Plantation

Eliza stood on the front porch of Omibala Plantation and kissed Ward goodbye. He was going to Montgomery, as an inauguration guest invitee of the governor-elect, William G. Smith. As much as Ward had never warmed to Brett's marriage to his mother, he could thank him for his financial advice back in mid-1861. Brett had said maybe it was an old salt's wariness, but no matter how much pressure was exuded on Ward and Eliza to invest in Confederate bonds and currency, they should keep at least half of their money in Union money in a safe Northern bank.

Having the foresight supplied by Brett had saved Ward and Eliza both from total financial ruin. So much so Ward still had the funds to help get Smith elected. Hastily passed recent laws prohibited ex-Confederates from voting but did not keep Ward from making campaign contributions.

Meanwhile in Virginia, at the prison in Ft. Monroe, Brett Travers was breathing the air as a free man for the first time in two and a half years. Brett's latter war services had taken a grand and circuitous route. It began in June of 1864 in Cherbourg, France. The notorious Confederate raider, *C.S.N. Alabama,* left the safe haven of the harbor to duel to the death with the Union pride of the fleet, *U.S.S. Kearsarge.* Capt. Semmes had ordered Brett to remain ashore for another Confederate raider to transfer aboard her within a month. Capt. Travers, with his vast experience and knowledge of the trends and traits of Yankee whaling ships in the Pacific, would lead this new unnamed raider on a hunting trip.

On his first day as Master of his new command and noting his crew was mainly Virginians, Brett correctly deduced that naming the raider, *C.S.N. Bull Run* would be a popular choice. He set sail south and west to round the tip of South America, Cape Horn, with intentions of plundering enemy trade vessels in the Pacific. Capt. Travers, known for getting the most speed out of his ships, made their next landfall in New Zealand in record time; only eighty-seven days. As he had never served a single day in the navy, Brett used his days at sea to read, study and learn the methods of sinking enemy vessels.

One thing Brett had become in his midlife years was a true admirer of talent. It mattered not if said talent in nature was American, British or even the Man-in-the-Moon. And so he read and studied about the best there ever was; Admiral Horatio Nelson. He learned while other European naval powers debated battle tactics such as, is it best to disable your opponent's rigging first or should decimating your opponent's leadership and officer corps first? Nelson kept it simple. To him, it mattered not if your enemy's sails were full or luffing. To him, it mattered not if your enemy's top brass was alive or dead. Nelson believed seawater quickly flooding into your enemy's hull trumped any and all strategy. Brett Travers would mimic that philosophy.

However, the Confederate navy was not sailing the high seas to do battle with Union warships. Precisely, it was the exact opposite. The Confederate navy wished to avoid the enemy's ship and concentrate instead on a campaign of public persuasion. The repeated sinking of private vessels, such as whaling ships, was an expensive proposition for those stingy, money-hungry Northeasterners. Sink enough tonnage, drop a few innocent sailors in shark-infested waters and pressure will be exerted on Washington to comply with the simple request from Richmond. If the Union Navy will cease and desist the blockade of Southern ports, the Confederate raids on all private shipping will also halt. A very simple tit-for-tat arrangement between governments.

Capt. Semmes had given clear, concise instructions to Brett and stressed that time was of the essence. Sink, sink and sink some more and do so quickly. Try and preserve life when and where possible, but do not tarry to assist any fatally damaged vessel or rescue survivors. Brett's orders should be carried out as follows: come alongside, show the flag, announce your vessel's name, make clear this is not a negotiation, advise the enemy of your intentions to sink, give five minutes to abandon ship before pumping two shells from your largest caliber gun into her waterline, then immediately set sail for your next target.

These tactics, a good crew, the new technology aboard the *Bull Run,* and Brett's seamanship ability made her a highly effective weapon. The rebel raider was very good at performing the tasks assigned what she was intended to do. From October 1864 until Brett lowered his flag and surrendered, she was the scourge of the Yankee whaling fleet. Completely devoid of any communication with the outside world, and especially the United States, Capt.Travers did not hear of the Confederacy's surrender until November 8, 1865. In that span, he sank thirty-seven merchant ships hoisting the flag of the United States, of which twenty-three were whaling vessels. More than a few of those whaling ships carried officers and crew aboard that recognized the distinctive silhouette and voice of one Capt. Brett Travers. Those survivors lucky enough to have an adequate supply of lifeboats and thus escape the cruel fate of snapping jaws of the Pacific sharks carried the alarming news back home to New Bedford, Nantucket, Boston and Gloucester. His name became well-known in the newspapers of the Northeast as a heartless butcher, a seagoing outlaw, and most hated of all, a pirate.

And so it was that with his reputation in the North and the fact he'd continued to fight and sink private vessels six months after Lee's surrender at Appomattox, a harsh and severe punishment must be meted out. It mattered not that news of his country's demise was impossible to hear of in the middle of the largest ocean on earth, nor that he was following military orders during wartime and thus not a rogue outlaw pirate. The Union Navy transported Brett from his surrender in Hawaii to San Francisco, overland to Virginia to be thrown in the same jail as Confederate President Jefferson Davis. Like Davis, Brett was held in solitary confinement without trial. Unlike Davis, who was released from incarceration in May, 1867, Brett was not freed until July, 1868. His hard time was simple retribution, meant to placate the Northern press and cause physical suffering, which it did. After all, the big Northern newspapers called him a bloodthirsty pirate, plus his Yankee captors had seen his mangled ear, his tattooed forearm and grossly scarred back. Only a pirate would carry such markings on their body. So, as he left the prison fort and trekked on foot up the road to Hampton, Virginia, Brett actually felt lucky he'd not suffered the fate of most privateers, a noose.

August 10, 1868
Ruins of Alabimo Plantation

He was thoroughly exhausted. If he'd had even the slightest ounce of energy, Brett would have grown angry. Instead, after his twenty-nine day walk from Hampton Roads to the southern tip of Clark County, he was indifferent. Let out of prison without a penny to his name, Brett Travers was forced to use his two feet to get home. Along his sad path he'd seen so many burned out Southern homes that he was numb to the sight of his wife's.

Standing at the end of the long drive, he saw no one, nor any activity, but there were *some* crops growing. It appeared the old vegetable garden had a little greenery, most likely beans, peas, okra and squash. He saw no animals like chickens or pigs. Gazing further west, the main stretch of cotton fields was barely recognizable. Probably 85% had gone wild and was overgrown with switchgrass and broomsedge. The remaining acreage closest to the pile of debris that once was the mansion did have mature cotton.

At around his halfway home point in his month-long hike to home, just outside of Raleigh, North Carolina, Brett had stepped in a hole and twisted his ankle. A kind old Rebel, by the name of Wesley, who was passing on his emaciated mule, saw his plight and not only gave him a lift, but allowed him two days to rest until the swelling went down. During his time in the barn, Wesley complained mightily of the state of affairs in the old Confederacy. He said many of his friends wished they'd been killed in battle rather than live to see the abuse they were subjected to by the occupying Yankee Army. When Wesley mentioned that in North Carolina, there were seventeen ex-slaves currently in the state legislature, Brett could not believe his ears.

Finally, just an hour before Brett was to continue on his journey. Wesley spoke of a new organization, the Ku Klux Klan. After explaining its roots south of Nashville, Tennessee, Wesley tried to convince Brett it was his duty to spread the word and beliefs of the Klan to South Alabama. After being out of touch with the outside world for nearly three years, Brett was shocked to hear the transformation of the South and her former ways of life. Brett agreed to consider Wesley's ideas once he returned home.

Much to his surprise upon leaving, Brett was met with a group of neighboring farmers. Wesley had bragged about the former captain of the

Bones of the Black Warrior

Bull Run being his overnight guest. He was gifted a new straw hat, a used, but decent pair of Brogans for his feet and a hastily collected $3.00 for expenses. It was the best the beaten North Carolinians could muster.

(Brett, Wesley and five other ex-Rebels were standing on a patch of ground at latitude 35.7 longitude 78.6, although they didn't know or about of that fact. Finding their next meal was of a much greater concern.)

Chapter 20
Gossip

September 22, 1870
Omibala Farm

Every paper wrote about it and it was true. Each major newspaper in Alabama's major population centers of Tuscaloosa, Mobile and Montgomery printed the same thing. The upcoming election, now less than two months away, would be the most important in the state's fifty-one-year existence. Here was the opportunity to right the wrongs and return the state's sanity. It was still shocking to every white man, woman and child that currently the state had two ex-slaves serving in the United States Congress. Outrageous!

The editors of the papers kept pumping out similar articles. The state had been readmitted to the Union and now ex-Confederates could vote. The people had to make their voices heard and overturn what these Yankee carpetbaggers had done over the past five years. It had been the Republicans who used their armed forces to not just win a war, but first devastate, then financially and politically ruin the South. Now, in this upcoming election, the Democrats had to win; had to.

There was strife in Clark County. What had once been one of the largest slave-owning areas in the state was, like Alabimo, a wasteland. Burned-out mansions and even regular homes still lay in sorry states of rotting lumber and blackened brick rubble. There was no money. Well, almost none as Ward, Brett and Eliza Travers by secretly remaining monetarily halfway loyal during the war, still had some wealth.

Ward had become intrigued with state politics after his experiences two years ago in Montgomery and a budding friendship with the governor. It was time for Ward to run for office and he'd chosen, with John Knox Douglass' help, to be the Populist candidate for state senate in their district. John Knox was his campaign manager and more. Ward had never regained his vision in his left eye after his wounding during the war. His right eye did work, but was subject to blurry spells after even short reading sessions.

John Knox helped in that respect also, by reading aloud to him. The choice to run on the Populist ticket was risky; both men knew that, but decided the family name, character, power and history meant more to the locals.

On the opposite side of the ballot was the son of the multi-business owner in the town of Stockton, Simon Bolivar Stockton, a brash, opinionated man of thirty-three years of age. While his well-known and now-deceased father had a sullied reputation, Simon had managed to rise above his family history and recently earned an architectural degree from the University of South Carolina. With a great need, especially to rebuild public buildings, there was quite a need for good architects. Pulling a few strings had landed Simon the plum job of reviving the university's many burned-out structures in Tuscaloosa, which Yankee cavalry had torched a mere four days before Lee's surrender. That thoroughly unnecessary act so enraged Simon, it pushed him into joining the Klan in January, 1869 when Brett secretly founded a chapter. However, Simon knew absolutely nothing of politics, but Brett did, and he'd taken a liking to young Stockton. Family connections wouldn't permit it to be openly known, but surreptitiously Brett worked behind the scenes as campaign manager for the Democrat, even though he was running against his stepson.

He had to be as extremely careful around Ward and Eliza; as cautious as he'd been when a prisoner around the anxiously cruel guards at Fort Monroe. Eliza still had not added him to the bank accounts, nor the deed to the land at Alabimo. No doubt, if she knew or even suspected, she'd divorce him instantaneously, scandal be damned. Brett felt good about John Knox and Ward's bold decision to run as a Populist, a party which, among other platforms, supported public schooling of ex-slaves. However, the name Travers was the most well-known surname between Montgomery and Mobile.

The deep coffers of Ward and Eliza would be tough competition, Brett knew. Ward, through John Knox, had taken out advertisements in some of the Mobile papers: *The Mobile Republican, The Mobile Daily News* and *Mobile Daily Tribune.* He also was running ads in *The Weekly Advertiser* in Montgomery. These were, not by all means, the top newspapers, just the ones with desperate owners to accept ad money for a Populist. The other half of the papers refused.

Douglass' tender on the grounds they were exclusively Democrats. Brett obtained copies of all the papers and noted John Knox shrewdly never mentioned Ward as a Populist, instead concentrating on the last name and historical roots going back to when it was known as the Mississippi Territory.

A month passed and the election was a mere three weeks away. The best method for Brett to gain insight as to how his candidate, Simon Bolivar Stockton, was faring was to hire intelligent young male students on college break for the harvest season. Brett had, on every Saturday and Sunday for the past month, sent his dozen fact-finders out to any town with over 500 residents and cordially converse with eligible voters. On Saturdays the young men loitered about the town square or saloons. On Sunday they waited after the church services to quiz them. By October's third week, the results were painfully evident for Brett. If his numbers were correct, Ward held approximately sixty to forty percent advantage.

After a sleepless night on October 22, Brett made up his mind. He called on Simon Bolivar Stockton, told him the shocking news *and* presented proof. Armed with cash, a good horse and precise instructions for the wording, Brett sent Simon out on a mission sure to swing the election in his candidate's favor. Once he'd decided to make his move, Brett had another helper make a fast, secret fundraising tour to the area's wealthiest cotton planters. He was planning a newspaper campaign of his own and it would be much bigger than Wards as *all* the newspapers in the southern half of the state would gladly participate.

Years back Brett had sworn secrecy to Eliza regarding Ward's secret. Old Ben Travers, in an effort to cover for Ward's future, had bribed the county clerk years ago to change the birth record. Ben had only been shown the "revised" copies of the 1830 Federal Census. Ward, a little orphan full-blooded Indian Ward, was still on the original file as Choctaw. Resourceful and snooping, Brett was able to obtain that record for a mere $5 gold piece. This very morning, Simon was galloping southward to Mobile to place his ads and shock the landscape: Ward Travers was half-Creek, half-Choctaw. The Alabama voters were fed up with non-whites in government for the past five years. The message of the ads was plain and simple. Stop the Populists and Republicans and their black and Indian candidates; vote Democrat, vote for Stockton as district senator.

Bones of the Black Warrior

It was old Ronald's son, Roy, who made the discovery. Roy had tried freedom and walked off the plantation with all the others a few years back but missed his parents and the honest labor of working the fields. He came to despise construction labor in Montgomery and returned back to toil in the fields for Mrs.Travers again, but now for weekly wages. Going for water mid-morning as he took a break from weeding the vegetable garden, Roy found Brett's lifeless body in Randon Creek with two gunshot wounds to the upper left chest.

Scared and not knowing what action to take, Roy looked for Ward, as this bad news that should be passed on to a man, not a woman. Later, Roy would believe it was a woman's intuition and that of a wife, that alerted Eliza not just that Brett was missing, but that he was dead. When Rev. Yarborough rode up on a surprise visit to Omibala, Eliza hid. It was then that Roy found Ward and told the two men of his discovery. The preacher and Ward wasted no time and quickly mounted up and rode east to the creek behind John Knox's home.

Upon confirming Brett was indeed dead, the reverend mounted up, and rode for Jackson and the county sheriff to report his death, or as it looked, murder. Within two hours, Sheriff Bob Dees was standing by the creek along with the Clark County part-time coroner, Dr. Abel Smithson. There was no firearm nearby, so it wasn't suicide. Someone had gotten very close, from the evidence of powder burns on the expensive silk vest and shot him twice in the heart. The sheriff also noted there was no blood on the scene. Capt.Travers had been shot, killed and then moved into the shallow, two-foot-deep creek. Further investigation even found two sets of footprints in the light brown sand, both bare and small leading up to the body. The prints, more than likely two women, struck all involved as odd. Was this direct evidence?

Many times, it is not what you did, but who you know. The circumstantial evidence and rampant rumor making the rounds was Ward shot Brett over the election and newspaper ads revelations. Also, everyone knew they never were more than civil to each other, and it was common knowledge Brett had revealed the secret of Ward's birth race to the public.

Yesterday, she'd gone to the sources, the census taker, who lived nearby Jackson, for a $10 gold piece, passed from the hand of Mrs. Brett Travers. Eagerly, he related how Capt. Travers had obtained the truth to the forty-year-old secret. Tomorrow the census taker would be making himself a local celebrity telling of his unintentional involvement in the big news.

When Sheriff Dees came to arrest Ward for the murder, Eliza stopped him outside the home, and they walked the grounds. Not wasting time, she directly told the lawman it was she'd shot Brett and with the help of old Ronald's wife, moved the body from the barn where he was checking on his favorite horse, to the creek bed. Her motive for the move was that she wanted as few sets of eyes as possible to see the corpse. Eliza made no hesitation to explain her motive, but she really didn't need to.

Sheriff Dees never liked Brett, either. In addition, the sheriff and Ben had been fast friends and both deacons at the same church many years ago. The sheriff told her, in light of her confession, he would not arrest Ward. Furthermore, it was highly likely the murder would *never* be solved. Also, Eliza should keep her admission to herself and never again mention it to anyone. He then mounted his steed and the investigation disappeared just as did the dust from the hooves of his horse as he headed back to Jackson and a silence that would last until he'd be lowered into his grave.

Another of Eliza's secrets, told not even to Sheriff Dees, was *her* dream. Upon paying the census taker and learning of Brett's betrayal to the family, that night, in between fitful bouts of on-again-off-again naps, Eliza dreamed her angel, Ben, said he understood Brett had gone too far and punishment was due his crime and the location of his old double-barreled pistol. Ben said not only was it justified to shoot Brett; she *must* shoot Brett. Eliza woke up that morning and was completely confused. Was that even a real dream? Or, possibly, like years ago from Ward's mouth, Ben's angel had visited? Or, had during her fitful night, had she dreamt that she dreamed of her dear husband's visitation?

Chapter 21
The Politician

November 27, 1875
2:45 p.m.
Randon Creek

It was the women who stated the fact. The life of the Populist party, south of the Mason-Dixon Line, had been extinguished. Dead. Completely lifeless. Eliza took Matilda Douglass by the elbow and backed away from the creek, "I've got the article. As soon as Ward finishes reading it, I'll have one of the slaves, excuse me dearie, one of the servants bring it over to you and John Knox."

Widow Travers, as most called Eliza now, had always been politically astute; realizing her best friend's husband and her own son's two-year experiment as Populist needed to end. Also, a voracious reader, Eliza always made time for the latest news. Although her copies of the Mobile papers were generally a week old, they were still informative. The latest articles were about the new state Constitution which people were saying was a landslide Democratic victory, those who'd pushed it, led the way were lumped together and referred to as "The Redeemers." The name fit. It had taken a decade, but this new set of state laws literally turned the clock back to 1860, the major exception of legal slavery. The outcome, once the delegates were elected to write the new document, was nearly 80% Democrats. Indeed, the Republicans, Populists and Independents weren't just beaten; they were annihilated.

(The real subject had only once really been openly discussed between the Travers and Douglass families, but it was always present. Brett's sneaky and conniving attempt five years ago to subterfuge Ward's political campaign had, and likely always would, cemented Ward's involvement in the political theater as merely a money donor or maybe an advisor from the cotton planter's perspective. Never again would he, nor should he, throw his hat into the ring, not even for the lowest county position. The shocking revelation that Ward Travers had been born of a Choctaw and Creek union was insurmountable.)

"Heavens yes, Mrs. Travers," Matilda said quickly. "J.K. needs to not just read the paper, but get himself up the road to the county seat, quietly unregister his affiliation and then register immediately as a Democrat."

"That's good advice, child. It won't be safe anymore for anyone to carry the Populist torch anywhere in the entire South. You've seen what has happened to the poor old darkies and the less fortunate whites among us, too. Their landslide will make it dangerous *not* to be a Democrat."

"I hate to think. Oh, and those awful Klan night riders, Mrs. Travers, you'd think we'd regressed back to the lawless days of a hundred years ago."

"True, true dearie and I'll make sure Ward does the same. For safety's sake, he and John Knox should even ride together to Jackson."

Both women felt better and that they could make their respective men understand the urgency to abandon the Populist banner. Satisfied, they moved back closer to the creek, their two simple chairs and resumed their fishing. The outdoor hobby brought Widow Travers great peace; being away from the everyday hustle about her recently rebuilt house and in seclusion, could engage in her new-found secret addiction; pipe smoking. Matilda cared nothing for it or fishing; but believed the widow needed someone's company and if a few dozen or so bluegills were caught, it'd be a nice change of pace for dinner.

(At the outbreak of the war, Ward's Omibala cotton plantation had accrued roughly one-third the number of slaves as his parents' operation. Before the War, both John Knox and Ward had been registered Democrats, after the War, at the point in time when they were allowed to register to vote, both had gone Independent. Two years later, feeling the prevailing political wind, both flipped to the Populists. John Knox had done so for moral reasons, but Ward for personal ones as the Democrat machine, and Brett, were responsible for keeping him out of a state senate seat. After the Federal government had begun setting up Freedmen's Bureau around South to assist the ex-slaves in their efforts to transition into free citizens, John Knox had given his secret support behind the scenes, but was certain any overt act would have brought down the Klan's terror on the farm, Matilda and Micah.

In a long held pleasant memory for John Knox, he recalled the day in 1867 when many of the ex-slaves from Alabimo and Omibala had walked to the county seat to register to vote. Roy had led the way and after they'd registered, it was he who called on Douglass Farm along with about two dozen men over twenty-one years old. Roy explained the Yankee soldier doing the registration had told them they all needed two names now, a first and a last and gave them five minutes to think of a last name. Roy announced to John Knox that out of the deep feeling of respect for him that most of them chose to be sons of John, or Johnson.)

Same day
6:25 p.m.
New Alabimo's porch

"Well, I thought, didn't you go fishing this afternoon, Mama?" Ward said as he exited the front door to join Eliza on the wide porch among the array of eight rocking chairs. "I was looking forward to some panfish actually. I'll never turn my nose up at smoked pork chops, but a little variety is nice, too." Ward extended his left hand to find the exterior wall of the house as his after-dark vision was extremely poor.

"Doing fine there, Ward. Just keep on. Three more steps and you'll be at the rocker next to mine," Eliza said but did not rise to help her adopted son. She'd learned he cared little for verbal sympathy or physical assistance over the past decade. "Besides, we have something to discuss."

"You made your point earlier, Mama. John Knox and I are riding up first thing in the morning to register at the courthouse."

"Glad to know that, but that's not what I want to talk about. It's been nearly three years since Becky's passing and folks are asking when you'll start courting again. Matilda said there's a new pastor expected at the Methodist church down the road in Stockton. Said he likes everyone to call him Brother Bryce. He's a bit older, close to my age I guess, *and* there's a widow's daughter coming to live in the parsonage with him. Matilda's met her and her name is Carla Boatner, used to be Gerald, anyway it seems she's about thirty-five and still extremely attractive. I'm even told she has exquisite alabaster skin, beautiful blonde hair and the deepest emerald green eyes in all of Alabama."

"Mama don't. Please don't. I'm too busy for courting, I take that back. I'm too busy for a wife. Women take time and time's something I find hard to make. Besides, any pretty woman sees my messed-up eyes and that's it. Those boys that stayed home out of the war are much prettier than us that fought."

Eliza resisted the urge to thump her grown boy's ear for saying those words but held back. A good draw on pipe tobacco would help soothe her nerves right now, she thought. But how could she get away with doing that? Oh well, tomorrow. Instead, they sat together and rocked the evening away, enjoying the humidity-free last days of fall weather and the fact the cotton was all ginned, baled and sold. They both just had to wait another six weeks for those brokers' ninety-day notes to be called and go cash in the fruits of their labor.

Chapter 22
Gone Fishing

May 1, 1878
New Alabimo Chapel

Reverend Yarborough signaled for the congregation to rise and the half black-half white solemn group, gathered for Elizabeth Delchamp Travers' funeral, complied. Six men; Ward, John Knox, Micah, their longtime family lawyer, Roy Johnson and Sheriff Dees left their respective pews and came forward. Each man took a huckle, lifted in unison and proceeded out of the front doors. The preacher led them around the back of the chapel, towards the old grist mill and the reconstructed cotton gin, which had also been burned by Yankee calvary in 1865. Ward did as always when he passed the western side of the chapel and looked at the black smoke scars on the whitewashed wood, still plainly visible from the Uprising of '47. Ulysses, many times in the past, had volunteered to paint over the scars, but was always rebuked by Eliza; she wanted the ugly black streaks to be seen and remembered.

Following closely behind the casket was Matilda, holding hands with Micah, with a silk handkerchief, a long-ago gift from Eliza, and her second of the afternoon, daintily held to her nose. None knew, but when she was alone with Eliza's body at last night's wake, she surreptitiously stuffed the grand old lady's favorite smoking pipe down the tufted edge of the coffin's interior and out of sight. She, of course, had no idea if smoking a pipe was allowed in Heaven, but just in case.

Fittingly it had been Matilda who'd been with Eliza when she passed away. The two were enjoying a lazy afternoon at the widest and deepest section of Randon Creek. Only Eliza was fishing as Matilda was knitting baby socks. All was quiet for almost a half of an hour, which was not terribly unusual for them, when suddenly Eliza's cane pole went flying out of her hand. Some big fish had struck, but she'd not fought back. Widow Travers had quietly gone to her reward, seated in a weather-beaten old chair that stayed creekside. Never moved. Even kept her pipe between her teeth.

Just as relaxed and at peace as if she was stealing a quick nap on a warm, still, pleasant late April afternoon, which it was.

Immediately to Matilda's left was Carla Boatner Travers, having been married to Ward now for two years. Off to her left were two servants. One carried their infant girl, Rebecca, the other her fraternal twin male, Ben II. Twins, but with many physical differences besides their sex. Rebecca, tow-headed with one thick mop of bright white hair and huge liquid green eyes surrounded by a medium-olive skin tone; was gorgeous and beautiful. Ben the second, was much lighter in skin tone, brown-hued eyes and without a single strand of hair, but nevertheless a handsome babe. It had been Carla's plan, saying at her age, that her child-bearing years were nearly over and that she quickly wanted to give Ward an heir. The fact she'd borne twins was a pleasant bonus.

Behind Carla was a bevy of faithful ex-slaves, some now servants, others now sharecroppers on nearby farms. Leading this group was old Ronald's ancient wife, still alive and loyal to Mrs. Travers. The group of mourners made their way in silence to the Travers' grave sites, a good thirty yards past a double row of dogwood trees, about half still in bloom, behind the cotton gin. The shade from the two gigantic cypress trees enveloped them long before they reached the family plot. Eliza's grave had been dug early that morning, next to her husband Ben's, who in turn was next to their son Benjie, who'd been in the grave since 1847.

After the reverend's last round of words and final prayer, each little group began to file their way back toward the chapel. At this time the blacks separated from the whites and were no longer silent. It was old Ronald's wife that started it. Her voice was weak but strong enough, that she announced at this time in the Home-Going that they should sing and led them in *Amazing Grace*. In reverence, all the whites paused, turned and listened in its entirety before continuing on. It had been Eliza's favorite hymn, and it brought a new river of tears to Matilda and many others' cheeks.

After waiting for an appropriate time for reverence, the Travers' family attorney sent word down from Jackson that Ward should come by his office. Not knowing the length of the meeting, John Knox went along with his eyes. Lawyer Allen had the will out on a table in the corner of his office. It was very simple. Ward received all 2500 acres, the house, support structures, livestock animals, carriages, cotton barges, tack and equipment necessary for farm operations. Also included in her will was a surprise business: E.D. Travers' Transports, based on Mobile Bay and owner of the schooner, *Dampier*, which ran daily packets of passengers and freight between New Orleans and her home port.

In regard to the $430,000 cash in the First Planters Bank of Mobile County, Ward's portion was 90%. Of the remaining ten percent, it was divided equally: Ben II, Rebecca, John Knox, Roy Johnson and to First Baptist of Mt. Vernon, which was Reverend Yarborough's base.

Ward was in a semi-state of shock as he and John Knox rode south back to the tip of the county. He knew Mama was wealthy, but nothing like this. Plus, there was a schooner? How had he not known? The truth was Eliza had secretly made the purchase and intended on gifting it to Brett on their fifteenth anniversary but shot him roughly two years shy of the mark.

When the two were about three miles from home, Ward spoke, "J.K. old friend. I need help, your help. Running Omibala is about all I'm good for or even up for these days. If I try to keep her and Alabimo *and* a schooner, I'll be in a plot next to brother Benjie within the year."

"That's a full plate, Ward Full and then some."

"Here's where you can help. Buy Omibala. I have no idea of your financial state, don't want to know, but you pay me what you feel is a fair down payment and I'll finance the rest. Plus, I don't want to be usurious or greedy, so the interest rate will be one-half of one percent. You'll repay me once a year, on February first, so you'll have your farm proceeds plus the cotton from Omibala in your account."

John Knox reigned up and reached over to Ward's bridle. "Whoa…whoa."

"Wait, I forgot the price! How can you say yes, no or maybe until I tell you the price per acre. There are 730 acres, by the way. Well, it's like this. I've always liked history. So did Mama. She was rooting around in a travel trunk old Ronald managed to skirt out of the mansion before the Yankees burned her. Turns out Daddy kept a diary. Not an everyday one, but it was more of what happened every quarter of the year going all the way back."

"Back how far?"

"Back to the day he bought the first acre from those silly Frenchies that tried making a go. Can you imagine? Raising grapes for wine in this stifling heat, Ha! Anyway, he paid $2 an acre, so that's my price, too."

"If I hadn't been with you all day, I'd swear you'd had a fifth of bourbon or fell off your horse onto your head. No, both!"

"That's my price so don't try and dicker me lower," Ward teased.

"I won't, I promise. Oh, and although I appreciate your offer of a ridiculous interest rate, I'll be paying cash. Tell me Ward, if these are the kind of business deals you make, how'd you not go belly up twenty years ago?" John Knox teased the generous man in return.

"Then it's a deal. We'll give lawyer Allen whatever time it takes for Mama's land transfers to go legal, then we'll make an appointment for the sale from me to you."

"Sounds good, Ward. Now, about this schooner? Matilda was always telling me about your mama and her love of fishing. Any of that rub off? When do we take your new boat out in the Gulf and try our luck?"

Chapter 23
An Education

September 17, 1882
Tuskegee, Alabama

Roy Johnson, Jr. felt blessed and cursed. The entire freshman class, of which this was the first and only grade level, had similar feelings. He and his best friend, Cleo Johnson, no relation, had shared the back of a single mule for a week-long trek north and east from Clark County to the newly established Tuskegee Normal School for Colored Teachers. So new in fact, on the 100-acre grant of a former Confederate officer's plantation, there was yet to be a single standing building. An excellent place to start, in the words of the first and new principal, Booker T.

Washington was for the students to earn class credit while learning construction principles. Washington envisioned, in the beginning, the basic structural needs for the institute. He told the freshmen they'd start with a combination of classrooms, an office for him, plus a dormitory to house no fewer than forty students and most importantly, a chapel.

Blessed in that the state had finally done the right thing, according to the late John Knox Douglass, a casualty of the 1880 Yellow Fever Epidemic, close and dear friend of Roy the elder. The college was long overdue. John Knox had long held the opinion that these children of the ex-slaves should have had access to higher education since 1866. Cursed in that in the white-ruled world that was the State of Alabama, never would enrolling freshmen at any white school be expected or asked to hoist tools and physically build their own academy.

The initial outrage of Cleo and Roy only lasted a few days as the class mindset came around. Here was an experience of a lifetime, a chance to change not only the state, but possibly the entire South. Sleeping on damp grass in moth-eaten, twenty-five-year-old Union Army tents, where a few days ago was cause for dissension, now was seen as a bonding brotherhood between young men that would last a lifetime. No other incoming class could ever lay claim to this unique exposure. Relish it.

The young men also knew, after a couple of days, that toiling under a hot sun, sweating side-by-side with Principal Washington was a great honor and again, something no subsequent class would ever experience. Roy, Cleo and the others, after the initial disappointment upon arrival, began to admire Mr. Washington. It was easy and he being only five years their senior increased their alliance. Another first for these first freshmen, who'd never seen a crop field other than the typical, were three acres set aside for a food new to their world; the peanut.

Roy, Cleo and two brothers from White Hall, a small village outside Selma, were tasked with designing, building and erecting an entrance sign for the school, formally: Tuskegee Normal School for Negro Teachers. Mr. Washington specified it to be readily seen by any passersby at fifteen feet tall and wide; with a crimson background and gold lettering. The four felt honored to have been chosen; toiling from dawn till sundown every day for three days to finish the project two days early. It had been Cleo's idea to secretly add each builder's name, the date and hometown to the bottom of the footboard, only to be seen at some unknown point in time when the sign would inevitably be replaced. A permanent record for some students to ponder in the future, as their collective reality ahead was the reason they'd not turned around, left and gone home upon arrival.

Roy, Jr. excelled in not just building the entrance sign, but with all things woodworking. His father's brief foray into the construction world in Montgomery, right after the war had at least given him rudimentary skills, which he'd passed on. The finish, the design, the work ethic and the rapidity with which Roy, Jr. and his crew had constructed the sign were not lost on the school leader. At the next meeting to discuss construction, Mr. Washington not only gave praise to the four sign builders, but after singling him out, announced Roy as student-foreman for the chapel project.

(Mr. Washington, Roy, Jr. or any others in the first class at Tuskegee Normal were aware the center of campus was 32.2 latitude, 85.4 longitude. They were too busy.)

Chapter 24
A Secret

June 11, 1884
New Alabimo Farm
Master Bedroom

"Ward, turn that lamp off and come to bed. What is it, after nine o'clock?" Carla pleaded, but didn't bother looking up. She was engrossed in the light of her own lamp, reading the latest rage, *Treasure Island* by Robert Louis Stevenson.

"Almost done dear. Just adding events from the second quarter of this year to Daddy's old diary." He paused, thinking Carla would inquire as to his entries, but she was spellbound by the novel. After a minute of silence of rereading his notes, he sighed and closed the diary, which was actually an old merchant's ledger about eighteen inches tall and eight inches wide.

"This Capt. Flint is an absolute monster, I say," Carla said as if Ward cared. "I was thinking about his book and maybe letting Elbee read it in four or five years. Oh, well I'll decide that later."

(Elbee was the nickname of their son Ben. Over the past couple of years he'd gone from Ben, to Little Ben, to L.B. to the now familiar Elbee.)

Trying to engage in conversation he tried, "Well, what about Rebecca? She's really a better reader than Elbee."

"Oh, no, no. This is a boy's book."

"So? You are reading it."

"But I'm an adult and familiar with- oh, why am I wasting my time explaining modern literature to you? Silly."

"Just asking about our children, dear. I'm beat anyway. These new spectacles that Dr. Toland made are helping me read better and my eyes don't tire out as quickly."

"That's good to hear. Dr. Toland and Father were friends from their childhood days and even went together and fought the Mexicans years ago.

By the by dear, his nurse told me the term spectacles is out of fashion now, Ward. Everybody calls them eyeglasses nowadays."

Ward's eye injuries from the War, as he aged, were causing more problems, but he never complained except occasionally in private to Carla. He turned the key in his kerosene lamp, leaned onto Carla's side of the bed, gave her a quick kiss and said good night. Carla told herself she'd stop at the end of the next chapter, join Ward and turn off her lamp, too. Just like she'd promised herself ten minutes ago at the end of the previous chapter.

Ward's sleepiness took a temporary sidetrack. Carla had mentioned her father for the first time in probably a year. There'd been a major falling out. Carla's mother had passed away in the same Yellow Fever epidemic of '80 that took John Knox. Brother Bryce lived alone quietly in the parsonage for two years. Brother Bryce wasn't the first old man for it to happen and he wouldn't be the last.

After Carla's mother had died, the church ladies brought meals by the parsonage every night for about two months, then slowly it faded from their collective memory. At that point another woman, and one the antithesis of the Methodist ladies, Sally Russell, daughter of the despised petty thief and rumored Mobile pimp, H.T. Russell began visiting. Prying eyes began to mention Miss Russell's carriage was seen at the parsonage sometimes as late as 10:30 at night. What could the two of them be doing in there?

Those prying eyes didn't have to wonder for too long. Brother Bryce's sermons went from condemning the sinners who drank, gambled, smoked and in general broke every Commandment, save number six, to saying forgiveness, help, understanding, praying and minding one's own business was what really being a Christian was all about.

The deacons called a meeting after the fourth sermon along those lines. Seventy-five percent of them were upset. The rest believe that, if given time to grieve and recover from becoming a widower, he'd return to the old Brother they knew and loved. Word of the deacon's meeting reached Carla Travers and she immediately took a carriage south to Stockton.

She purposefully timed her arrival mid-afternoon on a Friday, as that was her father's typical practice time for his upcoming sermon. After beating down the unopened door of the parsonage, Carla finally walked in and saw a half-naked Sally Russell asleep on the daybed in the parlor.

Bones of the Black Warrior

The house reeked of tobacco smoke and empty beer bottles about. Quietly, she tip-toed around Miss Russell to the main bedroom. Her father was asleep, or passed out, wearing only his long johns with more empty bottles strewn around the tables. Mortified and more than a bit angry, she left.

Carla, of course, never told a soul except Ward. A few weeks after her visit rumors began creeping up from Stockton to the tip of Clark County. Sally Russell's carriage had been seen four times lately leaving the parsonage just before dawn. Once more the deacons met. There was a tense debate about having Brother Bryce terminated immediately, but finally their leader convinced them a final attempt to right the ship was only fair. It failed miserably when the lead deacon arrived at the parsonage and knocked on the door, but was told to go away, first by a mocking Sally, then by a cynically laughing Brother Bryce.

Carla might have been able to eventually forgive her father, even after he'd been dismissed and evicted from the parsonage, but when the deacons found that their jointly held parsonage bank account at First Planters had been drained dry, she was shocked. Next was the Methodist Board of Regents defrocking him. Carla was deeply ashamed. The deacons decided there wasn't a large enough sum to recover and the bad publicity of throwing *their* ex-minister in jail outweighed sweeping the matter under the rug. Sally Russell lived in her father's old home and with nowhere to go, Brother Bryce, or now simply Mr. Bryce Gerald, moved in. Carla was livid, vowed to never see her father until the situation changed, and he gave up his unholy relationship with the deceased pimp's daughter.

June 14, 1884
Stockton, Alabama

Ward had lost enough sleep the past three nights worrying about his father-in-law. He had no real plan or if he had anything to offer and definitely would not tell Carla but decided to go see Mr. Bryce Gerald in person. The old Russell place was well back from the road and years of neglect had allowed tall grasses, bushes and wild sugarcane to completely shield the house from the public road. By most standards it was a large house, nothing like a plantation manor, but with probably eight decent-sized rooms stacked in a square configuration, with a detached kitchen and the remnants of two smaller structures that rot had defeated. The house itself was a depressing sight. Creepers and vines had practically taken over the bottom floor. The last ancient coat of whitewash was hanging on by a thread. Dirt, weeds, trash, and neglect dominated the entire setting.

The stench hit even before the shock registered in Ward's poor vision. Something was dead and the hot sun was flaming with a noxious odor. With a handkerchief covering his nose and mouth, Ward dismounted in front of the porch steps among the overwhelming buzzing hum of a hundred flies. Ward then saw the source, a dead goat. Quickly, he scanned about for a shovel to bury the rotten animal. Hopefully swinging his gaze about the decrepit property, he heard the sound of footsteps approaching from the open door and long dark hallway of the main entrance. Listening closer he considered their source. If they were human feet, they certainly wore very hard sole shoes.

The 'clomp-clomp' wasn't human, but another goat; a big male with impressive horns. He'd been inside the house and from his manner, the animal seemed more at ease inside the house, than out. Ward and the billy locked eyes for a moment before the goat turned back and disappeared into the shadowy hall. Once inside, on a humorous note, the goat bleated out a complaint as if to tell any human inside that company had arrived. Something of a goat-butler.

"Hello. Anybody home?" Ward took his first step up the wooden riser and his boot promptly shot a hole through a rotten board. Carefully, he extracted his right ankle, wary of cutting it on two exposed nails. He recalled seeing a lazy, malnourished swayback tied in the side yard when he'd come far enough up the overgrown drive. Someone was obviously home. Why hadn't they come to the door? A small gust of wind moved the cloud of flies closer to Ward and he sped up enough to escape through the front door.

As his eyes began to adjust to the contrast, he faintly heard someone singing, then the tinkling of an out-of-tune piano for a few awful bars, then back to some singing. The voice was definitely female, so Ward assumed Sally was home. Well, the music, or attempt at music, would explain her not hearing his arrival.

Bones of the Black Warrior

He tried again. "Hello it's me, Ward Travers. Miss Russell? Brother, I mean, Mr. Gerald? Hello?"

No answer, so he allowed his ears to lead him through the semi-darkness toward the room he believed to be the origin of the bad music. Even though Ward was not a big man, nor was he small, his boots made a resounding echo through the house. He stopped at what was likely the main parlor off the hall and looked in. Nothing but bare floors, no rugs or furniture. After a few more steps, looking to his left in the dining room; again, no rugs, chairs, tables, or wall art. The music source came from the far end of the hall where the back door was open, and suddenly stopped. Something told Ward to stop walking. Whew! Another horrid odor infiltrated Ward's nostrils and he took five more steps to be at the door to the last room on the left. He had a hard time seeing, but it looked like someone was lying in the middle of the barren room, face up. There were also furry creatures around whomever Ward assumed was sleeping there. Another wind gust parted the threadbare drapes as a shaft of blinding daylight illuminated the scene.

"Ahh, no, no, Brother?" escaped Ward's mouth before he could stop them. It was his father-in-law, dead and with five adult cats quietly eating away the dead flesh on his exposed face, hands and fingers. Ward felt his breakfast coming up. He shielded his eyes and turned and ran straight into Sally Russell. Her firm extended stomach made first contact. Sally was pregnant. Very pregnant.

August 17, 1884
Stockton home, Alabama

Carla, even though the day was scorching hot, wore her largest bonnet, not in hopes of shielding her fair skin from the blazing sun, but to hide from curious eyes. She drove not her best carriage, but an older, disused buggy. Beside her sat the fifty-two-year-old Ruby Yarborough, once an Omibala slave, now a paid cook, seamstress and just for today, midwife.

Carla had stayed away but sent an occasional teenage servant to walk to Stockton and the Russell residence. The latest report was that the birth was imminent, and it was indeed time. It had been a struggle for Carla and more of one for Ward. The easy choice would have been to ignore Sally's lonely plight, after all with her reputation, really that baby could be from any wandering male in south Alabama.

Two weeks prior, Carla had confided in her neighbor, Matilda, about the pregnancy as the two went down to Randon Creek, removed their shoes, hiked their skirts and slowly shuffled down the shallows to cool off. The debate swayed until it was Matilda who suggested they stop and take a rest in the rickety old fishing chairs she and Eliza had used years back. Further, she added, "Miss Eliza, it's me, Matilda. I'm here with Carla and we are thinking about you and all the good times you enjoyed right here. I swear I can even smell your favorite old Sutliff tobacco in that aromatic vanilla."

"I don't smell anything," Carla whispered and promptly received a shushing.

The brief interruption did not stop Matilda as she next asked Eliza's spirit to help give them, or really Carla, some guidance on the proper course of action for the situation. She even went as far as to explain the odd union of the defrocked preacher and the promiscuous daughter of a known pimp.

A few minutes later after leaving the old fishing hole and putting their shoes back on, Carla spoke quietly, "Well that settles it, there's a distinct possibility that Sally's unborn child is, I mean was, sired by Father. That leaves me no choice, Matilda. I'll help as far as seeing the innocent babe has a safe welcome into the world."

"And then the newborn will be taken to Mobile directly to the Protestant Orphan Asylum, like the three of us decided earlier."

"Three of us?"

"Never mind, dearie."

On this day, Carla and Ruby arrived at the dilapidated home. Carla, with a monetary assist from Ward, had been able to convince Brother Bryce's old board of deacons to allow him to be buried in the graveyard behind the church; they'd just had to understand why his tombstone could only have his two dates and his initials. They agreed and that's how he rested. In another show of kindness and generosity, Ward had sent a paid detachment of workers to the house to make a few improvements, like removing the live animals from the inside, placing them back in their repaired pens and burying the dead ones. Sally never mentioned it, either unaware or unappreciative of the act.

Bones of the Black Warrior

As Carla announced their arrival at the door and knocked, the recurring thought came again. How had Sally, who evidently had many men over the years, managed *not* to become pregnant, but then lay with a man twice her age, for maybe only three or four months and now is about to give birth? She was certain the same question permeated in Ruby's mind. Too late to solve that riddle now, after she deduced no one was coming, just entered, calling Sally's name.

Another thing Ward had provided was a decent bed with clean sheets in the house. Ruby had visited Sally just one week ago and knew the bed was in the same backroom as the piano. When the women entered the bedroom, Sally was sitting upright in bed with a gigantic grin on her face. A bottle of rum was on her nightstand along with a fine, brown powder, alone in a clean circle of dust.

"Well hello ladies. You're late!" she bellowed drunkenly.

Both visitors were stopped in their tracks and looked at a disheveled Sally, sleeping gown half-on-half-off, sitting nonchalantly in a wad of bloody sheets. They said nothing.

"Yea, baby boy was itching to get out in the world and couldn't wait so he decided the middle of the night was good-a-time as any."

"A boy? Where's the baby now, Sally?" inquired Carla, moving closer and scanning the room.

"Oh, he's in good hands. I've a cousin, right here in Stockton. We kind-a have an agreement, see, she's a respectable wife and church lady and me, well, you know about me. Our kinship is a secret and in return she does me a favor now and then; and slips me a few dollars on occasion."

"Your cousin, then, I see."

"She waited until after dark to send a couple of her women servants by. They told me she'd paid them well, otherwise they wouldn't have been seen dead at my place. Anyhow, they both had experience in the matter, sat me up, gave me the first of two bottles of rum and told me to start-a-pushing."

"So, you were assisted by trained midwives. That's good Sally. And the boy? He's hearty, healthy, ten toes, ten fingers, all in good order?"

"Well, la-tee-dah, thank you very much for asking about me! Just had my innards stretched from here to eternity is all."

There was total silence. Ruby was embarrassed at the reaction to Mrs. Travers' act of kindness. Sally took a sip of rum and continued by saying the boy was fine and taken down to Mobile where a young lady friend of her cousin and husband resided. Not to worry, she added the mister was a bank clerk, made decent money, belonged to the Episcopal church and owned a home somewhere on South Conception Street, near the same church.

"So, this Episcopalian family in Mobile has plans to adopt your son?" Carla asked hopefully.

"Uhh, not really, Mrs. Travers. See I'm flat broke. I ain't been able to make no money with this big giant belly. So, we fixed up an arrangement. I'd never track the boy down or hold no memory connecting us and they'd come back to town after being away for five months. That-a-way, it'd look like she'd been pregnant, left, birthed a boy, and came home. See, she can't have none herself. That mister didn't like the kinds of things that can follow a boy in life, once people find out he's adopted."

Carla was aghast and felt an extreme urge to strike out and slap Sally. Instead, she inhaled a deep breath, tightly closed her eyes, calmed herself and mentally told herself it was time to go home.

"So, a gift to them?" unexpectedly Ruby interjected.

"Now I didn't say that exactly. We kinda did a business deal. It was more like they wanted a newborn son without the orphanage getting involved. Me? All I wanted was cash money."

Chapter 25
Swindled

May 23, 1887
Omibala Farm
2:40 a.m.

Ruby's nose was probably her keenest sense. That night it saved multiple lives. The old plantation manor had hosted a significant party earlier in the evening and most everyone imbibed in a few glasses of wine and were deeply asleep. Mrs. Matilda Douglass had hosted a congratulatory party for a few locals of the first graduating class from Tuskegee College. Roy, Jr. Cleo, the White Hall brothers and their female escorts were among the guests. In a show of keen business acumen, Matilda had also invited some of the more prominent white educators from Clark County in an attempt to hold informal job interviews for the grads. Only a little passage of time would tell if her efforts would bear fruit.

Immediately hearing of the gathering, it spawned a sinister, resentful response from the local KKK chapter. In the Klan mindset, this kind of nonsense required their preferred method of retaliation, pain and suffering. Earlier, two Klansmen had stealthily approached Omibala Farm with pork scraps laced with rat poison and fed the five dogs that were in essence the guards. With the coast clear, the dozen hooded riders came on the grounds, quietly dismounted and as they approached near, lit their torches. They made one circle of the mansion, gently placed the torches through windows, most already open in the May heat and retreated running at full speed. It worked. The fire immediately caught the drapes and worked its way up the walls to the ceiling. All the bedrooms were on the second story. Ruby, sleeping in a guest sleep area where the four lady escorts of the graduates had retired, caught the first whiff of smoke, recognized the danger and ran about the halls signaling the urgent alarm.

In less than two minutes, the eight guests, Rebecca and Elbee who were also visiting, Ruby and Miranda were out on the front lawn. Immediately, Roy, Jr. and his friends began hauling water from the well near the stable.

It was a gallant, but fruitless attempt. Soon, it was evident there was nothing to do but watch and cry. The fire reached its zenith a bit later and the roaring flames shot fifty or more feet into the night sky. The mammoth roar, hard snapping, loud popping, occasional small explosions and constant crashing also alerted all the animals, domestic and even the wild, nearby in the east woods. Ruby came to Matilda, offered her a hug and pulled the edge of her nightshirt up to dry the lady of the house's tears.

After a minute of letting Ruby console her, Matilda suddenly brightened up and actually smiled. "I just remembered! You all know my Micah has his insurance agency in Jackson? About last New Year, he told me there was this new thing. You can buy insurance on your home for a fire. I bought it, see, I'm not wiped out. I have that insurance. Micah told me in case a fire burned down the house, his company would completely pay to replace it. All is not lost. I'll be alright everyone. I'm all right," as she dried her last tear and forced a smile.

May 27, 1887
Jackson Alabama
11:10 a.m.

Ruby stayed in the carriage. They rode north to Jackson in the good buggy today. Matilda was more than a little miffed. Two days earlier, she'd sent a message to her son via one of Carla's servants who had an errand for the Travers. When Micah hadn't shown up at the smoldering ruins of his childhood home, both as a matter of concern and secondly as the insuring agent,

Matilda began to worry. She'd patiently waited all day yesterday and still he did not come. Mrs. Travers' servant came back saying not only could she not find Micah Douglass, she couldn't locate Douglass Insurance Service at all. She'd walked up and down all six streets of the commercial section of Jackson and never saw a sign, a banner, or a name painted on any door or window. Matilda verified the servant was literate, so that wasn't the problem. Where was Micah?

Little did Matilda Douglass know they'd ridden in the opposite direction they'd have found her son in Mobile, where he'd been the past two months. When his lease had expired on the agency building, he'd packed up and moved. He didn't reopen in Mobile. No, Micah had been wooed to a different type of business. A type of which his mother, and especially his deceased father, would have severely disapproved.

Micah had developed a few strong habits in his latter teenage years while away at school in New Orleans. First, he'd become fond of tobacco and was never without a Cuban cigar between his fingers. Secondly, he liked good wine and whisky from the noon hour until he put his head on a pillow. Third, New Orleans had tempted him with the excitement of horse racing and was more likely to be found at the Louisiana Jockey Club than in class at St. John Lutheran Academy.

Lastly, Micah was quite the admirer of ladies, young or older.

After finishing at the university in Tuscaloosa, he'd returned back to Clark County and put a tremendous effort to avoid farming. The insurance field was a new, up-and-coming industry and he convinced his parents being first in would give him a tremendous advantage. They even helped him with a loan to open his doors.

Micah found quite a few willing customers and there was a fortune to be made if one put forth the effort. Not Micah. Once things were running smoothly, he regressed back to his four bad habits. Then, three years ago, his insurance career had the unfortunate happenstance of his chance meeting with Sally Russell around March. They shared those common interests and found each other's company heady and invigorating. But her pregnancy put a stop to most of it and so he lured a poor, innocent, alcoholic Methodist preacher to serve as cover.

Micah was actually the baby's father. In addition, there was no cousin, nor were there Episcopal parents to take the baby. Micah wanted the boy and hired a nanny, who had the misfortune of being deaf and dumb, but that was to be a plus for Sally and Micah. The two had reopened a new, clandestine business in Mobile, just like old H.T. Russel had years before. It was a line of work going back thousands of years and Sally had experience, while Micah's previous involvement was from the customer-side of the transaction.

Recently, he'd grown weary of his dull office duties of a respectable job in Jackson and had quietly closed his insurance shop before the devastating fire at Omibala. As his budding new business needed cash, and this was not the type of establishment one could visit the bank, he began stealing the customers' premiums which canceled all the policies. Not even his own mother carried one cent of coverage.

Micah's five years in New Orleans added to Sally's periphery tutelage at the knee of her infamous father, helped. Neither would use their real name plus for simplicity and good cover, pretending to be a married couple by the name of Case. In a show of disrespect to the law, and a little humor, Micah had chosen his name as Justin, while Sally had gone with a French flair and used Bazquette. Together they pooled their resources, mostly Micah's, and renovated a three-story older home in a perfect location to serve their clientele. Micah, or Justin now, would be in charge of the bar, securing protection and all gambling operations; Bazquette would handle the girls.

Independent of Micah, Sally had converted the home's pantry into an opium den. Curious about this new source of revenue, she instructed him how to "cook" the magic bullet before placing the mixture in a pipe bowl for the hidden den's customers. Curious, Micah soon succumbed to drug's draw. By the end of 1887, Micah was indulging daily.

(The house was on Old Water Street, almost exactly where the Mobile River met Mobile Bay and perfectly situated for its intended use, halfway between the railroad yard to the south and the city docks to the north. Latitude 30.6, longitude 88.0)

Chapter 26
Infected

August 9, 1888
New Alabimo Farm

The two old neighboring farms had always helped the other. For more than a year Matilda Douglass was a guest of the Travers. Ward had done all he could to help, but Micah's old company held firm and dismissed the claim for nonpayment. Carla tried her best to keep Matilda's spirits above water. The loss of her home was bad, but first, the betrayal of her own son's insurance scam and recent rumors of Micah owning a house of ill-repute in Mobile, was almost too much.

In the past six months, Matilda had likely lost a quarter of her body weight and her clothes, unattractively, hung on her frame. At night alone in their bedroom, Carla frequently said, "Before she can rebuild Omibala, she'll have to rebuild Matilda."

When Carla thought she'd seen her friend hit rock bottom, there was a dark turn. Frustrated with Sheriff Dees' inability to track down any of the Klan arsonists, Matilda began plotting her own revenge. Under the ruse of self-protection, Matilda tricked Ward into loaning her his Colt .41 caliber revolver. Furthering her ruse, she'd tell Carla her frequent disappearances to Randon Creek afternoon was to rest. In fact, it was for practicing her aim. If the sheriff couldn't mete out justice; she'd do it herself.

In her current state of mind, the widow Douglass felt like she had nothing to lose. She showed a reckless streak in September and October as she made a weekly trek to Mobile and the architectural firm of Simon Bolivar Stockton who had done well. He chaired the top firm in southern Alabama and held significant political clout in state politics. His nearly twenty years as a state senator not only provided connections, but a shield of protection. Simon secretly, was the Grand Cyclops of the Klan den that encompassed the bottom third of Alabama.

Simon Stockton's incognito guise of Klan rank was unknown to the majority, a few locals from his hometown area took an educated guess he was at least a member. Matilda would park her carriage directly in front of Stockton's office. From her seat, she'd firmly tell anyone entering that they should be aware the head man inside was a leader in the local Klan. Any other time,

Simon would have laughed her antics off, but there was an election coming in the first week of November. This nutty lady from Clark County might turn from more than a nuisance into a political liability. Even on warm days, Matilda kept a light blanket over her lap with a pistol just beneath.

On about her seventh trip to Mobile, after sitting for two hours and warning Simon's customers, she got up the nerve. Turning off Jefferson St. east on Delaware, twelve blocks later, Matilda was at the intersection of Old Water Street. The fine homes, brick hotels, smart business fronts and tidy townhomes had given way to the gritty side of a major port city. No brick structures here. The few that once resided in this section had been flattened by a huge ordnance explosion and subsequent fire just a few days after the surrender ending the Civil War. There was row after row of unpainted clapboard dwellings and cheaply constructed seedy businesses.

With her determined jaw set, Matilda pulled up in front of the only three-story building on the block, painted a deep purple with yellow trim. Inside, a piano was playing, and a few men were singing songs with full throats. If she was unsure this was her son's place of business, a young lass of about twenty came out on the front porch, clothed only in a corset cover and drawers that stopped at the knees, and with that, Matilda was certain. Pausing, she went over her prepared speech to Micah. The message in the Good Book is forgiveness and that's what Micah needed. Come back to Clark County, give up this life of sin, set up the agency again, and come live with the Travers until a new Omibala was built and she'd forgive her son.

Just as she was in the act of tying the reins to the post, she froze. A small boy, dressed smartly in an expensive corduroy suit came out, approached with a licorice stick in hand and stared inquisitively directly at Matilda. Although her late husband was nearly forty when they met, it took little imagination to see how John Knox would have been at four With sandy reddish hair and deep blue eyes, the boy was the spitting image. His sudden appearance and apparent willingness to approach, scared Matilda so, that she quickly untied and took her carriage at full trot again up Delaware St. directly to St. Stephens Road and north, nonstop for home.

September 22, 1890
244 Old Water Street
Mobile, Alabama
8:20 a.m.

Micah pushed his poached eggs around his plate next to his untouched biscuit. He had no appetite and hadn't for three days. He felt sick, but had few symptoms other than not being hungry, a rash on his hands and feet, plus hair that had been falling out in clumps for a week.

Sally plus the cooking and cleaning lady, Billie Jean, were the only other persons awake in their bawdy house operation.

Billie Jean was a relic leftover from the past. She'd once made her living on her back in the city of her birth, in 1830, having begun her prostitution days as a teenager during the Mexican War. Mobile's port had been a staging point for American troops bound for Vera Cruz and wide-eyed young soldiers were willing to pay handsomely for her time. Shrewd even back in the '60s, she refused to take Confederate money for her services and amassed a small fortune only to be beaten and robbed one night in 1878 and had to start over. However, by then time and hard living had caught up and she resorted to begging. Back when Sally and Micah opened for business, she sought them out, alas Sally laughed in her face for suggesting, at her age, she could still earn money for a madam. No, Billie Jean was hired instead to cook and clean for her and Micah. It was wise old Billie Jean who after observing Micah's condition, suggested he see a friend with a medical background.

Jake Jensen used to be a doctor, but after accidentally killing his fourth patient, lost his license. These days he could only treat the sick of Mobile's underworld. Billie Jean told Micah where to find Doc Jensen and ask for the dosing treatment. In her learned opinion, Micah likely had syphilis.

A little more than a week later, at dawn on June 1, Micah and six-year-old Andrew drove their carriage away, up Delaware St. to Saint Stephens Road toward Clark County and the Douglass Farm. Having sold his share to Sally for a song, Micah was going home to introduce his son to his grandmother, repent for his egregious sins, and hopefully find a permanent home for Andrew and die. An actual doctor told him the arsenic vapors and mercury baths were really worse than the disease and gave him a small chance of one week or so, before he'd meet his Maker.

Seven hours after leaving Old Water Street for the last time, Micah tugged on the reins at the drive of his family farm. The shingle attached to the brick pillar at the entrance was new, he noted. Without being told why, he understood it. The sign read: Douglas Farm, established 1852. The last name spelling was not an error. Matilda, in shame, had changed the family name in an effort to distance them from any possible connection to her wayward son.

The last name change was recorded in the ledger that Carla Travers had taken over the responsibility of keeping since Ward's eyesight issues. Every instance and happening worth recording at Omibala, the Douglas Farm, and of course, Alabimo was in the diary. It was with great sadness that she recorded her best friend, Matilda's, decision regarding Micah and Andrew. As her son and bastard grandson stood on the front porch, she refused to allow them entry, speaking through a closed door told Micah that not only had he been disowned, but so was the boy and to never come back. Micah pleaded saying he could understand, but only had a short time to live. He made an impassioned plea to Matilda to at least take in the boy. Thinking of John Knox and his honored memory, she'd flatly refused. (Micah returned to Mobile and Sally. He died three days later when his common-law wife took little Andy to the Methodist Orphanage where he was raised.)

Another of Carla's last recordings for the year 1890 included the major shifts in land ownership. All the legal documents were finalized and Omibala was no more. Alabimo was Ward's and he had absorbed his own previously separate lands into the original plantation he'd inherited on Eliza's death.

Matilda had no plans to rebuild a residence on Douglas Farm. Carla had agreed to allow her to raise a cottage and sell Douglas Farm. It had little worth these days. A terrific freeze, most said it went down to negative 13 degrees, on three consecutive nights in late December, 1889 had not only decimated the fruit trees, but killed two-thirds of the livestock.

Her last entry recorded the sale of the Douglas Farm to Roy Johnson, Jr. Adam Louis, a successful Negro businessman and admirer of Booker T.

Washington, had personally loaned Roy the money for the land and remaining livestock. However, Roy wouldn't be planting fruit trees, or cotton. Roy was going to follow the advice of his former principal at Tuskegee. Washington had written Roy about his recently promoted professor, George Washington Carver, the new head of the agricultural department, who strongly advocated the peanut and sweet potato as cash crops of the future.

January 1, 1905
Alabimo master bedroom
Mid-morning

Carla summoned the twins, Rebecca and Elbee to her bedroom. Ward's health was extremely poor but was having a good morning and wished to talk. Both children stood at the foot of the bed with Carla seated next to Ward's head to better hear her husband's weak voice. She repeated his words, "Your mother will be heir to all the property when I pass away, but I don't want either of you to leave. Do you understand me?"

Elbee and Rebecca both nodded directly to their dying father. Rebecca fought back a tear.

"Becka, you'll marry soon, but don't leave. We have the money to build you and your husband a separate house. I only ask you to marry a farmer...cotton planter, I mean, and he has to lean the right way politically," Carla said, sustaining a strong voice. She relayed Ward's wishes, even the notion of continuing his fight with the Farmers Alliance. (A popular political movement of the last five years, was the natural foe of the large operators and advocated radical ideas including government intervention in crop and shipping prices and regulation thereof)

Elbee spoke up for the first time, "I will Daddy. You've schooled me well. If the government starts making the railroads operate at a loss, the price for cotton shipments goes down. That's not good for Alabimo. Lots of time, money and sweat went into our slides and barges. They're some of our key advantages to setting the market price. I understand why we have to fight the Alliance and give you my solemn word I will, Daddy."

Ward Travers smiled and gripped Carla's hand with all his might. "Ward said he wants to take a short nap and he'll see us at lunch...and bye

125

for now," she added of her own accord. Carla understood what his hand was saying. This was it, and he'd rather the children did not witness his death.

(Ward, ever the fighter, held on the rest of the day and quietly passed away in his sleep sometime around midnight. Three days later he was laid to rest next to his beloved Mother's grave, in the shade of the mammoth twin cypress trees.)

Chapter 27
A Plague

December 15, 1913
Alabimo master bedroom

The elated Elbee couldn't be contained and rushed in to see Judith, his wife of six years, and newborn child. He so wanted a boy and had to find out. (Carla had given up the big house to Elbee as a wedding gift and moved into a separate wing she had added to Matilda's cottage.) The local doctor from Jackson had ridden down and was being assisted by Ruby's daughter, Martha, also a midwife who would wet nurse the baby. Rebecca and her husband, Frank McClain, waited outside the bedroom door, ready to congratulate the couple.

"Yee-hi!" exclaimed Elbee at the sight of his son. Judith had Martha pull down the blanket to reveal her child's nakedness to let Elbee's eyes feast upon him before her lips could even say the word. Martha quickly mumbled something about the room's cool temperature before covering up the infant just as Elbee came to the midwife and swept his boy into his arms for the first time. "Judith, dear Judith, are you alright? I love you dearly. We have a boy!" Elbee surprised himself as he'd almost blurted out "finally" have a boy. Judith had a pair of girls previously. Two years earlier than the new baby and another girl approximately one year prior to child number two. He moved about the room quickly, constantly staring at the newborn's face, unaware of where he was and luckily didn't trip.

Martha had been watching Judith's face, saw the unspoken signal of a rough and tumble manhandling a fragile newborn and gently moved to Mr. Travers extended her blanketed arms and Elbee complied. He then retreated to the doorway to invite his sister and brother-in-law to meet the newest family addition.

Then it dawned on the fair-skinned, brown-eyed Elbee, that the baby boy had green eyes like Ward, and the same olive skin. Then Elbee went back to the giant poster bed and looked at Judith just to confirm what he already knew. Blue eyes and a very pale, alabaster skin tone. As much as

Carla had tried to shield her children, Elbee and Rebecca, somewhere around their twelfth birthday, found out the gossip; their father was actually full-blooded Indian. There had been quite a few fistfights for Elbee during his teen years as he was regularly taunted at school.

At the same moment it occurred to Elbee that he'd yet to kiss Judith and thank her for delivering another healthy baby to the family fold. Pausing from his glee briefly, he did. In the excitement, the little boy's name, decided upon a month ago, was yet to be mentioned by the exhausted mother and ecstatic father. And so, the proud aunt, Rebecca said his name aloud for the first time: Benjamin Douglas Travers.

December 19, 1913
7:20 a.m.

Roy Johnson, Jr. walked up the drive to Alabimo with an overflowing basket of fresh eggs for the Travers family. His visit was not entirely of a social nature. He'd received a letter from Tuskegee's Professor Carver the day before the birth of Elbee's son, but out of respect for Judith, held his tongue about the contents until this morning. The letter was over two weeks old now, having first gone by stagecoach from the Institute to Montgomery, there to a steamboat onboard a U.S. Mail packet, to Jackson and finally to the southern tip of Clark County and a community lockbox for the locals' mail. The news was not good, especially for the Travers.

Professor Carver, known now as a peanut expert, had attended an agricultural seminar in Birmingham around the first of the month. He was a guest lecturer but sat in on the other speakers' turns at the podium, too. Three cotton farmers from their west, two from Louisiana and one from neighboring Mississippi, addressed the attendees. There was reason for Alabama cotton farmers to be concerned. The three had relayed tales of an awful plight on their once healthy crops; the boll weevil.

Twenty years earlier, this insidious insect had migrated up from Mexico into the Texas cotton fields. With each passing growing season, the weevil had multiplied and migrated eastward. Mississippi in 1911, the most recent statistics showed, lost one-quarter of a billion dollars in unrealized revenue or roughly four million individual bales, to the Mexican boll weevil. Surely, by now the destructive bug had infiltrated the fields of Alabama. The proof was just not available yet. Worse, there was no known defense. No poison could halt its incessant march east, nor did the invasive bug have any natural predators.

"That indignant darkie!" Elbee stormed to no one in particular. Roy delivered his message from Tuskegee, along with about twenty eggs and then was not so politely asked to leave. Elbee stomped back up the front steps and into the home's main hall before letting his emotions overflow. "Damn him, talking to me like that!"

Roy had passed along the bad news about cotton planters to the west of Alabama and suffered the wrath of Elbee Tarver. Elbee didn't need anyone telling him how to run his business. He'd almost blurted out to Roy that he'd turned a $22,500 net profit last year from cotton. Why should he listen to the son of an ex-slave, especially one who grew these strange little orange potatoes and odd little nuts that didn't grow on trees? Cotton was King and everybody knew it. "How dare him smart mouth me and try to tell me my business! Hmph! Plow under my cotton and plant peanuts, he said! Oh, I could almost strangle him!"

"Did you say something, Elbee?" Frank asked from the back parlor where he was taking his morning coffee, with a secret splash of bourbon. Elbee didn't answer and kept right on, stomping out the back of the mansion towards the stable. He'd take a ride on his Arabian horse which likely cost more money than Roy made last year. Maybe that would calm his anger?

November 22, 1915
Alabimo cotton gin
Manager's office

"Mr. Travers, sir, I'm sorry as I can be. I worked the men harder than I ever worked any men. They did the job, but they just twern't nearly close to the usual amount of bolls to harvest," farm manager Billings ashamedly said to Elbee.

Elbee was kicking himself. Deep down, he believed his mistake was allowing Judith to talk him into their four-week vacation in New York City during the harvest. Yet, she hardly ever asked for anything and when she wanted to see certain exhibits that were only in the city during October and

November, he relented. "So, what are the final numbers, Billings? Go on. I know they're bad, but I can take it."

Billings couldn't mouth the terrible news and instead pushed over his clipboard, or memorandum files as they were sometimes called, with the final tally of bales ginned, produced and now ready to shipment downriver to Mobile. After about half a minute, the clipboard went flying out the office's door onto the main floor, landing by the steam-powered hot air press that blew the cotton dry just before going into the bailing area. Elbee was furious. Not so much at Billings, but at himself. If Billings' calculations were correct, and they'd always been for the past decade, Alabama's production was off by 80%.

Quickly calculating the current market price per bale, Elbee found a pencil on Billings' desk, didn't even bother with paper and did the math right on the desktop. He knew the acreage, every bale weighed 500 pounds and the last quote from the broker, before his New York trip, was .13 cents a pound. Gross production for 1915 would be slightly under $60,000. This was bad. He completed the math. After fixed expenses, assuming nothing else went wrong, this year profit was practically nil, or $1166. Oh dear, Father Ward and Grandfather Ben would spin in their graves knowing the amount of sweat, worry and toil netted less than $100 per month. Equally as maddening was that Roy had warned him to diversify from cotton two years ago.

April 7, 1923
Southern tip Clark County
Postal Drop Box

Elbee opened the letter from Mobile. It was from First Planters Bank and like it was called, the demand letter not so subtly reminded Mr. Travers his crop loan for 1922 was in a serious state of arrears. He had used his ninety-day grace period and now had fifteen days in which to repay $30,000 or risk losing 1,000 acres of prime farmland he'd used for collateral. One thousand acres was approximately one-third of Alabimo's holdings. Oddly, his first reaction was relief. The bank loan officer also wanted Elbee to pledge the deed to the mansion in addition to the land to obtain the loan. Fortunately, an old friend of his father's, the retired bank president, happened to be sitting close by that day a year ago, and influenced the younger banker to only use the land. What was an awful predicament could actually be worse.

Elbee crushed the letter in his palm and remounted his horse. No longer did he ride a $1,400 specimen of horse flesh. These days he rode an old plow horse that plodded along at a snail's pace. Judith and the kids need not know of the direness, and he'd actually foreseen the letter's arrival and had a plan in place. He'd sacrifice 500 acres back to the bank and repay First Planters 50% of his debt in cash. That would nearly wipe out his savings. Still, oh thank heaven for little favors. What if he'd be riding home now to tell Judith to pack her things and prepare for foreclosure on the mansion?

Duty called and even though it was painful, Elbee fulfilled his traditional obligations and went to the family journal to record the dismal downturn of the family finances.

February 5, 1924
Johnson Farms (formerly Douglas Farms)
Front porch

"Roy, you don't know how much I appreciate you meeting with me this morning,"Elbee said with respect. "And again, please accept condolences from Judith and me about little Ronnie. Tragic, so tragic, so sad. May his soul rest with God."

Elbee Travers was referring to the recent death of Roy's five-year-old from diphtheria three weeks prior. Secondly, he was there to pick Roy's brain. King Cotton was dead. The brutal combination of the boll weevil and new foreign markets in India and Egypt had crushed the white gold's once-vaunted status. Elbee had committed to planting peanuts and sweet potatoes. He had to. His loan defaults in the past had wrecked his credit. No bank would extend him crop credit and he'd resorted to his last option for 1924. Elbee now owed a $12,500 loan mortgage against the mansion.

Roy offered Elbee a seat in an old family rocker on the porch and the two men sat in private at the modest 900-square-foot log house. Elbee gave his utmost attention and Roy was extremely cautious in giving advice. "Mr. Travers, sir, I only wish you could sit out a year and at least grow a bit of clover in your field to build up the nitrogen content. Going straight in two months' time is cutting it close, especially for your land. What's that cotton been on that soil? 'Bout near a hundred years, I'd bet?"

"Understand all that, Roy and I'm in full agreement, but time isn't on my side. I have everything at stake, and I have to come through with the bank, so I have to plant as soon as the weather allows."

And with the two-hour conversation and most of the contents of a pitcher of lemonade, Roy Johnson and Elbee Travers' once fractured relationship was back in good standing.

Chapter 28
An Ill Will

May 3, 1929
Mobile
Corner of Conti and Royal Streets
1:40 p.m.

Elbee and Judith were thoroughly enjoying their day away from the farm, the kids and the constant worries entailed in both. Elbee mentioned how much this day felt like one of those back when they began courting in 1906. As a horse-drawn ice wagon passed, he turned his head and smiled at his wife. There was pride in owning an automobile and his mood was uplifted as he drove into the city in their 1928 Ford Model A farm truck.

Judith had marveled at how quickly they'd traveled, making it from Alabimo to the Mobile city limits in only two hours via the new State Road 71. Leaving the driveway, they followed the gravel road for the first four miles on the old Federal Postal Road, turned south on the former St. Stephens Road, on a mixture of loose gravel and rutted dirt, for thirty-five miles until the outskirts of the city and that new phenomenon; a two-lane paved road. She'd laughed freely and broken into song as the wind had whipped through her hair as Elbee had pushed the truck upwards to nearly forty miles per hour once they'd reached the hard-surfaced highway.

Exiting his door after the wagon passed, Elbee smartly moved around the hood to open Judith's. They were here to see their first ever moving picture show, a matinee showing of *The Jazz Singer*. "Let's go honey. Don't forget we're going to eat after the show. Old man Allen, the lawyer, recommended we try Morrison's."

"I'm almost ready to skip the meal, go back to that paved road and see how fast you can get this Tin Lizzie going."

"I know that was exhilarating, wasn't it? Hate to correct your excitement, but the Tin Lizzie was Henry Ford's Model T. This is his newer version, Model A my dear."

Elbee's financial situation had changed for the better ever since he made the switch from cotton to peanuts. The soil he'd inherited, rich, deep and fertile, fed by hundreds of years of spring floods meant his peanut production out surpassed any other in Clark County. It meant he could afford not just a new automobile. In addition, he bought back 250 acres from the First Planters Bank last month. Profits were so good the year before that he paid off the mortgage on Alabimo with the 1927 harvest. Both of those triumphs had been joyfully recorded in the family journal as well.

Downtown Mobile
Corner Conti and Royal Street
Same day, 3:35 p.m.

Judith nearly pulled Elbee's wrist bone out of its socket, tugging so hard wanting to again experience the thrill of speed on the paved highway once more. She'd convinced him after the movie that a fast car ride was much better, but there was a slight problem, Elbee noticed as they exited the theater. The Ford had a flat tire. Correction, as Elbee made his way closer; two flats and he only carried one spare. This was a new predicament. Horses didn't have these problems. As he pondered a solution, a strange man he did not know, close to his age or maybe five years younger, wearing denim bib overalls, approached on the sidewalk.

"Hmm, well that's not good, is it? Maybe I can help?" said the unknown man.

"No, not good at all. I was just thinking about how my horses never had these issues," answered Elbee, with a quick light-hearted laugh.

"I saw your car tag, not a Mobile resident, I presume?"

Elbee nodded in agreement and said he was from up in the next county, forty miles north. He then asked the stranger if he knew where he could help with the location of the nearest Firestone Tire and Rubber dealer?

"I do and you're in luck it's only four blocks over. Look, I'm free right now. Why don't you and your wife walk over to the Cowthon Hotel, and have a sit down in the cool lobby? I'll make the walk over to Broad Street and get you a new tire."

Bones of the Black Warrior

Elbee glanced at Judith. She didn't want to be left alone if Elbee went, nor did she want to walk in the heat. She made a little signal that he should accept the offer and pay the man for his trouble. Elbee went to his wallet and, not sure of the cost, asked. The stranger said he'd replaced a tire last month and they were $17.50. Elbee gave the man $20 saying he'd err on the side of caution and that he was also going to pay him for his trouble. The stranger didn't say yes or no to accepting money, instead saying they'd discuss that matter on his return.

A little more than forty minutes later, Elbee and Judity returned from the Cowthon Hotel to their automobile, and he again went to his wallet. The stranger had not just walked to the tire dealer, but returned and fixed both flats on his own. In the process, he had gotten more than a little dirty and his hands were coated with axle grease, too.

"My goodness. You have gone above and beyond here. I feel very obligated, you are truly the chivalrous knight, sir. You must take this $5, you must," Elbee said with the money extended. "No sir, no. I refuse to be monetarily rewarded for something I enjoy doing. Besides, I'm in work clothes and for you to mess up a nice suit, well shucks, that'd be a shame."

Elbee tried again to pay the man and again, but the man kept his hands stuffed deep into his overall pockets. "Elbee, you've tried three times. This nice gentleman refuses to accept money over the $18 for the tire. So, I have an idea. The next time this gentleman is in Clark County, we shall entertain him at Alabimo. He's most welcome to bring a guest also," Judith interjected.

The man with the grease on his hands stood erect at Judith's words. "Elbee? As in Elbee Travers of Alabimo Peanuts?"

"Pardon my lack of manners, but you are right. Forgive me, but in all this dealing with the flat tires, we never did introduce ourselves. Yes, I'm Elbee Travers and this's my wife, Judith."

"Well, small world. I'm Andy, Micah Douglas's son. Matilda was my grandmother. I never knew her and barely recall my dad, but I've heard they were longtime neighbors of the Travers' up to the southern tip of Clark County."

The humid air of the sidewalk suddenly seemed to go away and Judith tried to conceal her face. Her worried eyes were wide as saucers and her mouth was agape. Elbee didn't know what to do or say. He just nodded in the affirmative and stayed silent.

December 1930
Clark County, Alabama

Soon after doing some snooping about his family history in Clark County, Andy Douglas was proving that in reality, he was no knight. For the past six months he'd been busy scheming and plotting how to get Johnson Farms away from Roy and regain his grandfather's legacy. Andy might, at times, be a better man than Micah, but unlike John Knox Douglass, he carried no sympathy for the Negro race. Instead, Andy was fueled by a deep and burning hatred for the black man.

There were not many men the Klan threw out for excessive violence, but Andy carried that distinction. Twelve years prior, Andy had discovered his heretofore unknown, cold-blooded trait. Leading men across No Man's Land and capturing sections of German trenches at the Battle of Croix Rouge Farm, in Chateau-Thierry, France, he personally dispatched eleven of the enemy into eternity in battle action. He took out four by bullet and seven by the cold steel of his bayonet.

Andy, still today, was terribly scarred from his violent war Croix Rouge experience. Not physically, but mentally. One minute he was the prince, helping others, going beyond the norm, overtly nice and hospitable. Then, never knowing what triggered his mood swings, he could flip, become very dark, surprisingly vicious and extremely brutal. Most of Mobile knew of his night-and-day behavior and in so, prevented him from ever gaining meaningful employment. It was only his war hero status that kept the police from throwing him under the jail for his occasional erratic, hotheaded actions.

(Andy really *was* a war hero. Blessed with a pair of tremendously fast legs, he'd used them at the beginning of the Battle of Croix Rouge Farm. A U.S. Army colonel, leading a different unit of American soldiers, who prided himself on his self-taught French, misheard the French general's commands and pulled his troops of Iowa boys out of a trench line in front of the German lines. A little later, German aircraft reported the American retreat and their infantry formed up to move and claim the unoccupied trench. An Alabama soldier hoisted in an observation balloon reported the enemy movements and down below, Andy overheard the situation and didn't hesitate. On his own volition, without any officers' order, he grabbed three bags of a dozen hand grenades each and ran full tilt toward the empty trench, dodging German bullets for half a minute until he reached the sunken safety of the elongated pit and immediately began lobbing grenades to his front. The unexpected resistance gave the Germans pause as Andy's actions allowed the remainder of the Rainbow soldiers, predominantly from Alabama, the time to reach safety and reclaim the vital trench. Fifteen minutes later, Andy and his bayonet led the charge that ran the Germans backward and cemented his war legacy to the good folks of Mobile.)

While the Klan was not so much opposed to the Negro existence, if they stayed in their place, as, in their eyes, they did have certain uses in regard to menial, outdoor labor in the hot sun, not Andy. When his mood turned, he wanted them either eradicated or all shipped back to Africa.

Having been forced to compete with them for jobs ever since he returned from the Great War in 1919, Andy's once latent hatred had boiled over. Many times, after heavy drinking, on the July 26 anniversary of the bloody battle, Andy would patrol the Negro sections of Mobile, the Oakdale and Africatown quarters, in the wee hours until he found an unaccompanied Negro male. He would make them beg for their life before putting a .45 slug from his 1911 Colt into the unfortunate's brain. His alcohol-soaked mind could recall killing two, but in actuality, he was responsible for six unsolved murders.

Another example of Andy's Jekyll and Hyde personality was just after the Great War. He'd walked down Old Water Street one-thousand times and seen the old whorehouse where he'd spent his first few years of life. Finally, after an entire day of drinking rum, he set fire to the giant wooden structure, but upon seeing the danger of his actions, felt tremendous guilt. Andy sprinted at full speed the nine city blocks to the Creole Paid Fire and Rescue building on Dearborn Street. He even participated in the bucket brigade that eventually extinguished the flames before they spread to innocent buildings next door.

Andy had started his campaign to regain Douglas Farms, back in August and September, by sending a series of anonymous letters to the Johnson house that suggested they should abandon the property or else face the Klan's wrath. On a Sunday morning in October, Roy and his family returned from church to a burning cross outside of Roy's door. The following Sunday morning Andy set fire to Roy's corn crib while no one was home. After seeing Roy did not respond to his threats, Andy used his old Klan connections with the Clark County Sheriff's Department. In November, he'd taken some hard-earned cash to two deputies with the promise of more to come if they'd assist his venture. The two deputies, no bleeding hearts themselves, gladly beat the tar out of Roy as he'd been caught alone, at the furthest point from his house, plowing a cornfield under. Still, Roy stayed put, resolute not to be bullied.

Roy never talked of his plight to anyone except his wife, Glory, not even Elbee or Rebecca. Instead, he endured his torture alone, but it paid off. Perpetually broke, Andy Douglas could not afford a car, and a bus ride would leave evidence of his movement, thus riding his horse forty miles to the tip of Clark County proved too daunting. Before Christmas of 1930, Andy gave up his quest and joined the merchant marines. A little more than a year into his seagoing life, while serving as an ordinary seaman aboard the coffee freighter, *The Raritan*, Andy lost his life in a collision at sea off the coast of Cuba, with a banana freighter ironically named, *Bull Run*.

Chapter 29
On Deaf Ears

May 30, 1934
The Citadel, Charleston

Benjamin Douglas Travers, better known simply as Doug, stood proud as he marched away from the podium. Elbee and Judith were beaming with pride at their son, the senior class valedictorian and his stirring speech. He wore his splendid dress white Citadel uniform for the last time and brought a tear to his mother's eye as he spoke. His speech had been of a personal nature of how in the past four years, he'd transformed from a nervous, skinny, broken-down freshman to a confident and able-bodied senior ready to lead men in battle if necessary. In wrapping up his speech, he glowed with the anticipation of becoming a commissioned officer in the U.S. Marine Corps and stressed his love of country.

Elbee didn't push, but hoped his youngest child, a son named Joey, and senior in high school would follow Doug's footsteps to The Citadel. Judith, who previously had not been so keen on the idea, knowing the majority of their graduates did pursue a military career, after hearing Doug's speech was now on board with her husband's wishes.

And so it was, that very afternoon after the graduation ceremony, the parents and Doug took Joey to the admissions office and filed his papers to enroll the next September.

December 11, 1941
U.S. Army Recruitment HQ
Montgomery, Alabama

Joe Travers didn't put a lot of thought into his actions that Thursday morning, a scant four days after the Japanese attack on Pearl Harbor. Something told him if he left Alabimo and drove south to enlist in Mobile, as a port city, he'd end up in the Navy. However, if he drove north, to Montgomery, he could find an army enlistment station. Ever since he was eleven and had a close call swimming in the Tombigbee, he'd tried to stay out of the water if he couldn't touch the bottom. Besides, he promised his parents that he would not join the Marine Corps, like Doug.

Something might happen to both of them simultaneously should they be in the same branch of the military. It was sound and rational thinking. Within two weeks he'd be in north Alabama, at Ft. McClellan, for basic army infantry training.

Joe was enlisting as a private, not an officer, like his brother. When Elbee's health had declined, Joe was needed back on the farm and had dropped out of The Citadel after his sophomore year. Doug had made it clear, seven years earlier, that he was going to be a career military man, not a peanut farmer. Joe never verbalized his joy at his older brother's decision, but after two years of the strict life at a military school, he'd had enough and was more than happy to quit school.

September 15, 1944
South Pacific Ocean
Off the coast of Palau Island

Captain B. Douglas Travers would be leading an entire company, part of The Fifth, this morning into battle with the Japanese entrenched on Palau Island. The third day of the tremendous naval bombardment was due to cease at 5:15 a.m. At that time, the Higgins boat landing craft where Doug and thirty-five other Marines were situated, would head south the five miles to the east beach of Airai Bay, Palau Island, part of the Marianas Chain and 550 miles east of the Philippines.

Captain Doug Travers struggled to keep his breakfast of steak and eggs down. The choppy seas added to the acrid smell of cordite from the big ships' guns and diesel smoke in his nose made a sickening trio. Gathering himself, he paused to take in the sight: five huge battleships, the *Tennessee, Idaho, Pennsylvania, Mississippi* and *Maryland* were blasting away at Peleliu and occasionally turning on Palau. The thunderous reports of the big guns from the line of battleships shook Doug to his very core, rattling every bone in his body with the deep, booming rumbling vibration with each terrific blast. Reconnaissance told the Americans the main enemy forces were concentrated on Peleliu, but they could not afford to leave the smaller threat at Palau in enemy hands.

Less than one mile to the east was another Higgins boat loaded with U.S. Army soldiers. In the 81st infantry division was Private Joe Travers. Unbeknownst to the Travers brothers, they were both in the same battle arena, despite their parents' attempts to separate the boys from shared harm, here they were. Joe's Higgins boat throttled up and began the thirty-minute ride to the north beaches of Airai Bay. He, too, paused and looked back at the fleet, in awe of the combined awesome firepower of the Navy, and then went into silent prayer.

Separately, both Joe and Doug took note of the massive invasion force heading towards the island of Peleliu, again by combined Marine and Army forces. They were part of an assembled group of Higgins boats roughly one-twentieth the size of the main Peleliu attack force. Fate had sent them both to the smaller neighboring island of Palau. "Get this alligator moving, pronto, sailor" Captain Travers yelled at the navy coxswain manning the helm of the LTV. He swallowed hard to keep his breakfast down and he too went into silent prayer. Halfway through his personal prayer the drone of a squadron of Avengers, Dauntless and Hellcat aircraft from the *USS Enterprise* came screaming in low, overhead toward Peleliu. Doug snapped back to the present and never finished his prayer.

Reverting back, he raised his binoculars and found his target. A line of four log huts housed what reconnaissance photos described as the communications and likely commanding Japanese officer headquarters on Palau. Doug's company had been assigned the task of capturing and destroying the huts, men and equipment. The salty splashes on his lens made vision difficult, but not impossible and he zeroed in on not just the huts, but a rocky pathway leading from designated Blue Beach to the huts. The Japs likely had, and he would have, trained a piece of light artillery or at least a machine gun on the pathway should the invasion occur. He mentally made note not to use the path and going around would be much safer.

Palau was Doug's baptism by fire. His wartime duty so far was as commanding officer of the drill instructors at Parris Island, South Carolina. His superiors had been so pleased with the job he'd been doing, even though he'd requested front line duty, Doug had been denied until the spring of 1944. During a staging stint in San Diego, he met a Mississippi girl, Peg Moreland. The two had immediately hit it off. Sadly, after only their fifth date, Peg was shipped off to Ft. Des Moines, Iowa. They promised to write to each other and so for each had lived up to the agreement.

The men, his men, in the Higgins boat, were quiet except for a few Catholic boys who'd formed a bond, circled together and were saying prayers aloud, but in a quiet voice. Doug wondered if Peg knew where he was. Not in a Higgins heading to Palau Island, but that he was about to go under fire for the first time. Her face materialized in his mind. She was gorgeous, but more. She had all the qualities he admired. Peg was no-nonsense, straightforward, intelligent, smart, funny, patriotic, and wanted to do her part to defeat the Axis powers, go home, get married and start a family. Doug wanted that also.

Not usually one for the realm of extra sensory perception, Doug gave it a try and concentrated on sending Peg a message. If she sensed he was in battle to know these things: first, he would do his duty and second, he'd return to the States, tell her he loved her, and they'd be together for good. Somehow, he managed to tune out the noisy chaos and briefly envisioned Peg. Almost as soon as he did, the first Japanese mortar round hit the water twenty yards to their starboard, she vanished as the reality of combat rattled his chest cavity.

Joe Travers, roughly three hundred yards away in his own LTV, was seasick. His breakfast did not stay down, and he held his head over the side, retching his guts out. The fact that his nasal-toned Boston-raised sergeant was yelling at him about his stomach problems didn't help.

Then, coming to his aid was his newest best friend, Andre Duplechain, a Cajun from south of New Orleans.

Growing up fishing and shrimping on the Gulf of Mexico, Andre knew about seasickness and in preparation had taken two ginger cookies from the ship's mess. "Here comes your Traiteur, (Cajun for healer), Alabama, eat this cookie, slowly and chew it all up," he instructed Joe with a reassuring hand on his shoulder, too. "And do this. Turn toward the island, find a patch of trees and fix your eyes on it and only them. That'll help calm down that flipping stomach of yours. Don't talk, just do as I say."

Bones of the Black Warrior

The Cajun's advice reaped near-immediate rewards and Joe's problem subsided. He took a swallow from his canteen, swirled the water in his mouth and expelled a stream of nasty water, along with the rotten taste, from his lips. "Thanks, Andre. It's bad enough here without my insides trying to come out," Joe said, and he managed a smile as water spray from an enemy mortar round splashed them both with the salty brine. "Say, Coonie, how deep do you think this water is?"

Paulu Island
6:30 a.m.

Capt. Travers pulled his binoculars away and peered ahead. Was this for real? Or did he wishfully imagine it, like he'd done an hour earlier with Peg? His company's first objective, the palm log complex of huts on a small rise on Blue Beach, was gone. It didn't exist. Ten minutes before his LTV landed, one last barrage from what he thought was the *USN Tennessee* had obliterated all four structures. All that remained were smoldering logs tossed about like a child's toy blocks and three gigantic craters fifteen feet deep. He'd been hearing small arms fire coming from Red Beach to his immediate right for the last twenty minutes, but Blue Beach was all quiet. His company had not encountered one single shot from enemy resistance. Doug had no way of knowing that his foe had concentrated all of their 200 men on Paulu into one area; the one the Americans referred to as Red Beach, leaving Blue Beach with no one for them to fight.

Joe was in the fight, and like his brother, this was his first time under fire, too. Being in one of the two platoons that had landed on Red Beach had their foe outnumbering them 2-to-1, but they were holding their own. Joe, along with everyone else, had heard of the famous Japanese Banzai charges and every US soldier on the beach was wondering if or when they'd be facing one. He was busy popping off rounds at what he thought were dark shapes behind the muzzle flashes in the tangle of bushes and leafy undergrowth one-hundred and fifty yards straight ahead. The nasal sergeant from Massachusetts tapped Joe and four others on the shoulder and motioned to follow. The five were going to reconnoiter the enemy's left flank for weakness. Andre Duplechain, who was the company radio man, was with them, too. (Andre, as many Cajuns could, spoke French fluently and when the situation called for it, he'd make a radio transmission so, as to confuse any Japanese listeners.)

Meanwhile, after Captain Travers assessed there was no one to fight, he had his radio man call his immediate superior, Major Treadwell, who instructed him to cautiously move north to Red Beach's left flank to assess and assist the Army who definitely had encountered the enemy. Doug sent word for his seventy-man company to follow his lead towards the north and the fighting.

Once in the battle, the first thing Doug noticed was similar to what Joe had become aware of earlier. The sound in flight and bouncing off the sand of the Japanese seven-millimeter bullets. Both men had gone under live fire during basic and were familiar with the sounds from the American guns. The Japanese rifle report was not as loud or deep, and the sound of the bullet in flight was of a slightly higher pitch, as was the ricochet noise as it bounded off the sand. They'd both heard it discussed by veteran soldiers and lo-and-behold it was true.

After the Army sergeant had his five men up and moving a Japanese machine gun, previously unheard, came to life and, just in time to be caught in the open, the men dove into a large bomb crater and safety as the machine gun's spray went overhead. Doug Travers heard the same gun and paused his advancing men behind a seawall of concrete and protection.

Red Beach
10:05 a.m.

Capt. Travers had noted the last burp from the Jap machine gun at 9:12, nearly an hour ago. The small arms fire from the jungle had also slackened to near nothing. His company was restless and there had been little interaction with the Army troops now less than fifty yards away. He'd heard they were from the 81st and recognized it as his brother's division. What if?

No way Joe was here. A division numbered 10,000 men and with all these widely scattered Japanese-held islands, it would be quite the coincidence.

The close proximity to the Army had raised his troops' fighting spirit. First, they all had been told the Marines did all the fighting and later the

Bones of the Black Warrior

Army came in as guard duty relief. Second, they were competitive and wanted Marines to be able to take credit for wiping out Japanese defenses on Palau. Most of his men were bored and sick of the sand flea bites from sitting still in one place. There was more than a ripple of dissatisfaction among the men. They wanted to fight. He had his radio man ring up Major Treadwell for the latest recon information. A pilot from the *Enterprise* had reported no reserve units were behind the patch of jungle Doug's men were facing. Also, one of his more experienced soldiers had estimated, by counting rifle reports, that the Japanese strength was more than 100, but less than 200. The combined Army and Marine numbers. With their M-1 Garands semi-automatic rifles able to squeeze off five rounds to a bolt action Jap's one, they had a definite firepower advantage.

His men wanted to rush the jungle, but one particular section in a history class back at The Citadel, kept coming to mind. A modern general had examined the results of troops charging, both Union and Confederate, during the Civil War. The results were overwhelming. The defensive line troops generally inflicted a four to one casualty advantage over the attackers, if not more. That fact, combined with this being his first time in action, made his decision. No, they would not attack, but hold the line. The aircraft would eventually come off Peleliu to Paulu, he felt certain. He'd been hearing of the Army Air and Naval wings' use of a new gasoline bomb called napalm. It would be his duty to keep the Japanese troops just where they were. Soon, perhaps those planes and their napalm bombs would swing over here.

Joe's unit was under the leadership of Army Major Wingate, a West Pointer, who hated history and had fallen asleep fourteen years ago in his class when the same statistical information from the Civil War had been presented. Those in the Army had heard the same talk about only being fit for mop-up duty after the Marines seized the day. They wanted to be the ones to proudly state, that we outdid the Leathernecks at Palau Island and captured the Rats' flag. His men were thirsty, bored and sick of sand fleas, too. Plus, he'd received the same recon there were no reserves behind the dug-in Jap troops. Wanting to grab a little glory and shove it down a Marine's throat sounded good and so the word was passed, attack at 10:15. One-third of the men would flank left, one-third right and he'd lead the middle third right up the enemy gut.

In the doldrums and then with a plan formulated, Major Wingate forgot about the crew of five led by the Boston sergeant. The tough Bostonian had heard the same bragging from Marines for two years and felt, as did the major, it was time for the 81st to grab a little glory. Not only had these five men continued moving forward in a flanking move, but over the past hour, they were completely behind the Japanese.

Helping, although completely unaware they were assisting at the perfect time, in came two by two, four Hellcat fighters screaming in at 400 feet and strafed the jungle at 10:14. With the Japanese hunkered down for air attack, Major Wingate rose up to lead. The men cheered and followed. They'd made it almost seventy yards before the first Jap rifleman returned fire. His marksmanship was dead on and Major Wingate collapsed with a hole twice the size of his thumbnail in his center chest.

Joe was excited, anxious and itching to kill Japanese. However, where he was located, he lost a bit of his spit and vinegar when the Hellcats came screaming in, discharging a burst of .50 cals, churning up lines of sandy soil less than two feet away, nearly killing him and Andre with over shots. Being behind the enemy had a major disadvantage as stray American bullets now were coming in a steady stream and with no regard to the nationality of the flesh they might penetrate. Wingate's men were firing wildly as they ran forward. A hail of lead drove the five to the ground and they were unable to see what was taking place. What was transpiring was bad. Especially dangerous were the six Thompson machine gun men who sprayed hundreds of .45s through the leaves and over the Japanese position into the five Americans. The Boston sergeant took it first. Anxious to escape the precarious position and curious to quickly find a solution, he half-rose to his knees to take a quick look and got shot. He was dead before he hit the ground with three bullet wounds from friendly fire to the face and head.

A portion of the Japanese defenders was sent backward to find an escape route from the onrushing Americans. The twenty or so were on Joe, Andre and the other two survivors before they realized what had happened. Faced with five-to-one odds, Andre, who held his radio receiver, not a weapon, threw up his hands first. The other two did likewise as did Joe when he saw fighting was no longer a viable option. Fate chose the soldier to Joe's left as he was swiftly bayoneted by two angry Japs despite surrendering.

"Damn you, we gave up. We surrendered you bastards," Andre yelled which drew attention to him and another Jap shoved a pistol in his face in retaliation and said something in a rage, but at least did not shoot the normally jovial Cajun.

Joe felt it. This was the end. He didn't see his life flash as was the common misconception. No, instead he saw his happiest of days. Oddly it was from four years prior when the peanut harvest was sold, and his Daddy showed him the final numbers. It was his second year as president of Alabimo Peanuts, which had been in business for thirty years, and the year's profits were ten percent over the previous best. Joe was good at this and had outperformed his father's top results. He was a success! Then, he took a rifle butt to the chin, and all went black.

Meanwhile, just a short distance away, Captain Travers kept resisting. The men were vehemently stating they needed to attack. But he held firm. His instincts felt right. The brash move by the Army was a mistake. Out of their cover, they were vulnerable and were falling like flies to the Japanese fire. Doug knew time was on their side. Eventually the aircraft would come in and take care of the troublesome Japanese soldiers. Why not? They were in control. Only hold the line and remain patient. What was keeping those flyboys, anyway?

The twenty Japanese who'd retreated had no use for prisoners and so the other unknown GI and Andre were quickly bayoneted to death also. Joe was not. Instead, he was going to be a pawn in a game with the attackers. Stripped to his underwear, Joe was tied to a nearby palm and a Japanese soldier who spoke perfect English was placed at his side. A small man, even by Far East standards, stood next to Joe and yelled at the translator. Joe could tell from the differences in attire, knee-high boots and sword at his side, the small man held some sort of officer status.

Strangely calm, the English-speaker instructed Joe what to say. "Lt. Ohogi demands you tell the other Americans you and four others are our prisoners. If they move forward, you will all be killed. They must cease firing, retreat back to the waterline and do so now."

Joe hesitated and his head was still spinning from the blow to the chin and pain racked his entire face. He wasn't even sure his mouth would work.

The small officer slapped Joe hard directly on his nose and the translator repeated his demand more robustly.

Joe tried, but it was too much to repeat, "Stop, don't come closer or they'll kill me," he tried to muster out weakly.

"Louder American dog, louder," said the translator. "Kill all five. Say all five!"

"Or they'll kill all five of us," Joe said with more conviction.

The little officer yelled, but Joe couldn't tell if it was directed at him or the translator, but there was immediate action. The officer unsheathed a knife with a four-inch blade and without saying a word or emotion, moved on Joe and stabbed him deeply once in the upper arm.

Shocked, Joe just stared at the little man. He'd said the words as they told him. Why did he do that? Then the pain of the wound hit and it was an intense fire like he'd never felt. He struggled against the binding rope but to no avail.

"They do not retreat, dog. Tell them again! Tell them to withdraw back to the beach or you and the four others will die."

The little officer came again and with a darting move stabbed once more, this time lower in Joe's upper thigh, just below the line of his underwear. There was no delay. The deep cut of the Kaiken dirk was intense, immediate and before he realized it, he painfully screamed out and promptly received another hard slap on the nose. To accentuate the threat, the little officer drew his pistol and fired three quick shots into Andre's corpse as if to signal his threats were real.

Leaderless, the Army attackers stayed put, neither advancing nor retreating. Joe's translator kept repeating his demands, and Joe kept saying them, but when nothing happened the officer would stab Joe again, never in a vital spot like the heart, neck or lungs, but kept on until Joe had a total of nine stab wounds as his cries of agony filled the humid air.

Nearby, the Marines had seen and heard enough. Orders would not be obeyed. Finally, one private yelled out, "Marines lead from the front." That did it. In groups of five to six, they rose, charged the jungle and as he saw his men go forth, Capt. Travers relented and joined the rushing melee. To their left, the Army saw the Marines going into tight quarters and they too rose up and ran to fight. Now close enough to see Jap soldiers, not just dark

Bones of the Black Warrior

shapes in the distance, their accurate aim and overwhelming firepower of the M-1 Garand and Thompsons quickly made the difference.

They rushed directly at the stunned, overwhelmed Japanese and it was over in four minutes. One-hundred and sixty Japs were dead. Thirty-two combined US forces were dead and another twenty-one wounded, of which there were more Army than Marine casualties. The translator had seen the close-charging Americans and ran away, only to be cut down in the back in a hail of Thompson machine gun fire. The little officer sensed that he was going to die, but at least take the tortured American with him. He shoved his Nambu 8-millimeter pistol barrel to Joe's temple, made eye contact with the young man from rural Alabama and without hesitation pulled the trigger.

Click. He'd emptied his weapon into Andre's corpse and never reloaded. There was no telling if it was a Marine or a member of the 81st that shot the Japanese officer. Joe saw the little man's unshielded head explode in a cloud of red mist right before his eyes, chunks of the man's brains hit Joe's face and stuck there.

Then and there, Joe thought he was dead and instead of seeing grandma and grandpa's faces in Heaven, he saw his older brother standing right before him, smiling and speaking, but he didn't hear a word. His ears were not working for some reason.

Joe had blocked it out when it happened. The puny Japanese officer, in between his nine stabs to his captive's arms and legs, right before a hail of .45 bullets took his life, had taken his fountain pen and jabbed it down the American's ear canal, puncturing both his eardrums and causing permanent deafness for Joe Travers.

Chapter 30
A Chance Meeting

February 19, 1956
Johnson Farm

Roy Johnson was an old man and old men, having experienced much of life, are not usually easily riled, but he was very much so. He'd just finished reading the editorial page of yesterday's edition of *The Montgomery Advertiser*. The writer had unequivocally stated the words of minister Dr. Martin L. King were not those of the Negro community and should be retracted. Roy disagreed and even at his advanced age of ninety-four, violently threw down his newspaper in disgust. His son, Cleophus, named after his best friends from the days at Tuskegee, heard the commotion and came into the same room.

"I'm guessing you just read the same thing I did an hour ago? The editorial, right, Papa?"

"It's a time long tima-a coming, son. Long time and this newspaper man's fighting it tooth and nail, ain't he?" When he got angry, Roy would stuff tobacco into his pipe, light it and take one puff before letting the flame die out, preserving the rest for later. His Zippo lighter wouldn't catch and heaped more frustration on him. He hurled his lighter on the floor next to the paper and it bounced up, hitting his son on the shin.

"Here's a book of matches, Papa," Cleophus said as he calmly walked over to the ratty old chair the old man refused to give up to the trash heap. "Give them back when you get your pipe lit. I want to light a fire. The radio said it was going down to thirty-nine tonight." Cleophus did as he said, as the kindling took fire he retreated to the center of the room, picked up the newspaper, folded it neatly and with the lighter, handed them both back to his father. "Here, find what's on the radio tonight. I'll sit in here with you and we can listen together."

"I'm flustered son. I thought things would be better by these modern days, but all they want to do is keep holding us down, hold us back and keep us down. Reverend King said it plain as day, but the ones with the power, they don't want to hear it and instead they smear him. I'm so disgusted."

"I know, me too, Papa, but right here tonight at five till seven, we can't do a darn thing. Let's listen to *Fibber Mcgee and Molly* for half-an-hour. You'll be calmed down by then and we can talk about Brother King and the newspaper after that. I'll get us both a hot chocolate, okay?"

Suddenly, the back door opened and slammed. The scurry of four feet was heard going into the kitchen, the refrigerator door smacked open, the rattle of a glass milk bottle, followed by the 'glug glug' sound of someone, they all knew who, draining the last of a gallon of milk down their thirsty throat. Roy's hearing was still good enough.

"What's that noise? Darry is that you or is that you, Jackson? Whichever one, come tell your old great-grandpappy about the game this evening."

The two teen boys stood in the kitchen for a moment. Darry poured a glass of tap water and without turning on the hall light, retreated down to the bedroom he shared with Jackson.

Shortly, the high school pride of Clark County's Negro School System athletics, Jackson Johnson, came into the den beaming a wide grin and a white milk mustache high up on his six-foot-seven frame. As he was asked, he told his grandfather and great grandfather about his 28-point effort against Crispus Attucks High, and the team's twenty point win against the larger school from Baldwin County in the varsity game earlier.

Darry was the older brother by a year and served as the basketball team manager. His only semi-athletic venture. While Jackson, a true physical specimen, played all the sports, Darry was more bookish and the intellectual in the family. Darry didn't care to relive his little brother's night as he'd recently been given a book about *Brown vs. The Board of Education* by a young lady he was seeing on the sly, Henrietta Grey, from down the highway in Stockton.

After a round of congratulations for Jackson and then *Fibber*, what was up for discussion, between Roy and Cleophus at 7:30, was the third month of the Montgomery bus boycott, stoked by Rosa Parks' refusal to give up her seat and subsequent arrest of the previous December. Rev. Martin Luther King, newly elected president of the Montgomery Improvement Association, had organized the boycott in response. The association's purpose was to air grievances with the buses empty seat policy, seating in the rear only and only making a few select stops in the black community, while stopping at almost every street corner in a white one. The newspaper editorial was downplaying Dr. King and the need for any actions, stating relations between the races were just fine and everyone needed to forgive and forget. The editor emphatically wrote the bus company was the innocent victim here, not Mrs. Parks or the Negro community.

Despite the newspaper's plea, the bombing of Dr. King's home and his subsequent arrest, conviction and one year jail term, the boycott did not lose momentum. The bus boycott garnered national attention and funds to set up carpooling services to assist the Negroes' vital need of getting to and from work. Later in 1956, the U.S. Supreme Court ruled the segregation of buses as unconstitutional and to desegregate immediately. Despite pressure to end the boycott, King and his group held strong until Montgomery's buses complied with the federal decree.

Darry, after Jackson's exit from the den, went back for more water, overheard his father and grandfather's discussion about Dr. King and the buses. While he and Henrietta had actually been introduced at a party, they both discovered a common interest, the civil rights movement, of which she held a more active view than most. However, Darry, in her opinion, was coming around to see the light. While Dr. King had good intentions and his Mahatma Gandhi approach might work. Henrietta's recent readings were changing her thoughts. Dr. King's methods were too slow moving and more aggressive acts were necessary.

The news of the boycott victory which ended just before Christmas, 1956 filtered down to Jackson Farm. Dr. King and the MIA's victory in Montgomery seemed to be the salve of inner peace old Roy had been waiting on. Seemingly more pleased with the world and happy for the bus-inspired victory, he died in his sleep during his after Christmas dinner after enjoying a rare full pipe bowl all the way to the end.

February, 1957
Alabimo Farms
7:30 p.m.

Bones of the Black Warrior

Doug Travers had mixed emotions. Joe was being allowed a visitation release from the VA Hospital in Gulfport, Mississippi tomorrow. He hadn't seen his younger brother in four years as Joe had been secluded in a wing of the hospital, for the past three years, for the violently predisposed and was not allowed visitors. Supposedly, he was better. Not cured, but incident-free for two full years and pronounced fit to visit family. In a series of letters with the chief of staff, Doug had been given permission to host Joe for a twelve-day visit. Doug thought February being somewhat of a down month on the peanut farm, would be the best time to give his brother the most attention. Still, the farm work demanded much of him and Peg, his wife, would make the two-hour drive over to Mississippi. Accompanying her would be their eleven-year-old daughter,

Liz, who'd earned a day off from school by way of her straight-A report card for the year to date.

Biloxi, Mississippi
Whitman Hotel Restaurant
Next day
12:10 p.m.

"Mama, Mama, they have cocktails on the kids menu. Is that what I think it means, like Daddy before supper? Look, it says shrimp cocktail?" Liz asked innocently as she read the menu.

"You are very observant, my dear, but no, it's not like your father having his evening toddy. A shrimp cocktail isn't something you drink. It's boiled shrimp all in a fancy bowl and there's a tomato-based sauce, sort of like a spicy ketchup, that you dip the shrimp in. No, if it was a real, well anyway, I'll tell your father this story tonight. He'll get a kick out of it. Waiter, we're ready to order now," Peg said as she opened her purse for her pack of cigarettes.

The busy waiter smiled and gave a quick non-verbal signal he'd be right over after he filled the water glasses at the next table. Liz took it all in as she was enjoying her day and feeling of self-importance. She was dressed in her Sunday best and her new Christmas present, white gloves. Peg, likewise, was in a church dress, high heels, stylish hat and elbow-length gloves.

Then, a surprise.

"My oh my, Peggy Moreland from Gulfport, Mississippi? Prettiest head cheerleader the

Commodores ever produced," a tall handsome man, her age, in a business suit said from her left. He was her old high school beau, Scotty Gorenflo, from one of the Coast's most prominent and affluent families. Peg was caught off guard especially when she saw Scotty wore a black patch covering his right eye.

The small talk grew beyond a mere greeting and when the situation became clear Scotty was alone, Peg invited him to their table. He'd had a business lunch and already eaten but sat and had a piece of pie and cup of coffee and caught up on old times. Liz didn't like it one bit, but she was powerless and sat with a scowl affixed. The eye patch explanation came up immediately. Scotty had lost its use back in January of '45 in the Battle of the Bulge but quickly explained he'd adapted and could still shoot even par at the famous Great Southern golf course.

Peg was at first excited to see her old friend, but his familiarity, especially in front of Liz, began to work on her nerves. Scotty explained, mostly directly to Liz, that he'd planned to ask Peggy to marry when she came back home after the war. Then, he said he'd been heartbroken to hear she'd married a Marine officer from southern Alabama. In response, Peg tried to control the conversation and keep things in the present, but Scotty was much more interested in reliving the past and their glory days from high school.

Soon Liz's fried shrimp and her stuffed flounder arrived, and they both ate quickly as Scotty did all the talking. When he finally asked about her business on the Coast, Peg paused. If Liz hadn't been there a quick white lie would have sufficed, but instead she told of Joe and the VA Hospital. Scotty, being from Gulfport knew that the local VA housed mostly mental casualties from the war with minor physical wounds. To the more crass, in their word, crazies.

Little Liz then spilled the beans that Uncle Joe would be on a short visit, and that she and her Mama planned to bring him back at the beginning of next month. That was all Scotty needed. He immediately insisted that on their return trip they should arrive early, go out on his yacht to Ship Island, see the old Civil War fort, and have a picnic, after they dropped poor old Joe off, of course.

Peg quickly went to work building an excuse why that couldn't be done, but when Scotty said he played golf every weekend with the hospital's chief administrator and would know of Joe Travers' comings and goings, if he asked, Peg felt trapped. She didn't commit by saying she'd see Scotty on her return, but she didn't say she wouldn't either. Scotty then ended it by saying he'd arrange for his twelve-year-old niece to come on his boat also, as March 3 was a Saturday, so Liz would have a playmate her own age. Scotty added the location of his docked yacht and how easily identifiable it was, being twice the size of the next largest vessel and in honor of his eye patch, flew the Jolly Roger pennant from the main mast.

To make it worse, when Peg asked for the check, Scotty said he had a standing agreement with the manager. If he ever saw Mr. Gorenflo take a seat at a different table, the bill would go directly to his standing account, not his guest. Peg protested, but her old boyfriend pleaded innocence and it was customary on his home turf.

Peg could not help watching Scotty as he excused himself and left the restaurant. For some reason, the years and the salt and pepper hair had only added to his rugged good looks, and the eye patch, well, it added a flair of mystery to the successful man of the world. A frown creased her lips as she quickly thought; her Doug seldom was seen out of his dirty denim overalls, plaid work shirt and muddy boots, these days. Isolated in the boondocks, she found it difficult to recall the last time she and her spouse had dressed up for a night out on the town.

February 25, 3:20 p.m.
Four miles east of Alabimo Farm
Rural Route 5

Doug was wringing his hands with worry. After a late morning lunch with just him and Joe, he'd gone to the office in the old cotton gin to write checks for some bills that were due. He'd made it clear to Joe that he'd be back in thirty minutes, which he was, but Joe vanished. The long-time maid, Arlivia, said she'd seen Joe walk down the front drive, but assumed Mr. Travers was okay with it and took no action. After going around to the back and calling for his brother, with no response, Doug went to the separate garage building, hopped in the International Harvester pickup and tore out down the driveway. That had been three hours ago without results, he'd driven up and down Route 5 and 4, but never found him. Around 2:00 he'd come back, parked and sat on the front porch and watched the drive for Joe's return. His plan was to call the sheriff for help in an hour, if necessary. It was then that he saw Joe coming up the driveway.

Doug leaped directly off the porch, sprinting to meet his kid brother. When he'd approached within forty feet, he had a flashback to 1944 and Palau Island. Joe wasn't in as bad of shape as that awful day, but nonetheless a mess. Joe's shirt was ripped, torn in three places and he had half a dozen fingernail scratches on his neck and face. His left ear had bled, and a crimson string of dried blood was caked to his neck.

Doug inquired if he'd been in a fight or tangled with a wildcat. Joe's speech pattern had deteriorated badly and was difficult to understand. All Doug could be certain was the phrase, "paid her back." He quickly took Joe upstairs to shower and put on fresh clothes. After that, for the rest of Joe's six remaining days at Alabimo, he never spoke, nary a single word. Joe ate, slept and walked the grounds alone those days, silently got in the car early that Saturday and stayed mute the entire way with his sister-in-law.

In Doug's opinion, the mystery of Joe's disappearance and his haggard look upon returning had a likely cause. The local radio, two days after Joe wandered off, reported an unheard-of atrocity for Clark County: a murder, nearby on Route 5, Tensaw, only four miles from Alabimo. A forty-two-year-old woman had been reported missing from her job as a cocktail waitress at a cowboy honky tonk, called Mamie's. She lived alone and when a deputy investigated, found her badly beaten body, atop a dirty mattress in the old sharecropper shack where she had died. The radio announcer said the crime scene had shown signs of a fearful struggle as the woman had vainly fought her attacker or attackers.

March 3, mid-morning
Gulfport Small Craft Harbor

Peg Travers drove up in her immaculate-looking car, a 1955 Chrysler Imperial, freshly waxed by Jackson Johnson for some pocket money for the teenage boy. Liz had not been able to come back due to an upset stomach and after dropping Joe off, Peg was prepared to meet Scotty, decline his offer of a boat ride and return to Alabama. Easily towering over all the other docked vessels, she saw the Jolly Roger flag smartly snapping in the breeze and veered toward the pier which only had one huge yacht. The boat was a magnificent specimen of 1930s craftsmanship, from famed Dutch builder, Feadship, with intricate attention to detail, just like he said, she easily stood out. Before Peg even had her declination speech worked out, she parked. Scotty had recognized the car approaching and was on the pier, unseen behind a utility building. In a flash was at her car door alone, without the niece.

In a little more than an hour, Scotty flipped a switch by the ship's wheel, as they heard the clank of the metal chain deploy and the heavy anchor splash in fifteen feet of clear, green water on the north side of Ship Island. Scotty had explained he normally employed a full-time captain and first mate, but today had given them the day off. They were not just alone on the yacht, Scotty pointed out, there wasn't another boat within two miles.

If Doug had done just the slightest bit to shave, shower and put on decent clothes over the past few days, Peg might not have taken such an interest in Scotty's sporty, magazine ad appearance and overall clean, healthy look. The feelings of guilt were becoming less and less the further the yacht sailed out of Gulfport Harbor. Peg felt like she was on a vacation and maybe even in a Hollywood movie, just a bit.

Not much of a drinker, Peg did have an occasional glass of wine on a holiday or special event, but something got into her as she tossed back her third delicious Fuzzy Navel cocktail of the young morning and felt warm all over. She also felt uninhibited, a tad sexy, as Scotty put on a Frank Sinatra album and did a funny little waltz over to her.

March, mid-morning
Empty sharecropper shack
Rural Route 5 Tensaw

The bent-over old woman swore to it and the two deputies had no reason to doubt her word. The nearest neighbor to the deceased bar waitress had called their office and said she'd witnessed something disturbing last week, the very day of the murder. The woman said she'd seen a black boy of probable high school age arrive at the shack, go inside and leave three or four minutes later, in a hurry as he ran full speed down the dirt driveway to a bike and took off due west on Route 5.

Furthermore, she described him as abnormally tall, probably six-foot eight and wore a red and white leather jacket, like those of Clark County Negro High athletes. One of the deputies had played some high school basketball and occasionally would find a pickup game. There was only one exceptionally tall local black boy always on the local playground. The deputy knew his name and where he lived. The boy was extremely talented and had a good chance for a scholarship to Tuskegee or Alabama A&M. The old lady's description fit Jackson Johnson. At the very least, this new information warranted him questioning the boy.

Chapter 31
A Mob

March 6, 1957
Alabimo Farms
Master bedroom
9:35 p.m.

"Look Doug, I found this today in the attic under a stack of boxes filled with old shoes that belonged to your mother," Peg said as she exited the bathroom and approached the bed. Doug had already settled in and was propped up with his book, *Don't Go Near the Water*, a humor novel about the US Navy during World War II in the Pacific Theatre. He didn't respond at first, until Peg stood bedside and shoved the old journal directly in his face.

"Is that it? The old family history?" Doug said with excitement as he swung his legs out of bed and stood up to hold the heirloom. "What in tarnation were you doing in the attic?"

"Don't play coy with me, Captain Travers. You know why. We're going to Mobile weekend after next for that Order of the Aztec Mardi Gras party. I found a few dresses in your mother's old cedar chest and you sir, you cannot wear a black coat and white shirt to Mardi Gras. It's all about bright colors, you know."

"Yeah, okay, I remember now, the Mardi Gras party, Corporal Moreland. I guess out-ranking you won't get me out of this silly Mardi Gras shindig? But anyway, this is great, the old journal has been lost for I don't know how long?" Doug said as he took it in hand and grinned broadly.

Peg tried to stay tuned in and listen, but her mind drifted back to the past Saturday. As Doug was reading aloud from journal entries from years prior, however, Scotty Gorenflo kept entering her mind. Oh, three days ago, yes, she'd been alone on his yacht and the scenario kept popping up, but nothing had happened. Scotty sure thought something would and made a move during a slow dance, when he attempted to kiss her, but she stood her ground, rejecting his advance and vehemently stating she was a one-man-woman; completely faithful. Then added that one war veteran should respect the wife of another, to please pull up the anchor and take her back.

Talking about the old days, yes, she had enjoyed his fancy boat ride, but that was absolutely it. Scotty apologized, blamed it on the booze and ran the boat at full speed back to the harbor. He begged forgiveness and hoped it wouldn't ruin their friendship. Peg didn't respond either way as she got off the boat, walked briskly to her car and drove off.

Doug didn't even realize Peg had closed her eyes and was asleep as he read aloud. "Wow, this penmanship is really hard to read; not just that it's faded, it's so loopy and frilly." Glancing over after a half minute of no response, Doug continued, but read it to himself and he flipped back in time.

The exact year was too faded, but he did see the "18" part, and after a moment, deciphered the first sentence of a paragraph, "The railroads keep trying to corner the cotton transport market, but our slides and barges, even though they are now old, still do the job admirably. We sent…"

A circling ring of a water spot had obliterated the rest of the paragraph, so Doug dropped his eyes further down the page. Picking up again, "Paid $22 for tickets by steamboat for 4 passengers from Travers Landing to Selma to see my acquaintance, Mr. Bill Keene, about buying 3 of our older slaves. The first night we hit a snag that pierced our hull. Waited three days on a remote sandbar to be rescued by a second steamer. After another two days upriver to Selma, Mr. Keene had assumed I was not coming and bought three slaves elsewhere and no longer needed Ned, Velma and Hertiseen. The market for slaves is now drying up and we must sell before we lose this accursed war. Complained to the ship's master who lowered our return fare to $16 for all 4 of us."

"Peg, this entry is from the Civil War," whispered Doug to his wife, "someone is writing about trying to sell the slaves." After turning the page, he read a new entry, "Roy and Cleo claim to have seen the ghost ship of the Tombigbee last night. The Elizabeth Battle caught fire and sank ten years prior just off Travers Landing. Thirty-eight souls perished. Old ghost tales make good campfire talk, however I've never believed in such nonsense. I allowed Roy to tell me his tale and did not admonish him. I hear them sometimes, talking among themselves, scaring the bedevil out of each other relaying tales of the spirits of the old human bones we continually dig up around the plantation.

The water stain bleeding through from the previous page made the rest of the long paragraph illegible. Doug thought he might be up all night reading the old journal and decided to stop there and turn off his lamp for some much-needed sleep.

March 12
Main bedroom
5:35 p.m.

"Doug put down that old journal and try on this coat for the Aztec party, please," Peg said. "I'm picking up my dress from Mrs. Marshall's alterations tomorrow, so I'm set. You need to decide tonight what you're wearing so we'll have time to get it dry-cleaned. Try on the green jacket."

Reluctantly, Doug placed the journal on his bedside table, stood up and walked to the far wall where Peg stood, jacket in hand. "I'm at a really interesting part, Peg. I'm not sure who's writing, and I think the year is 1932. It mentions the death at sea of Andrew Douglas, oh, and get this, it brings up the question, was he really the son of Micah? It says Matilda had always harbored thoughts he might secretly be a Travers half-brother?"

Flustered, Peg ignored her spouse, "Try this on, you can solve some old mystery after Mardi Gras, right now you need something to wear to this party. I want you to look nice. Got it Marine?"

The livid green coat's sleeves were too short, although Doug protested he could wear it anyway, Peg wasn't having it. Together they went up the utility stairs and pulled the wire string on the naked light bulb in the fully floored attic. Peg headed for a rack of clothes, all under a protective sheath of plastic, but Doug saw something else of interest; a sword leaning up in the far, half-lit corner and covered in cobwebs. Attached to the hilt was a string and a paper tag measuring about three square inches. Doug pulled his Zippo out used the flame and read, "For gallant services rendered by Col. John K. Douglas, Alabama Militia, veteran of The Creek War. Posthumously awarded to Mrs. J.K. Douglas by Clark County Ladies Temperance Chapter, August 11, 1886."

"Peg, we have to take this down and put it over the fireplace or somewhere. Look. This is a great find."

"Admit it, we're never going to make this party, are we Doug?" she said, before an involuntary sigh escaped as she turned toward him.

Even in the semi-darkness of the poorly lit attic, he saw her disappointed face and realized he needed to give his wife the attention she deserved. They and the peanut farm were still isolated and opportunities for social interaction were far and few between, he reminded himself. He laid the sword down and walked over to the rack of clothes. "Black or dull colors won't do. I know that, so how about I take this bright red coat down to the bedroom and try it on in the light? I hope it fits," he put his arm around her waist, gave her a hug and kissed her gently on the cheek.

"Babe, we're going to enjoy ourselves this weekend in Mobile, aren't we honey?"

Peg smiled and pulled the light's chain and together they carefully found their way to the stairs and descended. Before they reached the bedroom to try the coat on, they both heard knocking at the front door. It was not a casual knock, but one of haste and urgency. "Who could that be?" Peg said before Doug could. They bypassed their bedroom, tossed the red jacket on a chair in the second-floor hall and quickly together rushed to the front door.

"Mr. Travers, they got my boy, Jackson. We got a phone call from somebody, a white woman's voice all I know, but they got Jackson," a frantic Mrs. Cleophus Johnson said in the waning daylight on Alabimo's front porch.

"Who?" Peg blurted out before moving aside to let Doug come closer.

"Lutilly, are you alright? Who? Who's got your son? Where's Cleo?" the words spewed hastily from Doug.

"Come inside Mrs. Johnson, come in," Peg asked in a calm tone as she extended her hand to hold the black woman's. But she hesitated and instead put her hands to her neck in anguish.

"The man said, the white man on the phone said they, the KKK, they got Jackson and some Catholic boy. They gonna have a double hanging off a bridge over Horseneck Creek as soon as it gets good and dark. He said the Klan knows Jackson killed that waitress woman from Mamie Martin's place back in February."

Doug's blood ran cold. Jackson was a good kid as Lutilly and Cleophus were wonderful parents. How did he get mixed up with the Klan? The waitress from Martin's bar had a name: Tilly Hoskins. Doug had seen the multiple newspaper write-ups last week and every time he did, the mental image of torn clothing, the bloody ear and neck of Joe staggering up the driveway came back to haunt him.

"Where's Darry? What about Cleophus?" Peg interjected to which Lutilly replied they were together in their car riding about Route 5 searching.

Half an hour ago, someone unidentified, a black person, called the Johnson house and said they saw Jackson's bike abandoned by the side of that road. Jackson never missed supper and he was now over two hours late coming home from basketball practice. Darry said his little brother stayed a bit after practice to work on his free throws, but said he'd be home by 4:45. Then she volunteered that she'd called the sheriff's department, but they said her son was probably over at some girl's place on the sly and besides it was much too early to report a missing person, told her to relax and they hung up on her.

Lutilly then backtracked and mentioned a deputy had visited last Sunday afternoon and taken Jackson out to his patrol car, alone. When Cleophus asked Jackson what it was about, her son said it was only about playing ball in a semi-pro league. Now she believed Jackson lied and hid the real purpose behind the deputy's visit.

Doug instructed Lutilly to come in and sit by Peg as his wife called the sheriff. Maybe being a Travers still carried some weight with the law in Clark County. He announced he was going to check all three bridges on Horseneck Creek as he flew to the kitchen, grabbed the keys to the Chrysler and his always-loaded Colt revolver from behind the bread box on the top of the refrigerator and was out of the house.

The Chrysler's big V-8 powered down the gravel road due east of Route 5, six miles east of Tensaw. Doug knew the bridges' locations well from his numerous fishing expeditions on the creek. They were all in a row and with approximately one mile of separation; all three very secluded from prying, curious eyes as only the scant few residents of twenty or fewer people in the Jayford Community used this road sparingly.

Fifteen minutes after leaving the house, Doug was approaching the last of the three bridges.

The loose gravel and deep ruts on the little-used road made it dangerous to go over 40 mph. There was no evidence of any recent human activity in the first two. The phrase 'good and dark' kept coming to mind. It was straight up six o'clock, the sun had set, but there were still a few streaks of orange light high in the western sky. Doug said a quick prayer he'd not be too late as he leaned into the glovebox and retrieved the best flashlight he owned.

Arriving at the west side of the old narrow, rusted third bridge there were a few dozen empty beer cans, a couple of empty whisky bottles in a messy pile behind three older model cars and two pickups. Slamming on the brakes, he threw the car into park and jumped out. With the help of his strong flashlight, Doug saw the assembled crowd of ten or so white men, all in work clothes of those men who labored outside for a living. A stark reality hit Doug, the men were without hoods, meaning they cared not that their faces were uncovered, signifying there wouldn't be any witnesses. Swinging his light to the right, just by the southern edge of the bridge railing were Jackson and the young white man, both clad in only their underwear.

"Hey all you! Stop! You all know me, I'm Doug Travers. Not gonna be any hangings!" He jogged up the wooden planks and prominently displayed his Colt pistol and moved it about, pointing it directly into the Klan crowd as he scanned the men and quickly deduced he was the only armed man on the scene. Jackson Johnson already had a noose around his neck and his hands were tied behind him. Two Klansmen, who were in the process of looping a noose around the neck of a thin white boy, halted and stared.

The entire Klan group stopped moving about, grumbled, mumbled among themselves and stared hard at Doug, but didn't say anything, nor did they move away from Jackson and their other captive. All were locals from either southern Clark or northern Baldwin Counties and knew the Travers name.

Doug summoned up his best Marine drill instructor voice and yelled, "I said there won't be any hanging!" With that, he pointed his pistol over their collective heads and squeezed off a round. The loud gun report broke the still silence, ran down the stream and echoed back. The Klansmen, all in a singular pack, bolted, running past the far side of the bridge and scattered into the adjacent woods.

Doug was left standing by Jackson and the young Catholic man. With no time to waste, leaving their hands tied, he took the noose off Jackson and instructed them to run to his car. In a flash they were in the Chrysler as Doug quickly jockeyed the car, in two nimble moves, to turn around on the narrow, gravel road. He floored it as the dust flew; rocks, ruts and danger be damned. It was time to flee. Doug felt sure the Klansmen had weapons, just not on their person, but in their cars. He wasted no time getting back on the flattop, driving his wife's car hard as he sped upwards of 90 miles per hour northwest, towards Alabimo and Jackson's mother and father.

Once home he'd report the two attempted murders, not only to the county sheriff, but the state's criminal investigation department in Montgomery. If that got nowhere, which was likely, he'd personally drive to Birmingham and request a meeting with the field office commander of the FBI.

Arriving on Route 5, he felt a touch better, was a bit more composed and then grew angry. Good God, this was 1957! This was America! Trying to kill a young man just for his religious beliefs? Then their vigilante justice tried to hang a teenage boy on mere suspicion of murdering a prostitute? A prostitute more than likely killed by his kid brother, not Jackson Johnson. Both hangings would have been barbaric acts that harkened back to the lawless days after the Civil War.

Feelings of guilt washed over Doug. Why had he not gone to the VA Hospital director, a Dr. Urie, or the local law and reported what he suspected about Joe? Inside, he knew precisely the reason; shame. He didn't want to know the truth and was afraid to find out. His act of cowardice had nearly cost two innocent young lives at the end of a noose, murdered by an ignorant, liquored-up mob.

Once within sight of his farm, he deliberately drove slowly, thinking. Could he tell Peg the real truth, or what he suspected to be the truth involving his brother and the deceased Tilly Hoskins? Finally, under the fluorescent shine of the big light pole behind his house where he parked, Doug let himself off the hook. It could have been much, much worse. Instead of delivering a scared, frightened teenager back to Cleophus and

Lutilly, he could be informing the Johnsons that one, they'd lost a son, two, he was terribly sorry and three, he'd pay all the funeral expenses.

Chapter 32
History Lessons

March 17, 1957
Alabimo
Master bedroom
8:40 a.m.

Doug sat alone in the corner chair of their bedroom and read the journal. He still had almost an hour of time before church. The Johnson family had asked the Travers to attend their house of worship with them this morning, in honor of Jackson's rescue. They'd be going to the little African A.M.E. church, not far down Route 5, planning to arrive at 9:45. Sleep had been hard to come by last week, constantly thinking how his inaction almost meant Jackson's funeral. An old habit from childhood had even returned; biting his fingernails, and all ten were down to the quick. Reading the journal would at least occupy his mind as right now, along with the steady, tick-click-tick of the grandfather clock in the hall that was driving him mad.

Opening the journal midway, the more time he spent with the journal, the better he could decipher the busy, loop-filled script. 1878. The nameless entry after the date started, "Received second letter from North Alabama businessman, Mr. H. Eugene.Hargraves, requesting backing in exchange for shares of stock in a new business venture. Replied via post, again declining the offer. The ambitious Mr. Hargraves' idea is to create high-temperature furnaces located in Jones Valley next to Red Mountain. Stated has already employed experienced workers and managers from Sheffield, England to guide his venture. Additionally, Hargraves' bold plan will found a new city around his venture of steel production, stating in his letters this area of Alabama, particularly Red Mountain, is rich in coal, iron ore and limestone. He seeks a limited number of investors at a $100,000 minimum investment. Alas, being versed in farming the matter atop Mother Nature's soil, not the lifeless rocks and elemental veins of minerals underneath, harkens my cynical nature to bear. Hargraves confidently predicts a $100,000 investment would recoup $350,000 in four years, possibly less.

The funds are available, however, tempted by such prospects of fabulous returns, cannot risk such a sum and therefore respectfully declined Hargraves offer a second time."

He turned four more pages, as they were stuck together and began reading the next entry on a new page. "I, Carla Travers, record this to advise any future reader to take precautions because all banks are not the same. The horrid events in the year 1893 have taught the Travers an extremely harsh lesson. We've all seen the newspapers and the troubling instances, nationwide, since the War Between the States banks are now being robbed. In that precautious air, the Travers have spread the family money around between five different institutions: two banks in Montgomery, two in Mobile and one nearby in Jackson. The best explanation my late husband's friends gave me was The Panic began in the financial centers of Boston and New York. Fueled by wild rumors spread by unscrupulous newspapermen, people began to hoard their currency, quit spending and depositing money as they had before the squalid gossip. The hoarding created a shortage of available money which in turn caused bank insiders to worry and whisper of the possible danger of a severe cash shortage. This proved to be kindling for the growing fire. The lucky ones with the information provided by those with the connections withdrew their funds. Those coming in later to get their money, with a growing feeling of justification about their worries, were told there was none left to withdraw. Many of the banks had nothing in their vaults. The Panic was no longer felt only in New York and Boston. As the Travers' money was roughly evenly divided among the five, when two went under; the Second National of Montgomery and the Savings Bank of Mobile County, the family fortune was depleted by $140,000. I am a simple woman trying to do my best for God, my family and possess no insight into the complicated world of finance. However, whomever you may be, at some future time, read and heed this warning - be fully certain your bank of choice can stand up in hard times and not cost you half of your hard-earned, life savings. April 2, 1894."

Doug reread the last half of the previous paragraph and let Carla Travers' words sink in for full effect. Then, he took his pen from his dress shirt pocket and quickly calculated the worth of $1 from 1893 to 1957 values. The math gave him a jolt. The Banking Panic of 1893, in current values, had cost the family approximately $500,000. Before he realized it, he was standing up and pacing the room. How different would his life, the farm and their future be with that kind of money?

His vision then returned to the same page. Just after the 1894 date someone had taken an eraser to a short entry but did a poor job trying to rid the paper of the writing. Curious, Doug remembered an old schooldays trick; place a paper atop the erased section, turn a pencil point sideways, rub the side of the point to cover and the once-hidden words should reappear on the new, clean piece of paper. Once finished, Doug took the paper to the window and used the incoming light to reveal the erasure. "If only the old rumor of De Soto's lost treasure on Alabimo's grounds would prove true and replace the lost bank money. Would love to be pulling carrots and stumble across a horde of valuable gold coins. Maybe, just maybe, the Good Lord willing, one day."

Doug incredulously read aloud to himself then paused and reflected on the back-to-back recordings of the family's history. One, probably a pipedream of wishful thinking by gaining fortune in finding Spanish gold on the property, the other an overcautious decline of investing only to miss the boat of the ground floor of the fabulously profitable Birmingham steel industry.

"Hon, need to be in the car and ready to leave in five minutes, Doug," Peg yelled from downstairs at the base of the stairs.

After responding, it struck Doug that he'd never made an entry into the journal of his family history. This little window of time was as good as any and he retrieved a fountain pen from his bedside table and began. In keeping with the news of the farm's economics, he thought back to the subpar production of three years prior. - It, the year 1954, was a poor harvest Alabimo's main crop, which is peanuts. The last rain of any consequence fell in early April. Farmers in Georgia, Mississippi and Alabama all felt the pain. Our net profit was just under $800. Luckily, due to a long run of good years and our own vegetable garden, pigs and chickens, we had the resources to survive the great drought. Contemplated investing in an irrigation sprinkler system as our soil is too sandy (and absorbent) for the furrow method of irrigation. As of this writing in 1957, it has not been necessary to resort to an artificial water supply as the Good Lord has supplied ample rain.

Doug White

Doug put his pen down and checked his watch. Glad he'd broken the ice and made his first-ever journal notes, he decided to keep future recordings more succinct. Hustling down the stairs, it dawned on him there was another segment of 1954 history he may or may not add to the journal, it was landmark and would have tremendous ramifications for his native South: Brown vs. Board of Education of Topeka.

March 27, 1957
Downtown Jackson, Alabama
Sidewalk outside Beckham's Grocery

"Well, hi there. Good morning, Darlene, so nice to see you. It's been awhile," Peg Travers said to the county's librarian, Darlene Thurman.

"Hello Peg, yes it certainly has been a while," the librarian replied. "Haven't seen you in a month of Sundays, but I did see your husband just yesterday when he came in."

"Doug? My Doug came into the library?"

"He certainly did. Spent the better part of three hours I guess and was full of questions, too."

"Oh, was he? What could my secretive husband be inquiring about?"

"Well, I guess there's no harm, but he was really interested in some books about local history and the Spanish conquistadors coming through Clark County four-hundred years ago and about Spanish gold coins; like what they'd be worth today."

"Hmm, my Doug the treasure hunter? Oh boy, am I going to have a little fun at dinner tonight."

5:35 p.m.
Same Day
Alabimo Kitchen

"Doug, dear, I ran into our county librarian, Darlene today. She was coming out of Beckham's Grocery as I was going in. Oh, side note they had pork ribs on sale, so I bought two racks if you want to cook out tomorrow. Weather forecast is supposed to be good."

Bones of the Black Warrior

"Hate to ruin your surprise, but she told you I was snooping around for books about Spanish coins, didn't she?"

"Yes, how did you know Darlene said exactly those words?"

"We went to school together from seventh through graduation. Darlene was known back then as quite the gossip. We even had a little corny saying, 'telephone, telegraph, tell a Thurman', because if you wanted to get the info, Darlene was *the* source."

"So, are you going to tell me what you were doing there?"

"Better than that. Come back here to the back porch." Doug led his wife through the huge well-stocked pantry, into the back hall, then out on the screened-in back section. "What do you think?"

There it was, leaning against an old chair Peg had wanted to trash, but Doug had only made it so far as the porch. The item was an old World War II Army surplus metal detector. Peg, from her military days, recognized the distinctive long handle, rectangular metal head, the backpack that supplied the power and the headphones for feeding the tell-tell signals to the operator.

"Please tell me you didn't buy a metal detector?"

"Okay, I won't. I'll just show you *our* new prized possession."

"Promise me you won't get obsessed with becoming a gold prospector or treasure hunter, I guess, is a better way of putting it. Please, promise."

"I will promise. Besides, I was reading in the library that the actual battle site between Chief Tuscaloosa and Hernando de Soto has never been found for certain. All I'm going to do is occasionally go around the place, play amateur archeologist and sweep it around a bit. Maybe I'll find a bunch of bones from a mass grave of the conquistadors that gave up the ghost in the battle, or hey, even better, find the chief's skeleton? All the books said he was freakishly big; seven feet tall."

"Cheaper hobby than golf or owning a boat, I suppose. Go for it,Doug," Peg replied sarcastically before leaving him alone with his new toy.

May 17, 1958
Montgomery
Columbus Street Baptist Church

Henrietta Grey and Darry Johnson sat quietly in the corner of the church's finished basement and were among the other fourteen listening to the speaker, a New Yorker, Al Feinstein. Darry had been hesitant to attend, but his crush won out. Besides, if there was danger, he should be alongside Henrietta this Saturday morning. This was a secret rendezvous of Freedom Riders and local blacks to which they'd offered their help. Feinstein was a young law student at NYU and along with two others like him, had come to assist and encourage voter registration for blacks of Montgomery.

The gathered group had plans to walk about, knock on doors and attempt to raise funds to place a large, full-page advertisement in *The Tuskegee and Montgomery Current Times* newspaper. Their ad would hopefully spread the word of a rally this upcoming Sunday night at the church. The Freedom Riders would also be in attendance and do some basic teaching on the actual legal aspects of voting and registering. Many whites opposing their voting spread falsehoods such as there being extravagant fees and long, written exams one had to pass, required to register.

When Feinstein stepped aside, Rev. Dickinson of the church took over. He explained a whole page ad in the black-owned newspaper would cost $225 per and would run only twice, in the Wednesday and Friday editions. The preacher encouraged everyone in attendance to purchase as many copies as they could afford and then drop them around town at places such as groceries, barber shops, other churches and common gathering places. Feinstein stood up and announced the Freedom Riders had pooled $35 to contribute to fund the purchase of newspapers and received a round of applause.

Crash! A brick came flying through the small window of the basement, showering Henrietta and Darry with small shards of glass. Feinstein broke for the door yelling he was going to get whoever had thrown the brick, but Reverend Dickinson instantly moved over and blocked the doorway. "Mr. Feinstein, you're new here. That's exactly what they want you to do. There are probably twenty-five Klan members out there with nightsticks and chains to beat anyone who dares come outside on the sidewalk. In here, we're safe, in here we'll stay."

Al Feinstein looked around the room then said, "That's just wrong, where's a phone? I'll call the cops and..."

Bones of the Black Warrior

A roar of laughter shook the basement as all in attendance knew the futility of a Negro church calling the local police for help from Klan wrongdoings. It wasn't funny, but it was, if only for the fact the New Yorkers thought their laws applied to 1958 Alabama! "He's got a lot to learn, huh Darry?" Henrietta said as she smiled at him, picked small pieces of glass off her skirt and placed them in a nearby waste can.

Early the following Saturday morning Darry jogged out to meet Henrietta's car at the end of his driveway. First, they were going to Jackson to catch the commercial bus to Montgomery, walk to the Columbus Street Baptist Church for newspapers and be driven around by the Freedom Riders to distribute free copies. It was a two-hour bus ride, hoping to arrive at nine.

Henrietta was using her grandmother's old 1939 Plymouth, only half-repainted a deep hue of purple while leaving large circles of brown rust on the hood and trunk. She trusted the old jalopy only for the twelve-mile trip from Stockton to Johnson Farm; she had been repeatedly warned the car likely wouldn't go further.

Darry was excited to be with her as she felt strongly about the movement. Even though they were both too young to vote, they felt by doing this errand today, they were contributing. Where before the horrible events and close call for his younger brother on March 12th, Darry would likely tell a fib to his parents if they inquired as to what he was doing by going to Montgomery, now he told the truth. After Jackson's attempted murder and subsequent foot-dragging by law enforcement, both Cleophus and Lutilly's neutrality about civil rights had vanished. No longer could they sit by and accept South Alabama's societal racial norms. Action, like Darry and Henrietta's, had to be taken. Doing what she could this morning to support the teens, Lutilly had made two fried egg sandwiches for their ride up to the state capital and Cleophus drove them up to Jackson to catch the bus.

Chapter 33
Torched

June 10, 1958
Driveway Alabimo Farm

Frank McClain, the widower spouse of Rebecca, Elbee's twin, was now 80 and lived by himself behind Alabimo's old cotton gin in a small one-time guest house. He stayed to himself most of the time, reading magazines such as a new publication called *The National Review.* Peg used to make a habit to try and include old Frank in the family activities, but almost always, he declined. She had to practically drag him to attend Roy Johnson's funeral two years ago. True, Frank had inoperable lung cancer and numbered days, however, Peg still tried.

The only things he had in common with the deceased Roy Johnson were old age and the ability to sometimes become downright angry. He was watching with concerned interest this thing the Negroes were calling "the civil rights movement" and didn't like anything he was hearing. This radical preacher, the mouthy Dr. King, and the near ruination of the innocent Montgomery bus system had bothered him immensely. Now, there were more Negroes becoming involved, getting much too uppity and organizing to vote with the help of Yankee rabble rousers.

Just one week prior, his favorite state politician, George Wallace had been defeated in the Democratic Party primary, the real race for governor, as Republican candidates in the General election usually polled in single digits. No time like the present was Frank's thinking, along with other staunch Wallace supporters. Four years from now the next Democratic Primary for the governor's seat would be held and while it seemed like a long time on the calendar, preparation took time, and money, to be ready for 1960. Frank McClain knew he didn't have a lot of time left and he was going to put every penny he could spare into seeing George Wallace win next time.

Wallace had lost by five percentage points. Respectable for a first timer, he'd been very close.

Bones of the Black Warrior

Now was the time to get going and erase those percentage points.

This June evening at dusk, 8:45, he stood at the end of the farm's driveway with a brown paper bag of money; all small bills, like $5 and $10. In a grove of pecan trees across the road, thousands of cricket chirps sent a deafening chorus through the thick, humid air. A sheriff's deputy patrol car should soon be arriving for the stash of $95 and take it to the South Alabama headquarters of the Concerned Citizens Council in Mobile.

The CCC was a quasi-white supremacy organization. They did not meet in extreme secrecy, wear hoods, nor have violent tendencies, but shared many Klan philosophies. Well-received by the white citizens in most communities, the CCC sponsored teenage bowling leagues, Little League baseball teams, Confederate general and battle victories essay contests statewide. The CCC strongly supported George Wallace and was shocked when John Patterson defeated their man. It was a sign that the outside agitators, like these Freedom Riders, were gaining voting power. Frank was hesitant to contribute more than $100 at a time, being well aware of Doug and Peg's ambivalent feelings about the CCC and their fiercely vehement opposition to the KKK. If they found out he was actively contributing; he'd get the long lecture from Peg, again.

Frank saw the patrol car approach and stepped back off the paved road. The tan and black cruiser slowed down and the driver's hand extended. The car barely made a full stop. In the dark and under the rim of an officer's campaign hat, Frank could only make out the bare traces of the middle-aged deputy's face. He grunted thanks, rolled up the window, took off to the east, spitting up a tail of gray dust and leaving Frank alone in the dark to wonder if Peg was watching. Even if her eyes did not, his near-constant cough usually gave his position away.

Neither Peg nor Doug was watching or listening for anything from the driveway. Frank had become such a recluse the past year or so, that they hardly thought of him lately. The only Travers Frank kept communications with was Joe, over in Mississippi. Frank had felt terrible about his nephew's injuries in World War II and had secretly even made the trip over to Gulfport occasionally, until he no longer felt comfortable driving and had given up his license. But he still wrote Joe. Maybe it was only three or four times a year, but that was more than his brother, Doug, did, according to Joe's return mail. It hit him, Peg had sent daughter Liz out to the guest house that very afternoon as a letter had arrived for Frank, but he'd been busy prepping for the cash delivery for the CCC and forgotten.

Arriving back at the guest house, Frank went straight for his desk, saw the letter and instantly recognized the handwriting. It was from the VA hospital and Joe. In actuality, it was Joe's only friend, Eddie, at the mental hospital who did the letter writing. They were pals and over time Eddie had learned to translate Joe's garbled speech pattern. Now, Frank was somewhat excited as his last letter to Joe had posed a great question and eager to see if the answer was inside today.

A little more than three months prior, on a very cold late afternoon, Frank had gone into the big house and raided Doug's bourbon supply for a tall tumbler glass full. As he aged, his joints and bones bothered him when it went below freezing, so he wanted to be prepared for later and not have to bother Doug or Peg for the nightcap. As Peg and Doug were prone to do, they sometimes would carry on an entire conversation and not even be in the same room. That afternoon Doug was in the main parlor reading and Peg was in the kitchen. Doug said he'd been wanting to get an albatross off his neck about brother Joe and the murder of Tilly Hoskins. He then said he truly believed his violence-prone younger sibling, when home on visitation in February of 1957, had killed the waitress. That was enough to draw Peg out of the kitchen, into the parlor and Frank's old ears couldn't hear the rest of their conversation.

Instead, in his last correspondence to the Gulfport VA, after the general niceties and generic how are things, he'd bluntly written, inquiring if Joe was aware of Frank's help regarding the whore waitress, Hoskins, from Mamie Martin's bar and his alibi? Now Joe's reply, dictated to Eddie, was here.

Eleven months later
Montgomery
Columbus Street Baptist Church

Darry and Henrietta, now engaged to be married, exited the church after attending another voter registration training session. Both were experienced enough now on the subject that they, not white Northern law students, co-led the instructional meetings. After high school graduation, both had taken local jobs and continued dating. It was their joint desire and dream to both get their college education at Alabama A &M, the Negro college there in Montgomery. However, for them, their minimum wage jobs in Clark County, saving tuition funds was extremely difficult. Using a few connections both families had, they were both able to move up the employment ladder by landing federal jobs in Montgomery and receiving substantial pay raises. Darry was with the USDA and Henrietta outside of town at Maxwell Air Force Base. Each found roommates in Montgomery and began saving money for tuition in earnest.

It was on this pleasant, sunny Saturday in May of 1959 that hand-in-hand they walked east towards South Court Street, their destination. Together the two would distribute political flyers all the way up until West Fairview Avenue and hoped to complete their task in two hours, leaving time for a late afternoon movie.

Half an hour into their rounds, they both stopped at a car parked on S. Court. It was almost identical to Henrietta's old 1939 Plymouth in color and rusty condition. It brought a smile to both their faces. Suddenly, the rumble of V-8 engines, from three cars, coming up behind them grabbed their attention. The second vehicle, a 1950 Mercury sedan, stopped by the two and both the front and rear passenger doors flew open. A white man was at the wheel and two more white men were in the back. "Get your ass in, troublemaker," one said firmly as he displayed a black pistol, as did the other man in the back seat. They both hesitated briefly then when the first man with the pistol cocked his hammer back, they complied. "Stop, woman, not you," he said. "Just him. Get in boy!" Quickly now, Darry was in the backseat where he was rudely pushed to the floorboard, had a pistol barrel shoved up under his left ear and was ordered not to move or make a sound.

Darry had been kidnapped by the Klan, driven south to Troy where he'd been secretly transferred into the trunk of a different car, then further south to Andalusia and another car. From there he'd gone in a cargo van into the Conecuh National Forest, along with five different Klansmen.

Two days later, after watching a huge flock of buzzards circle his fire tower post, a forest ranger descended and took off on foot to the north and the likely scene of whatever stoked the massive bird activity. Deep in the Blue Springs area of the national forest, down an old, abandoned logging road, not used since the park's formation in the 1930s, the two Klan vehicles had stopped. Tied and gagged, Darry was dragged 200 yards off the road and up a small hill with one lone gigantic pine. The Klansmen tied Darry securely to the tree, gagged and pummeled him with fists for a good five minutes before delivering their coup de gras. One member was a welder by trade. Funneling funds to the KKK from the Mobile chapter of the CCC surreptitious contributions, he'd purchased the cutting torch from a second-hand shop in Brewton, just for this type of purpose, hopefully should ever a situation like this, arrive. His new possession was a portable acetylene torch, capable of cutting through hard metal and he was anxious to see how well it worked on uppity troublemakers.

Darry succumbed to the piercing 4000-degree torch burns after about ten minutes of unimaginable torture, and his lifeless, nude body hung limp, tied tightly to the lone pine. After about a thirty-minute hike from the tower, the forest ranger found Darry's body. He counted over two dozen deep circular cuts and burns of pink and white exposed skin on the corpse, cut him down and used his jacket to shield the body from the scavenging birds. Next, he walked into a clearing and made the radio call back to headquarters, telling of the murder scene, requesting law enforcement and the coroner's presence.

Chapter 34
Playing Ball

April 4, 1960
FBI Field Office
Birmingham

Doug rarely ever used his former military rank designation but had done so in letters to the FBI headman, by signing off as Retired USMC Major Douglas Travers. (During the last days of war Doug had been promoted, somehow overcoming the "it's-who-you-know" philosophy that permeated the armed services However, once Joe's mental and physical disabilities had been confirmed, Doug realized his chosen career was over - he would be a farmer.) For some reason, he thought the FBI might be more willing to work with a former military officer than the head honcho of a peanut outfit from some unheard-of unincorporated village in south Alabama. As he'd predicted, neither the Clark County sheriff nor the state crime investigator's office in Montgomery had given him the time of day about progress on the Darry Johnson murder.

So today, he had an appointment with the bureau head in the heart of downtown Birmingham. His name was Sam Shuffert and still relatively new to the post. Doug's first letter had been to his predecessor who never responded, but he'd written Shuffert twice now before today's in-person meeting. Twenty minutes after his meeting in the ugly, squat, three-story building that screamed government low-bid construction, Doug was back in the parking lot to leave. All the FBI knew was, of course, it was KKK activity. They'd traced the blow torch back to the pawn shop in Brewton, but it looked like the perpetrator had purchased it under a false name. The tire track impressions had yielded positive identification, but the two vehicles involved were two of the most common on the road. Shuffert did say they had something more currently in review but wasn't at liberty to divulge details.

There was a second reason for today's visit to the city. There was a VA Hospital downtown and the former head administrator, Dr. Urie, previously at the Gulfport facility, was now in charge there. Feeling he owed the family name some soul cleansing, Doug had new, pertinent information regarding Joe to pass on to the doctor. Yesterday his brother-in-law, Frank, upon hearing that Doug was going to Birmingham to meet with Dr. Urie, divulged a secret he'd been hiding for almost two years about Tilly Hoskins. McClain's cancer was now wasting him away and his end would be soon. The Travers' had been good to him, and he wanted them to know the truth.

Per the old letter, Joe had not wanted to go off to war as a virgin and visited Tilly between enlisting and shipping out to Ft. McClellan. Well, Tilly saw an opportunity, and after having a Travers in her bed, seized it. Tilly began blackmailing Joe stating she was carrying his child and if the prominent Travers family didn't want that knowledge to leak out to the good people of Clark County, he had to pay up.

Joe may have been young, but he wasn't completely naive. He began to suspect Tilly was lying about being pregnant. Now serving in the Army and in need of a local, dependable spy, Joe had convinced Cleophus Johnson to keep him abreast of Tilly's so-called pregnancy. It turned out she was quite the inventive actress, shoving a series of ever-larger false, round pillows up her dress to give the outward impression of being with child. Facing fatherhood, shame and embarrassment, Joe had no recourse but to comply with Tilly's demand for hush money and secretly used Cleophus as his go-between runner with the cash.

Cleophus' first few letters to Joe had confirmed her growing belly, until one day while spying on her, the fake disguise slipped out, revealing itself to Cleophus. On to her ruse, he confronted her. Challenged with the discovery of her contrivance, Tilly's best weapons of sex and blackmail fizzled. Tilly's scam had begun in 1942 and lasted for six months. Joe's isolation in a world of silence went on for years. On and on, her dishonesty collected a toll on Joe and his pent-up anger consumed him, but it wasn't until 1957 that Joe had his chance.

During that visit by Joe to Alabimo, Cleophus had the idea to send a jar of pickled okra over to his neighbors, to be delivered by Jackson. On that very day, Joe wandered off and came home bloodied, Frank had intercepted Jackson, the okra and for $20 sent the teenager on a bicycle errand to Tilly's place.

So, now with the full knowledge of the story, Doug felt the need, in person, to confirm his previous statements to Dr. Urie about Joe's violent tendencies and connection to the death of Miss Hoskins. Joe Travers was guilty.

Keenly aware of the fact he'd never set foot outside of his VA, prison-esque unit, Joe had neither the reason to lie, nor the mental capabilities to. The letter from 1958, dictated to Eddie and sent to Frank McClain revealed as Joe had left, he'd actually passed Jackson Johnson, on the teen's way up to Tilly's that fateful day and walked back to Alabimo. Joe had exacted revenge and "paid her back" just like he'd said.

Fifteen-year-old virgin, Jackson Johnson, curious about sex, knowing nearby there was a local prostitute. Nice old Mr. McClain footed her fee, saying he was about dead and just thought all boys should get the experience before they turned sixteen. The only catch was Jackson had to wait his turn. Joe Travers was there now, so Jackson had to wait, watch, and then approach Tilly Hoskins' shack.

By the time Joe had staggered back to Route 5, Jackson rolled up, went inside, saw the dead woman, and briefly went catatonic before he high tailed it off the premises. The bent woman neighbor, alerted by an anonymous phone call, never saw Joe. Only Jackson's approach and exit, of which she was only too happy to report to the law.

Doug drove his car back from Birmingham to Alabimo, with one giant question, but no answer, bouncing about his head. To whom else besides Dr. Urie should he come clean?

When Jackson Johnson graduated high school, he personally told Mr. Travers he was getting out, not just of Alabama, but anywhere in the South. Due to his great height, Jackson could only enlist in the Army, which he did. Doug knew he was somewhere at a base out west in California and that so far, true to his word, he'd never come back to the area. Now, knowing the full truth of Jackson's innocence and close call with prison and the electric chair, he knew precisely why the young man vowed to never return.

Retired USMC Major Douglas Travers pulled up the driveway, paused, after determining he'd let sleeping dogs lie, at least for tonight, as far as Jackson, Frank, Joe and Tilly Hoskins were concerned. Instead, he considered his own future. Here he was, forty-seven years old. The farm operation would need a good man to replace him somewhere in the next decade and a half. Peg had given birth to their only child, Liz in 1947, making her fourteen now. Whomever she married was the only, obvious choice to take over the business. Well, girls in the area, since the war Doug understood, were no longer getting married at sixteen. In these modern days girls were going to college. More than likely, Liz would court, find a suitable man, get engaged and eventually marry sometime around 1968 or so. Clever enough to recall his own teenage days and how doing the exact opposite of your parents' wishes was customary behavior, Doug told himself he'd have to be alert, on guard, and quietly cunning in choosing the right son-in-law.

But that was in the future. He had something else more immediately pressing. Recently reading the old family journal struck a monetary nerve. First, he needed to diversify the family savings out of just one bank, the Clark County Savings and Loan. Second, he'd read of recent peanut processing machines that interested him. If he could convert Alabimo not to just grow, but to process and package the crop for wholesale distribution, there could be tremendous growth opportunities. Unlike the unnamed ancestor whose timidity eighty years ago had missed out on the beginnings of the steel industry in Birmingham, Doug would not make that mistake.

Sept. 16, 1963
Birmingham

Liz Travers, a high school senior, read the newspaper headline with her mouth agape. The day before, the Klan had set off a bomb in a black church, the 16th Street Baptist, in Birmingham. Four young girls were dead from the blast of nineteen sticks of dynamite; three were fourteen years of age and one was only eleven. Recently, Liz had been babysitting for a young married couple out on Route 5 that had a ten-year-old daughter, soon to be eleven. Liz adored the little girl and often thought she'd come and sit with the child for free. How could anyone murder children, much less one at the tender, innocent age of eleven? How cold and black-hearted were these monsters to commit such a horrendous, despicable act? The more she thought, the more sickened she became.

Struggling to answer Liz's questions of why, Peg tried to find the words, but felt inadequate. Taking Liz by the hand to the main parlor she seated her daughter on an antique loveseat. Peg retreated to the bookcase and took out the old family Bible, one purchased at great expense at the time. Turning the front cover page, she paused to re-read the faded handwriting: Eliza Delchamp Travers, October 1858. Much to her surprise, turning the page, again in the same handwriting, a list of major sins was written. Scanning the sentences she stopped on one:

20th Book - To Combat the Hate in the World - Proverbs 10:12.

Peg thumbed the brittle, thin pages carefully and found the passage, 'hatred stirreth up strife, but love covereth all sins' and read it aloud, twice.

"Liz, dear, does this make sense?"

Seeing a quick shake of her head, Peg tried, "Love is the healer, if the bad men who bombed the church had love in their hearts, they could not have committed such an act. If the men realized hate only brings on more hatred and that love has the power to heal and even prevent sins that cause misery on Earth and then condemns a person's soul to the eternal fire and damnation of Hell."

"Those men who did that will burn?" with hope.

Peg paused, familiar with how the law enforcement and justice systems in Alabama usually turned a blind eye to Klan atrocities, "Yes, dear they will burn in Hell eventually and maybe sooner in the state's electric chair, if…"

"Mama, I know I'm just a teenager and you're the grown-up, but all the love in the world isn't going to do those poor four little girls any good now," Liz interrupted and then showing no emotion stood, left the room and out the front door.

Peg couldn't argue with her dry logic, closed the Bible and took Liz's spot on the loveseat. The quiet stillness of the house was palpable. Alone with her unhappiness and evidently, the lack of healing from her response, Peg instead had thoughts for the suffering of those four mothers of the Birmingham girls. Tears welled up in her eyes as she hoped her daughter would not return to the room before she regained her composure.

March 10, 1965
Atlanta, Georgia
Heart of Atlanta Motel

Henrietta Grey thought her eyes were deceiving her, so she paused before speaking. After Darry's murder she, like so many of her age and race, wanted no part of Alabama. Upon graduating from Spelman College, in Atlanta, she'd taken the assistant manager position at the Heart of Atlanta Motel. (This place of lodging was one of the few in Atlanta to accept blacks as guests in these segregated times.) When understaffed, like this Wednesday afternoon, Henrietta would work the front desk. Once the group of eleven young men and four middle-aged ones completed the check-in process, she double-checked the guest register to confirm what her eyes questioned. The last name fit; not the first.

"Excuse me sir, Mr. Johnson? May I please have a moment?" Henrietta inquired of the tall, lanky member of the San Diego State basketball team. Quickly, she darted around the desk to block his path to the stairs leading up to the second floor where the team would be staying.

"Yeah, okay, sure," drawled his unmistakable Southern accent.

Taking him by the wrist, Henrietta tugged him out of the main path by the wall. "I have to ask. Aren't you Darry's brother, Jackson Johnson?"

Then, the team assistant coach turned, saw the two talking, grinned and gave a nod of approval, so the six-foot-eight forward sat down with Henrietta. "Uh-huh," was all he allowed.

"Your name is Jackson. Why did you sign in as George?"

Over the next five minutes, he explained. Back in 1958, when he enlisted in the Army, he requested everyone call him George, his middle name. He had first been based at Fort Hunter Liggett, in Jolon, California, but later was moved to the base in Los Alamitos. Always playing ball on the base's team and making new friends, he followed on to San Diego City College after his military time expired. He excelled in the league and was named two-time conference Player of the Year. After two years there, he accepted an athletic scholarship to San Diego State. Presently, the team was in Atlanta for the National Invitational Tournament and matched up against Georgia Tech.

Henrietta, after listening with interest, wanted to inquire about his middle name use, but decided to wait. Instead, she revealed she'd never lost contact with his parents, Cleophus and Lutilly, writing a couple of times a year and even dropping by when back home for Christmas or Thanksgiving. George said he'd been drilled by the Army to correspond monthly and still continued the habit, adding he hadn't been back to Clark County since 1958, but didn't elaborate.

'Ding-ding-ding,' went the bell ringer on the front desk. As she rose, Henrietta told him they must exchange addresses and phone numbers and to please keep in touch. George smiled and said he definitely would. As she walked away, he could understand why Darry had fallen for her.

Chapter 35
TheLawyer

Jackson, Alabama
Law offices of Allen, Dees and Jefcoat
11:50 a.m.

It was Liz Travers Demaret's first visit to downtown Jackson since it happened three weeks prior. She and husband Tony left the lawyer's office and headed for the drug store around the corner for lunch, as previously decided. Their mood was sullen, yet relieved. It was something that had to be done, just that to Liz, it was all…so fatal, so final. That previous downtown visit, twenty days ago, had been to Hill's Funeral Home to purchase not one, but two caskets.

Tony leaned forward to grasp the handle of the glass door on the town's only drug store to hold open for his wife. Five steps inside they grabbed the first open booth and slid in on slick, green plastic seats to be on opposite sides of the table. "Liz, I know you never thought of it, because you'd have mentioned it to me. I knew sometimes people were compensated for losses, like yours, but I never let myself think things out all the way."

"Me either, Tony. It's one of those awful thoughts you just never let enter your mind," Liz said softly so others nearby would not overhear.

The two were discussing a proposition from their attorney, Davis Jefcoat. In late June, Doug and Peg Travers had been killed in an auto accident, not three miles from home, out on two-lane Route 5. They were in their IH pickup truck, traveling north towards Jackson, when a southbound, fully loaded log truck suddenly veered over the centerline and smashed into them head-on. The investigating law enforcement officers deduced the truck's driver was extremely intoxicated and the collision was so tremendous, at least the Travers had been instantly killed.

Davis Jefcoat had proposed to sue the big paper company that owned the truck for a sum of $150,000. Of that amount, should they win, his firm's fee would be 12%.

"It would never be about the money," Liz whispered. "I'm just angry. Daddy worked so hard all those years and Mama told me he was planning on cutting back his hours so they could begin enjoying life to travel and take vacations. They never could before. The farm always kept them tied down. But once Daddy felt like you had enough experience, he could slack off a bit and treat Mama like he'd always wanted."

"It's not fair. Not at all. Isaac Paper should pay. I'm like you, Liz. It's not the money. Don't they do any kind of qualifying, like who's sober and who's not, before putting a man behind the wheel of a giant eighteen-ton log truck? I'm still shocked that damn truck driver came out of the wreck without a scratch. One of the patrolmen told me, in his opinion, that trucker had to be doing over 80 miles an hour. Drunk as a skunk."

"Guess I never told you, but he said the same thing to me over the phone," Liz paused and took a sip of the water the waitress had supplied, along with two menus, before moving away. "I want to make them pay, Tony. I feel as if I've been robbed."

"You just said the word I've been searching for since the accident. What you said is one hundred percent correct. You, me, Peg and Doug...all robbed."

January 18, 1971
Law Offices of Allen, Dees and Jefccat
2:55 p.m.

"Well, like I said, sorry Tony couldn't make it today, but I understand. My father and both grandfathers were farmers, and they never could seem to find any free time. It was always something popping up. Anyway, please give Tony my regards and here's the check. The firm's share, as we discussed, has already been deducted, so we're all settled up. I wish we could've landed that full amount on the settlement figure, you know, but we got pretty darn close."

"Thank you, Davis. You did a great job. I had no idea any of these types of things went on behind the scenes. I guess all I know about the law and lawyers came from watching *Perry Mason* on TV."

"Good old Perry. Yes, we all get a good laugh out of that show. The criminal always breaks down and confesses to the crime when he's on the witness stand, right when there's two minutes left in the program."

"I never knew cases were settled out of court, never. But like you said, Isaac Paper knew they were in the wrong and fighting it out in front of the world would just make them look bad."

"Public perception is strong medicine. They still need people to keep buying their paper towels and using their paper for their typewriters."

"Well, I for one, will never buy anything they make, but I'm just glad it's over. Mama and Daddy can rest in peace now. Tony and I can get back to our lives and running Alabimo."

"Alright, Liz, take care and we'll see you back here in ten days for the final signatures of closing your parents' estate. We'll make it all official for the farm, the house and everything else, too."

They shook hands as Davis walked Liz out to the sidewalk and said goodbye. Liz looked at where she was parked and decided, since it was a pleasant, although cloudy 62-degree day, she'd make the short three-block walk to Clark County Savings and Loan and deposit $112,000.

Arriving home roughly an hour before the winter sunset, Liz felt the urge to visit them and complete her little project. Exiting her 1969 Lincoln Continental, she smartly moved to the back porch, found her rubber boots, a well-used old hammer and a brown paper grocery bag with her recent handiwork within. If she was going down to the family burial plot, a few hundred yards away, near Randon Creek under the two towering cypress trees, it would be a muddy walk as this time of year the ground stayed mushy. Arriving, she gingerly passed the family headstones of Joe Ward, Carla and others, to the two fresh elongated mounds of deep orange dirt covering her parents. Their headstones were still being engraved, so in lieu of them, Liz had fashioned two simple, small wooden crosses that she had cut, painted, hammered and nailed herself. The soft ground easily accepted the two crosses. She stood and as a light mist began to fall, said a silent prayer.

December 31, 1976
Alabama
Kitchen table

Bones of the Black Warrior

4:45 p.m.

"I'd like to thank you, Davis, for driving down from Jackson and bringing the paperwork," Tony Demaret said wholeheartedly. "I really thought I'd be able to find a couple of free hours and make the drive to your office."

"Not a problem for me, Tony. Glad to," the attorney said as he pulled the stack of now signed papers and placed them in his briefcase. "Seems like I remember telling Liz a few years back that my daddy and both grandfathers were farmers so getting them off the farm to go and do anything, except Sunday morning church, was near impossible, I completely understand."

"Yes, Davis, that was so nice of you," Liz added. "Are you sure I can't interest you in something to sip on? How about a cup of coffee or maybe eggnog?"

Davis Jefcoat extended his hand and waved a negative, said it was time to go, stood, thanked her for the offer and shook hands with both of his hosts. They both walked him down the hall to the front door, where Liz stopped, but Tony continued outside to the edge of the front porch as their attorney got in his 1975 Mercury Grand Marquis and pulled away. The Demarets then retreated back to their kitchen table and continued their discussion of what had just transpired. Davis Jefcoat had drawn up papers first, for changing the company name, licensing and other legal processes in moving from merely a peanut farm to also a snack company. Second, for Davis to review and say Grace over a big new contract with a professional sports league.

It had been with Liz's blessing. She saw how the national media was making such a huge fuss over the country's most famous peanut farmer, President-elect Jimmy Carter, who hailed roughly 275 miles to the east, in Plains, Georgia. Never shy, she was like her father, and believed in striking while the iron was hot. (After his lessons learned from the family journal, Doug Travers had, indeed, both invested in the peanut processing machines for wholesale distribution *and* giant irrigation sprinklers.) The company was poised to explode. It had come to Tony and Liz leaving the movie theater in Mobile one evening two weeks ago, when they'd seen the boxing movie, *Rocky*. Jimmy Carter's connection to peanuts and their chosen

189

business would never be at a more fever pitch. The Alabimo Peanut Company was in prime position to transform from a small, local player to a larger regional one. But how?

Tony had a couple of ideas. Liz was the company president, after all. She was the direct connection, so she'd make the final call. Tony wanted to change the company name. The title, in his line of thinking, Alabimo could be misconstrued and twisted around to Alabama and Alabama, to many, only meant George Wallace, the KKK, Selma and the 16th Street bombing; generic bad connotations and not the things a snack company wanted to be associated with. But there was pride and worth in the brand name. Alabimo Peanuts was the sixth oldest producer in the state and fifteenth oldest in the entire United States. Tony suggested taking the A from Alabimo and the A from Alabama to keep it simple, renaming the company Double A Peanuts.

There was more. Double A was a designation of minor league baseball and baseball fans love peanuts. The Southern League, he'd learned, only allowed one brand of each concession item to be sold in their ballparks. One had to win the bid on that exclusive right. At first, he was hesitant, thinking it would probably cost many hundreds of thousands of dollars, but was pleasantly surprised he could put in the bid, and obtained sole rights for $35,000. With his wife's blessing, the family business was rebranded Double A Peanuts. They'd be supplying nuts to the stadium concession stands in Asheville, Birmingham, Orlando, Montgomery, Savannah, Knoxville, Jacksonville and Columbus, Georgia. His conservative projections, with each team playing 130 games, he'd get back the $35,000 from their bid expense somewhere around game number twenty-five.

For the upcoming fall, after the minor league baseball season ended, Tony had the idea to pay for rights and contract with all the sports concessionaires serving the forty-five or so high school football stadiums between, and including, Montgomery and Mobile. All in all, the new ventures went so well, that Double A Peanuts started buying more nuts from other local growers to keep up with demand.

After a decade passed, trusting that the farm and new ventures were secure, Tony and Liz both agreed to expand the house and install a swimming pool and tennis court in 1987. Initially, thinking the idea of lounging around the pool and swatting a tennis ball around would only be done sparingly. However, after hiring competent operation managers, they found themselves with not just more leisure time, but time to spend with their kids. Liz had given birth to twins, a girl and a boy, in 1976.

Little did Liz or Tony know that shelling out money for a tennis court, in the long run, would turn out to save them the expense of two college tuitions in 1993. Their kids were both excellent players. So good in fact, Anthony, who at fifteen-years old began regularly thumping top college players, went pro right out of high school and Beth accepted a tennis scholarship to a mid-sized state university that athletically competed in Division II.

Chapter 36
Bad Hombres

July 27, 2008
Grenada, Spain

Beth Travers Demaret wiped the sweat from her brow with her shirt sleeve. Her suitcase was way over-packed. This had to be the hottest day of her European recruiting trip. It was over. She exited the taxi on the Avenue de Andaluces, in downtown Grenada, to board the bullet train on her three-hour ride to Madrid and a flight back home. After the obligatory Atlanta layover, she'd catch a puddle jumper to Mobile and almost be home. Well, her old home anyway. Beth currently leased a small mid-century craftsman just off campus at Alabama Polytechnic Institute, also known as A.P.I. where she served as the highly successful women's tennis coach.

Her upcoming flight would wrap up driving seven days, alone, around Spain to recruit high school tennis players. At least the Spaniards drove on the correct side of the highway. Was her trip worth it? Not only worth it to her but the athletic director, school president and numerous alumni. As A.P.I. only fielded the less expensive, minor sports programs and didn't even have a basketball team, the tennis program was presently basking in its recent success. Under Beth's tutelage, the college's tennis team had made headlines winning their third consecutive Division II national title just this past June. She needed to replace three seniors and of the ten slots on her team, half were girls from the Iberian Peninsula. Si, si, most definitely worth it.

Roughly halfway across the Atlantic Ocean, the lady in the seat across the aisle from Beth finally had enough of wondering and asked, "Pardon me, but I've been peeking a glance the past few hours, as I know I have seen you," the professionally dressed, attractive, dark blonde, green-eyed woman, somewhere about thirty-five years of age inquired.

"Hmm, let me see," Beth said nicely. Her flight had been boring and absent-mindedly left her current copy of *Tennis Monthly* in an airport restaurant. The movie was a rerun of one she'd seen, remembered as beyond terrible and she welcomed a little conversation. She immediately picked up the lady's accent. Although she spoke English well, it was not her first language. There wasn't anything wrong, per se, she just had an accent. "I hope this comes across in the right way, but I did do a few TV interviews about a month ago. One was even on the national news, well national sports news, I guess, for a total of fifteen seconds..."

"Oh, tell me more, please."

Beth explained in as few words as she could get her message condensed that she coached women's tennis, back in Alabama, her team had won the championship, a few outlets had covered the game, the biggest had interviewed her and she'd briefly been on national TV for a day back in June.

"No, it's not from TV, but now that you mention Alabama and tennis...how do you say? Bah-da-bing, the light bolt goes off over my head."

Beth stifled her laugh, nodded and listened as the lady, who introduced herself as Vicki Cuevas, explained her younger sister had played Division II college tennis. Furthermore, she'd attended a marathon singles match in a 1996 tournament held in Memphis, where her sister lost to a fiery brunette from Alabama Polytech. The final score escaped her, but she remembers reading in the newspaper later that it set a record for the length of the match.

"Four hours and nine minutes, for a three-setter; six-seven, seven-six, ten to eight. Whew, makes me tired even today just thinking about it," Beth said as she returned the water bottle salute from Ms. Cuevas. "How can I forget that score? That was your sister?"

Vicki Cuevas recalled the tennis match and then surprised Beth, "As much as I remember the back-and-forth of your match, I also recall thinking this one thing, over and over. I'm a geneticist by trade, so people and their physical characteristics have always intrigued me. There I was, at a tennis match between my sister, a native of Espana playing an American. But to me, I hope I am not offending here, my blonde-haired sister with her green eyes and medium skin tone looked more the part of a typical American, while the American, you, with your beautiful dark hair, olive skin tone and brown eyes appeared, well to most, appeared to the be...well, like most would think the Spaniard would look. No?"

Beth nodded, but stayed silent, not that she was offended, not in the least, but it had been years since contemplated her twin brother's physical appearance to hers. Anthony was like Vicki Cuevas' sister; blonde, somewhat fair-skinned and green eyes, while she had described Beth to a T. Growing up Beth had always wondered why brother and sister, especially twins, could have such opposite features. Realizing her silence might be misconstrued, Beth again gave the water bottle salute and checked her watch. They still had five hours left of airtime, she introduced herself and the two women got lost in conversation and soon exchanged each other's cell phone information.

Beth soon discovered her new friend was actually Dr. Cuevas, having earned her doctoral degree from Tulane. She dared not immediately jump into her physical differences with her brother but decided to give their getting to know each other a little time. Maybe a bit later? But then the conversation took a turn to a more present-day sharing of facts.

A few hours later, mentally Beth made note to start getting out and seeing more of the world.

Listening to herself she realized it in her own words; raised in rural Alabama, college in a small Alabama town, working career in one place, again in a small central Alabama town. Contrasted with Dr. Cuevas and her upbringing in the Galicia region in northwest Spain. A native of Vigo, her father owned a fish cannery and her mother worked as the city's head of tourism, North America division. Personally, two years at the University of Barcelona to hone her English skills before coming stateside in the school's exchange program. Vicki had the luxury, she explained, and encouragement from her father to take her time, learn, grow and explore the vast United States.

She had done so by dividing her years in half and transferring to different colleges in different regions. Vicki had started in the Northeast beginning at Smith College, in Massachusetts, then on to DePaul and the city life in Chicago, and further west to Colorado State before all the way to UC-Davis. Her California experiment didn't last long, less than one month later, she withdrew, moved to New Orleans and took a job in the tourism industry as she waited to enroll at Tulane. Once there, she found her true passion, genetics. Again, with her father's blessing, there she stayed and got her doctorate. In fact, she was currently on the teaching staff there, she revealed, much to Beth's delight. New Orleans was an easy four-hour drive away from her current residence.

Beth felt her spirit renewed after leaving the plane and conversing with Dr. Vicki Cuevas. Their talk had eventually gone to the casual phase and Beth felt comfortable enough to tell her about her physical differences from her twin brother. The doctor had been strangely unimpressed, Beth remembered later. Oh well.

After an unexpected detour by the college and once arriving back at her rental home, she went to work online and made a decision. Encouraged by the enthusiasm for knowledge her new friend evidently possessed, and her obviously generous father, Beth decided to follow her heart. Besides tennis, growing up, her passion was digging for relics in the soil of Alabimo. It had thrilled her heart to spend time with her father, just the two of them, as Tony used his late father-in-law's metal detector, scanning the earth for keepsakes. Back at the old house in Clark County, she recalled, shoved in some closet, there was a big box of her personal findings like arrowheads, oddly shaped unidentified metal items and even a few coins well over a hundred years old. Inspired, she researched universities in Alabama to earn a master's degree in archaeology and needing to keep her present job, of course, she decided it was imperative to remain close to her present employer. Auburn, Alabama and UAB were too far away to drive, but there was one school, a good one too, near enough. Beth began preparation to apply and attend Tuskegee University's night class program. Neither woman realized it on the plane, but their new connection had been an accident of fate.

Next day, July 28
Mobile International Airport
Short-term parking lot

Beth paid the attendant and waited for the bright yellow arm to rise and let her drive off. It was good to be back in the USA. As she'd experienced a few times flying in the past, the strong summer thunderstorms of the Deep South can be prone to postponing one's flight. That had happened to her ten hours ago when the airline desk clerk in Atlanta informed her all flights into Mobile were canceled. No matter, her schedule didn't push her this

195

time of year and there was a hidden plus. If she'd landed last night as scheduled at 10:15 p.m.it would have been too late for her to get her bag, find her car and drive up to Alabimo announced or unannounced at that hour. She all too well remembered the early-to-rise, early-to-bed routine on a farm. At least this way, as it was presently 8:30 a.m. she could call home and alert Liz and Tony their favorite daughter was coming by to visit.

Once she got through the worst of the traffic, Beth made the call. First, to the landline she'd been telling them to ditch, but hadn't, no answer. Then she tried both her father's cell and her mother's. She left a message on Liz' saying she was going to drop by for a bit around 9:00.

She drove north towards Clark County, enjoying the ride in her still-new-nearly 2006 Tahoe. With her bonus for winning the national championship two years earlier, she'd made the plunge for the big SUV. Many times the need for a seven passenger auto was necessary in her role as coach due to none of the Spanish girls on the team having a car. Beth felt responsible for taking them around en masse when necessary; the girls loved the American malls and especially Walmart. Another reason to celebrate being home was the wide road and big powerful, roomy car. In Spain, she'd rented a tiny Fiat 500, and although she had no experience of being *in* a phone booth, thought the little car's interior likely possessed somewhat the same cramped amount of room.

Beth debated having a little fun, but when brother Anthony answered his cell and sounded half-asleep, she couldn't bring herself to joke, almost. "Yes, I'm trying to reach the fifty-second ranked US male professional tennis player that should've made the quarterfinals in Ft. Worth three weekends ago."

"Elizabeth, very funny, Beth. You do realize our country has more than just your Central Time Zone, don't you?"

"Oh, no, Anthony. I'm sorry. Where are you?"

"I'm in L.A. and no, not home in lower Alabama. I'm in the Western Time…"

"Go back to sleep. I apologize brother."

"No, no, I'm awake now. I'd be getting up in twenty-five minutes anyway. My agent got me scheduled for a meet-and-greet with some racket manufacturer's son or some bullshit. The complex is only ten miles away, but they told me to allot a good hour for traffic. Anyway, have you talked to Mom or Dad lately? I did and heard you were galivanting around Spain last week."

For the next few minutes, they talked mostly about their tennis-centered lives before coming back to the subject of their parents. Anthony coughed, took a sip of water and paused before asking, "Did you hear about all their trouble, the bank thing and the law?"

Beth gave a negative response and reminded Anthony she'd been out of the country. The news almost made her pull off the road and vomit. Liz had admitted Tony was too angry to be on the phone and felt like he'd been shot in the stomach with a double-barrel shotgun. First, despite their so-called friend, Gary Conelly, the bank president in Jackson, Alabama, telling them two weeks ago their money was safe, it wasn't. The bank, their only bank, the Clark County Saving Bank had failed last week. The FDIC would bail them out to some extent, but it appeared they were going to lose a couple of hundred thousand cash.

Anthony again coughed and took another sip, "hell if that wasn't bad enough, get this." Their mother told her son two days ago what had happened. The background went back a couple of years ago. The monopoly on peanut sales to the minor league ballparks vanished and there was no way to get it back. Nepotism had raised its ugly head as the league commissioner's son-in-law somehow mysteriously got into the wholesale peanut business and like that, Double A Peanuts was out. But it got worse, as belts got tightened, Tony had let go of some of the old help which he'd given annual raises in the good times, but now couldn't afford them. Against his better judgment, he'd hired some Mexican Nationals. The good news was they were hard workers and cheap. The bad news was most had forged documentation and thus were one, illegal and two, he'd discovered also last week, criminals.

Beth assumed they were stealing and said so, but Anthony said he wished it had been that simple. No, they had slyly started a large-scale marijuana growing project in the fertile soil of Alabimo. There were dozens of acres far from any road access, back towards the river, hundreds of yards off Burnt Hawk Trail. In that isolation, the Mexicans had felled select trees, cleared some plots and managed to keep them hidden by leaving a stand of thick tree cover and the always present jungle of tangled briars, vines and creepers in impassible undergrowth. They were decent farmers evidently,

197

as they plowed, fertilized, weeded and even irrigated the little plants until they were mature enough for harvest.

Tony had said he believed they'd been operating their sideline crop for two years before a bit of blind luck intervened. A pair of Alabama State game wardens had been alerted to an albino deer from game trail cameras just north of their property boundary. One fine April afternoon, the two agents were tracking it to the northern edge of Alabimo and lo-and-behold, after plowing through the wall of bushes, they spotted a huge field of two-foot-tall marijuana plants on Travers-Demaret property. The law didn't move on the illegal plants or workers immediately and set up surveillance. Finally, here in late July they came to the decision that their criminal quarry had been spooked away, it was time to move in and destroy the now mature plants before someone harvested it and put the product on the street.

The crew of DEA agents that came to the farm to destroy the weed also broke the shocking news of the operation to Tony and Liz. Bombarded with questions, the agents had been through many similar scenarios evidently, they adroitly dodged any good solid answers and only suggested the Demarets obtain an experienced attorney. While *they* believed the Demarets' innocence in the matter, it was, after all, their land that the illegal marijuana was being grown for distribution. One agent did throw in a semi-helpful hint, "Juries can sometimes do crazy things, so take this seriously."

A loud car horn blast jolted Beth back into reality as she saw her speed had dropped down to forty as the awful news had sapped her energy and attention. What a terrible turn of events had occurred to her parents. She threw a few more questions at her brother about the police and the ramifications of the illegal crop on their property, but he didn't know any more than he'd told her and said he had to run and shower.

Beth regrouped and recovered speed back to the sixty-five mile per hour limit. After a few deep breaths she dug her phone out of her purse to call her parents again, but before she could, she took an incoming call. Answering, she heard gasping, frantic pleas of Isabella Diaz, a talented senior-to-be on her squad. This time of year, the campus was fairly deserted, and she'd been out alone, practicing her serve. A nicely dressed middle-aged man had approached, said he was from a tennis magazine and wanted to take a few photos. Isabella explained she was flattered, at first, then noticed how cheap and amateur the man's camera equipment was and how he began putting his hands on her to pose. Finally, when he grabbed her breast, she hit him hard in the shin with her racquet and took off running for the dorm. That's where she was now, in the lobby, but alone and did not know if the bad man had or would follow her. Isabella then started crying and said she was very scared.

Angry, Beth told her to immediately find somewhere to hide, but find a way to see if a security guard was around. She explained that she was on the road but would push it and be on campus in less than an hour, to stay on the phone and give updates of whatever happened even if it was nothing. Isabella was firmly told to remain in hiding and stay on the phone with her coach.

Sidetracked with Isabella's issue and then dealing with the campus police, Beth forgot about calling Alabimo. The following day her morning was busy with catching up on bills, filing her expense report, dirty clothes, a meeting with the athletic director and the like. Around 4:00 she tried calling again, but neither answered so she left a message. It crossed her memory how, unlike her generation, Liz and Tony's cell phones were not carried about at all times.

After lunch the next day and not having received any word from her parents, Beth began to worry. A quick call to Los Angeles also went to voicemail, but knowing Anthony's tournament schedule, she'd have been surprised if he had answered. Telling herself if her folks didn't return her call this evening; she'd get up early and make the one-hour drive south to the farm.

Next day, July 30
Alabimo
1:45 p.m.

Agent Tee Bullard, the forensic investigator, told Beth she believed her parents were murdered two days ago, likely sometime between sunrise and noon. Beth pulled the tissue away from her runny nose and looked at the staid female agent from the state crime board in Montgomery but said nothing in response. Beth was thinking, two days ago mid-morning, that was just about the time of Isabella's frantic call, diverting her side trip to Alabimo. If not for that call, Beth would have driven up and, there was a good chance, she'd be stuffed into the closet of her parents' bedroom, killed in an execution style manner with their hands zip tied behind them, gagged and two bullets apiece to the back of the head. The agent had stated the obvious earlier, this was first-degree murder and not some random act.

"Hey, Agent Bullard, I found this casing. It must have hit the floor and bounced up and into this shoe, hidden," the other investigator revealed. "We know four shots were fired and our perp picked up his casings, except this one."

"Bag it, Mark and let me have a look," Agent Bullard asked and was brought the brass outer casing of the spent bullet. Beth took a step back and let the male investigator pass. The agent held the plastic container at eye level and studied it for a moment. "So, it's a typical nine-millimeter, but look here, see that "A" on the base of the brass? Mexican manufacturer."

Beth squinted hard and pushed the moist tears out, "Mexicans? Mama and Daddy had a whole crew of them working here. My brother told me that the law discovered a number of marijuana plants growing on our land and it was a lot. Anyway, what you found makes sense. They, or someone, executed my folks because they could identify them, didn't they?"

The second agent, named Marks, spoke, "Mam, that's a highly probable scenario. These bigger drug ops are run by organizations, Mexican cartels, and they don't play. They'll kill anyone, anywhere, anytime for the slightest of provocations. If you all had a crew here and they were in any way cartel connected and they suspected your poor parents could…well, it does add up. Oh, and my sincere condolences, also."

"Marks and I've been teamed up for three years now and unfortunately, we've investigated way too many of these scenarios, but they don't get any easier, Miss Demaret. It's tough, I know it is and it's gonna get tougher on you and I'm sorry for that."

Beth glanced down the closet again and saw the two dark red stains on the light brown carpet. Thankfully, the crime investigators had arranged for the bodies to be removed before Beth had come upstairs the second time. She was right, it was tough, very tough. Normally, she would've given a verbal excuse or quick explanation, but this day, she just walked out of the bedroom, down the hall fifteen steps and into her old childhood bedroom. Backward, she fell across the bed and stared at the ceiling in silence before starting a silent prayer as her tears flowed.

Chapter 37
Dry Bones

Friday, June 17, 2015
Behind Alabimo
Travers family graveyard

"This is where they all are, right here in this little square, well, all except my Mama and Daddy. The county said we couldn't bury any further towards the creek, so Anthony and I decided we'd go around to the other side of these cypress trees and start a new plot," Beth said quietly to her good friend, Vicki Cuevas.

"This is a very pleasant place, Beth. So very peaceful."

"Who knows, I'll probably end up here, too."

"We just hope and pray that it will not be until a long, long time, my friend. These two great trees must be very old."

"We, or really Anthony, saw this fellow that was out this way working for some timber company, this was a few years back when he was still playing, well he asked him to come by the property. So, the fella did, and my brother asked him, in his opinion, how old did he think these two trees were?"

"Oh, that was a good idea, to ask an expert in the field," volunteered Vicki, as she gingerly walked around the section of older tombstones, placed her hand on the nearest cypress and gazed straight up the trunk, marveling at its great height.

"He told us, without the benefit of being able to count the rings, it was his estimate that these two trees were the same age and had sprouted from, oh these are Bald Cypress, by the way. He said they likely came out of the same cone, worked their way out of the dirt about one-hundred years before Columbus' discovery of the New World."

"Really, so around the year 1400 and today is 2015. That would make these two about five, no six hundred and fifteen years old! My such a long time ago, very old," gushed Vicki.

"I said the same thing. Six-hundred-year-old trees on *our* property. Can you imagine? If these trees had eyes and ears, what wonderful things they could tell us, absolutely astounding I bet."

"Thank you, Beth, for bringing me back here and showing me this. I get a sense I'm back in the old country when I'm here. The wonderful peace and quiet. Oh, not easily found in the noise of New Orleans. It's so beautiful here."

"Why thank you for saying that, Vicki. How nice. Yes, it's pretty here. I didn't much appreciate the beauty growing up, but then again, I did appreciate we had something unique and special. Mama told me the first Travers settled here in the1820s, so we are almost at the 200 year mark."

"For America, I believe, that is a long time. You should be proud. In my country, things are much older, so a 200 year mark, not so much," Vicki added in a light-hearted tone. "If I recall my Abuela, sorry that's my grandmother, she always taught us little ones lessons about the old days. Our family line extended back to the Romans conquering Galicia. She always said we had lived there for 1500 years. Abuela told us the name Cuevas, which translates to English as caves, that our ancestors lived in mountain caves and would come down to fight the Roman invaders. But who knows? Old women are very much likely to exaggerate, no?"

"That's very informative. I had no idea about your last name. Hey, cave woman, I bet you're starving. Tell you what I have in mind. There's some hamburger meat in the refrigerator. And it's not just the regular grocery store variety. Just over the line in the next county, there's a small little butcher shop. His specialty and the reason folks drive out of the way for him is that they process local beef, and they don't believe in freezing. Twice a week, on Tuesdays and Fridays, he and his two brothers slaughter a cow first thing in the morning. So, if you go in there on those afternoons, you can buy super fresh burgers, ribs and steaks. So, my guest of honor, tah-dah, tonight we're having the freshest burgers you'll ever bite into."

"You Americans and your beef burgers! I will admit, I'm here now going on sixteen years, I have been converted. However, I have a funky, wait…finicky taste so I am looking forward to these. We will get so much protein, I think."

Bones of the Black Warrior

"We're going to need that protein and a good night's sleep, friend. Tomorrow morning, bright and early, we get out the metal detector, old jeans, work boots and our shovels to go to work."

"It will be a fun adventure. I am anxious to get started tomorrow, of course, after the delicious hamburgers tonight."

They strolled back towards the house as the sun went below the western treeline. Beth was itching to reveal her secret but did not. The past weekend, she'd come down to Alabimo, alone, and bored started digging into a dirt mound about one-hundred yards behind the old, small guest house. Luck had smiled on her. Using her archaeological training method, she had a small pit with numbered, string grids for reference. In the foot-wide trench, just barely visible, and still

75% dirt-covered, there was a human skull. Vicki had been curious, but so far, Beth had pulled it off, not revealing why she'd insisted her geneticist friend bring her portable DNA-test equipment with her from New Orleans.

July 18 – Alabimo
Main parlor
8:15 a.m.

"So here it comes, here's a repeat of the weather I saw an hour ago, Vicki." The two stood in front of the ancient cathode ray TV in the den area. "Look at that line of showers. All that yellow and the red coloring is *not* good. That's the heavy stuff."

Vicki watched a minute more then moved to the front window and watched as the raindrops beat against the glass. It wasn't so much falling as it was being driven sideways by strong winds. "If it would slack up somewhat, I'd be willing to visit your find. A little rain has never bothered me. Growing up we surfed all the time in the rain. However, this, my friend, I cannot call this a little rain," she bemoaned, never turning around.

"No, this is a full-blown summer thunderstorm. I'm not going out…" BOOM! A great clap of thunder, apparently atop of them, shook the whole old, wooden house, rumbled on for a few more seconds as the lights flickered and the TV turned itself off. "Well, that sure settles things. Time to find the flashlights, get another cup of coffee, curl up with a book and wait this out," instructed Beth.

203

Doug White

This Saturday storm wasn't just a steady downpour, but complete with thunder, lightning and a howling wind that tore around the house all day and into the early evening after dark. That night the two ate sandwiches off paper plates. Due to the storm the electrical power situation had been spotty all day, it went out just as they finished eating. Vicki left to retrieve a large candle in the den. Upon returning to the kitchen as Beth was handling the light cleaning-up duty, she asked about the current status of the farm and about her brother, Anthony.

Beginning with her brother she gave Vicki the synopsis version of her twin's adult life. Somewhere around 2004, he'd given up his professional dream and instead began the path to where he was now, in the financial sector. His falling out of the top 100 rankings and the never ending, grueling travel had thoroughly worn him out. Southern California is a tennis hotbed, Anthony landed a spot as a teaching pro at one of the posh country clubs and got his bachelor's degree in business at the same time. After that, he became a stockbroker in the Los Angeles area.

Five years ago, he'd met a successful, divorced songwriter and while handling her investments, fell in love and married. Her career contractual commitments made it impossible to move and there he was, happy with his chosen life he said, but always struggling to, "Cope with all the darn people and damn traffic", to quote him verbatim.

As far as the farm, Beth explained after her parents' death, there had been a few low-ball offers to buy the property, but she and Anthony had declined them. Eventually, another neighboring peanut farmer leased the facility and used it up until two years ago, when he died and had no heirs to succeed his business. Afterward despite her attempts to find a new tenant, none materialized. So, the entire farm operation was sitting idle.

The next morning's rain had slackened, but the ground was a muddy mess, despite the elements, umbrellas in hand, they made their way back to the mound to inspect Beth's discovery.

At a distance of ten yards, they were disappointed to see the problem caused by the heavy rain. Beth had left a makeshift plastic tent over the pit. It was gone and nowhere in sight. Her string grid was missing and upon arriving for a closer inspection both easily saw the sides of the dig had collapsed into the hole and refilled the vacancy.

Bones of the Black Warrior

"Well, sadly I know from experience you can't shovel mud. We'll have to let the sun do its job. I just hope the artifact is still under there and didn't get washed away," Beth said as she looked down, noticing the swift rivulet coming off the mound and heading toward Randon Creek. The sun made a brief, one hour appearance later that morning, but it was disheartening when both ladies heard thunder rumbling to the west just before noon. They both expressed hope this storm would miss them, but soon it was again pouring at Alabimo.

Surprisingly to both ladies, the Sunday storm for two hours at least, almost equaled in ferocity the day before. Even with the sun shining, it was still a quagmire and there was no reason for Vicki to stay too long after Sunday breakfast. While Vicki packed, curiosity drove Beth to walk out back. To her ears, yesterday's tremendous jolt of thunder seemed to have originated at the family graveyard. Dodging a myriad of puddles, she approached the area. Coming into the clearing, from twenty-five yards away she saw the damage. A lightning bolt had struck the nearest of the two cypress trees; revealing a huge, long streak of whitish-brown inner bark, contrasted with the other water-soaked, almost black bark. Deciding she was ruining her shoes, Beth turned around. On her way back she veered over to the mound of her digging and checked on things.

The tremendous rainfall runoff had caused the rivulet to grow substantially, and it had tripled in size. Her dig site had completely vanished, the mound's exposed soil had eroded by a third and had been carried down towards the creek. Where was the skull? Last weekend, she knew enough just from seeing the very top, or calvaria, that it was not a recent death. The signs of age were obvious in the discoloration of the bone color. She took one more brief look at the mound, but saw nothing of interest.

Out of the corner of her eye a sharp glint of light caught her attention. Once more curiosity took over as she studied the area where the bright flash originated. Then, there it was again! She started exploring in the direction of Randon Creek to investigate the alternate on-and-off flashing. When the wind blew the overhanging tree limbs enough, the sun would illuminate the object. She walked halfway to the creek and realized she was on the same path as the rivulet flowing from the mound. Then, almost at the creek's edge there it was and more. The fully complete old human skull had worked itself free and was lying in a sandy, tea-colored puddle. Next to it was some sort of old deteriorated bag-looking object, blackened by time and partially eaten away in a few places by something unknown. Just as a gust of wind moved the cedar tree limbs, sunlight hit the skull and the weather-beaten pouch and the glint of flashing revealed itself in all its glory. Standing atop the puddle, umbrella in hand and inspecting the scene, Beth found herself talking aloud, "God Almighty, that's a gold coin!"

There amongst the deteriorating pouch was indeed a gold coin. No mistaking that beauty. Further inspection revealed it to be the only one. On her walk tracing the rivulet's path, she had noticed, strangely in her silent opinion, a trail of nearly two dozen, round, smooth, river rocks that were all approximately one inch in width, strewn about by the rushing water.

Four days later, back at Alabama Polytech, Beth took a phone call from Vicki. "Beth, my friend, I've got the results from the tooth I took back with me. Also, I took the liberty, as long as I was in the lab, to have it radiocarbon dated."

"I'm so glad you did, because I did the same thing. We'll have two independent test results to compare for the age of the skull," Beth gushed with excitement. "Tell me, please go on. What did the DNA test reveal and what time frame did your people come up with?"

Vicki knew, talking to a trained archeologist, like Beth, she could use some basic industry jargon and not have to explain most of the terminology. Quickly, she revealed the tooth belonged to a Native American, to wit, Beth interjected her visual observations along with calibrations of the eye socket, race typical shovel-shaped incisors and the zygomatic, or cheekbones, she also felt sure of that. She then added it was likely a female between twenty-five and forty years of age. Then, Vicki said her people at Tulane estimated the time of historical death was the mid-sixteenth century.

"That's great, Vicki. My own findings have come up with a similar time frame. Oh, I also talked to the head of our history department. He told me, from historical tribal maps, she was likely a Choctaw Indian that died somewhere around the year 1550."

"So, my friend, we've both received similar findings," Vicki said, now with equal excitement. "But now, tell me this, we take off our scholarly robes and discuss the part with the fun. Can you please tell me what you've learned about the gold coin?"

"Remember seeing it and that the coin didn't have an exact date? So, according to a numismatist I called in Birmingham, he called it an Escudo by the way, that kind of actually helps with its age."

"Escudo, now that's a word my ears haven't heard in quite some time."

"I'd shot him a pic off my phone and later on, he texted me back. He said the script was in Latin, the large lettering translates to 'Ferdinand and Isabella', yes one in the same, oh it's hammered-out by hand as a standard run-of-the-mill circulation coin and that this particular kind was produced between 1497 and 1566."

"Those dates fit perfectly for us, don't they?"

Beth partly dodged the question with one of her own. "I've checked the long-range forecast, and it looks hot, but good dry, digging weather. Can you drive back over to the farm this weekend for another crack?

July 24, 2015
Behind Alabimo Guest House
11:25 a.m.

"What type of large tree is over our head, a cedar?" Vicki asked as she took her red bandana and wiped her sweaty brow. In the brutal heat, the two women had been carefully excavating the opposite side of the mound from Beth's earlier dig. "Oh, this heat of your American South. It's almost unbearable. Growing up in Galicia, rarely did we see a summer day over 26."

"Math was never my favorite, but I recall from my recruiting trips that 26 Celsius is just under 80 degrees. I guess growing up here and then spending half my life standing on a concrete tennis court in the midday heat, I'm not saying I'm immune, but it doesn't bother me as much as other people," Beth answered as she grabbed a plastic water bottle and poured a minute amount on a clod of dirt. "So that helps and the shade of this tree over our head. Yes, it's a cedar tree by the way, since you asked." The packed-on filth came free of the object in her hand after the wash. "Well, I'll be, I think I have dug out a scaphoid."

"That is a bone in the wrist, no?" asked Vicki, maneuvering herself more under the limited shade.

Beth congratulated her on the correct assumption and then told her comrade she had another surprise. There'd still been enough daylight for her to begin yesterday evening and start excavating again. Beth said in her first ten minutes she made a major discovery; another complete human skull. It was in the house now, but she'd cleaned it and studied before going to bed.

Vicki had to ask, "Another Native American female?"

"No, and this is the interesting thing. My grid records showed me they were both at the same depth level. The discoloration due to age looked almost identical, but we've got different sexes and ethnicities. The second skull was male, likely the same age range of between twenty-five and forty, but not Native American; I found a European."

"Excuse my jumping off to a conclusion, but back in the old county, we all learned as school children of the great Spanish explorers, conquistadors and their routes of exploration. If the carbon dating is correct, at approximately the year 1550 you discovered a European…"

"You're too good, Vicki. You'd have no way of knowing, less than two miles from where we are right now is a little island in the Tombigbee River named De Soto Island."

"One of the great heroes from the history books of Espana."

"I'll take it a step further. The Native Americans knew how to tan buffalo hides, but did not make or know of leather, in the way we do. That beaten purse the coin was in? I had it examined, and it was, excuse me, it is genuine cow's leather. Look down, see this pinkish tint to the soil right there? That's cedar resin leaching into the soil and a little internet research told me Ph level of the sap is an excellent preservative. That's why a coin purse from almost 500 years ago hadn't dissolved away into nothingness."

Chapter 38
Changing Course

May 29, 2018
Alabimo
Kitchen table

    The academic semesters and graduation ceremonies for both Tulane and Alabama Polytech were done for the spring and Vicki and Beth were afforded valuable free time. Beth's tennis girls had unfortunately been eliminated from the postseason, too. Nearly three years had transpired since the discovery of the gold coin and the two human skulls. Beth had spent the first year reading the history, learning about the expedition of Hernando de Soto. In late 2016 she'd approached Vicki with a colossal favor.

    Beth, during that year, had learned most of the translated journals and extensive writings recording de Soto's journey through what is now the Southeastern United States, were in the Library of Congress and the University of Wisconsin. Luckily, she was able to access them both online. Additionally, school connections from a friend led her deeper into the history dept. at Wisconsin, where she learned of a little-known journal that quite possibly could be of importance to Beth and Vicki. The only problem was it was located in Spain and protected under lock and key at the main library in Salamanca, Spain. Here is where Beth needed help and luckily Vicki's now retired mother not only had the time, but energy and curiosity to be her daughter and Beth's eyes across the Atlantic Ocean.

    Over the next two years, Vicki's mother made the five hour train trip from Vigo to Salamanca eight separate times. Each time, showing her credentials in addition to being under the watchful eye of a live security guard and cameras, she studied under a strict time limit of thirty minutes and took notes from the original, private diary of Vasco Etchevarria: born Extremadura, 1524, died Salamanca 1590. Vasco Etchevarria, before settling down there and marrying, had explored the New World twice. The first time was with the ultimately ill-fated de Soto Expedition in 1539, of which he miraculously survived and returned to Spain. Later, he then accompanied the Pedro Marquez expedition in 1561 to explore the area that Americans know today as Pensacola, Florida west to the Mississippi River.

As Vicki's mother reached this one particular section deep into the Etchevarria Diary, she took meticulous notes, as Vicki had alerted her to be aware. Etchevarria had received permission from the leader, Marquez, to venture north for two days and search for someone from de Soto's exploration party twenty years before. In 1562, at the junction of two rivers, not far from the site of the great battle with Chief Tuskaluca and the still visible remains of his gigantic, burnt fort, Vasco discovered a native widow woman and her odd children. Over the years, the savage girl, as the diary referred to her, had learned rudimentary Spanish and recanted to Vasco how after the famous battle, a young Spaniard was left behind due to his wounded legs. Her name was Cantea and the two had lived together until his recent death. This man, first recorded by name, as Iacomus, made her a mother of four, twin girls and two sons, both of whom bore the same yellow hair and greenish eyes as their father. Further on in Vasco's writings he expressed relief in finding someone named Tiago's widow, but the simple savage female could not comprehend, or did not want to, reveal the location of the purse of Governor de Soto's private treasury. Vasco wrote that he knew this other man, named Gemmes, had been entrusted with the gold purse before the great battle with the Indios of this region. Vasco went back to Spain without any gold; only with the strange knowledge of Cantea's lineage of two blonde-haired boys and that a Spaniard had been buried in a simple earthen mound, two hundred paces east of a set of large, twin trees, alone in a clearing.

Now, here in May of 2018, Vicki had a lengthy letter from her mother that gave the intricate details of Vasco Etchevarria's diary. In those years, Beth had become steeped in the knowledge of the de Soto expedition's time in present-day Alabama, or as she was prone to intentionally call it in private, Alabimo. This evening, at the kitchen table over a bottle of imported wine, the two ladies toasted Vicki's reading of the informative letter aloud.

"I am forever indebted to Mother Cuevas, Vicki. She's a saint for all the fantastic work she did. I know that was quite a job and I can't thank her enough. I must send her a gift, be thinking of what she'd like, please. Ah, but, of course, now you know what's next?"

"Well, my madre has always enjoyed a challenge, especially where a biblioteca, I mean library, is involved. However, can it make sense that an extremely wealthy man like de Soto would go around with only one coin, I mean, Escudo?" Vicki said as she topped off her wine. "There will be more, no?"

"Yes, there has to be. We know for a fact there aren't any more in what remains of the mound. But you know what else? The exact spot of the big battle between Chief Tuscaloosa and Hernando de Soto has never been 100% verified. I think we can find it, my friend, and maybe the rest of the gold," Beth said as she saluted with her glass of Spanish wine.

June 2, 2019
Southern property edge of Alabimo Farm
7:15 a.m.

"Don't worry,Vicki, the cart got a full charge of electricity last night. We'll be fine out here. Besides, I brought Anthony's old .22 rifle. I keep it loaded, by the way, the safety is on, but still be careful."

"A rifle? Why?" Vicki asked as she held on for dear life in the front seat of the bouncing all-terrain four-wheeler. She turned in her seat to check on their equipment, behind them, in the small trailer. Beth had placed two shovels, two trowels, a metal detector and her hand-powered dirt sifter back there.

"I didn't want to say the 'S' word, but you're forcing me to...snakes."

"Oh, I could have done without hearing that, but I am anxious to try out the new metal detector."

"You're gonna like it, I did. It's a great improvement. Besides the wi-fi feature and built-in GPS, it will pick up size, depth and give us a 3-D image before we waste time digging up an old soup can," Beth said proudly of her new investment. She then pulled the off-road vehicle to stop under the skimpy shade of a lone, young pine tree, proceeded to pull out a crude map and lay it over the steering wheel. With her index finger, Beth traced a faint pencil drawing she'd done by overlaying an area map from 1830 to one her grandfather had at Alabimo. "See this, here's the Tombigbee today or in 1970 anyway. I did my best to draw in where it flowed in 1830. Sometime along the way it changed course and shifted west about two tenths of a mile."

"They have that ability?" Vicki asked.

"I'm no expert, but I guess the shifting of the river, or maybe *rivers*, is why no one has been able to find the site of de Soto's clash with the Choctaws."

Beth took her finger off the map and pointed out to the now grassy open plain where up until a decade ago her family had tilled and planted crops for almost 200 years. For Vicki to get the full effect of where they very well might be standing, she gave her a quick overview of the momentous battle between the Old and New World in October 1540.

As de Soto traveled looking for gold, he had subjugated, enslaved and killed thousands of Indians he encountered. Hearing of these strangers and angered by their brutal customs, Chief Tuscaloosa had gathered his entire nation, forming a huge army of warriors to stop the invaders. The actual fighting all started with an insult that prompted one Spanish officer to take his sword and slash off the arm of one of Tuscaloosa's emissaries.

Well-versed in the battle particulars, Beth told how Tuscaloosa divided his forces in an effort to surround de Soto, but the chief had no knowledge of the might and power of his enemy's technological advantages, such as armor, crossbows and guns. Nor could he have imagined the overwhelming strength of soldiers mounted upon war horses nor the deadly, highly trained war dogs.

Even with Tuscaloosa's numerical advantage of ten-to-one, the Choctaw forces were annihilated. Written accounts from de Soto's scribes told how the Indians sent 1500 men out of the fort and disappeared into the thick forest behind the stronghold. De Soto then marched upon the fort. The remaining 4500 plus Choctaw warriors preferred to battle man-on-man, eschewing the safety of their palisade and strode out into the Spanish trap where the cavalry and armored soldiers decimated the braves. At this time the hidden warriors from the forest came forth to the rear of de Soto, where his camp laborers, priests, porters and other non-combatants were positioned. They did great damage to the conquistadors' supplies and accouterments, but for the most part, the governor's personal guard protected the religious men and others. After de Soto had wiped out half of the warriors on the plain, the others retreated back to the fort. The witnesses said then the Spanish conquistador split his forces. His cavalry rode to the back and dealt with the 1500 native fighters to their rear. The rest of his soldiers deSoto used to surround and set fire to Tuscaloosa's wooden base. Some fled the flames to meet their end by the sword, including Tuscaloosa's only son, but the vast majority stayed with their revered leader and died in the fire.

"See, Vicki, this could be it. We very well might be standing where Hernando de Soto massacred 6000 Choctaw Indians."

"Six thousand?" echoed Vicki incredulously. "That's half the present enrollment at my school!"

"That's the number I kept reading. They now call it the Battle of Mabila, between de Soto and the Choctaw tribe in 1540. A couple of authors even went further saying that the number of Native American corpses de Soto's men counted after the fight might even be low, due to the great fire."

Vicki froze as she visualized the gruesome scene and instinctively, from her childhood upbringing, made the sign of the cross and in Spanish, softly whispered, "En el nombre del Padre, Hijo y del Epirto Santo." Beth paused from her map and even though not Catholic, crossed herself out of respect for the dead. No translation was needed.

"Here's the really incredible part of the battle; the Spanish losses. The witnesses recorded that every last, single Choctaw in the battle died but, get this, only twenty-two Spaniards lost their lives. Just twenty-two! Shows what gunpowder, horses, metal swords and armor can do against wooden clubs and bare skin."

The two exited the vehicle and using the patchwork map, Beth guided them. "Okay, not only did Vasco Etchevarria's diary mention it, but most of my other research did, too. They wrote that the huge palisade fort of Chief Tuscaloosa was located at the bottom of a "V" formed by two rivers. So even giving an error in my measurements by saying that two-tenths of a mile, we might possibly be the site of the battle…right here!"

"I'm with you," said Vicki, leaning in to see the map. "Should I begin with the metal detector?"

With an enthusiastic yes, the two slowly walked in grid-like pattern over the vacant field, only broken by the semi-eroded furrow humps from previous crops. Beth had packed an ice chest with water, protein bars and two peanut butter and jelly sandwiches. After utter exhaustion set in around 3:00 p.m. they started their ride home. Vicki was careful with their cardboard box now on her lap.

They had quite a productive day of finds. There were a number of lead balls, many small unidentifiable metal artifacts, a few glass beads, a couple of half-dirt-cake burned pieces of wood and some pottery shards. Carefully laid on a bed of two beach towels were a total of nineteen long bones, all human and four complete skulls. Carefully propped in the corner of the box were also two Mason jars of bone fragments. But the best find of the day had been the rusted, triangular metal blade of what appeared to be some sort of weapon. Beth made sure they used the GPS function on the metal detector when it was discovered to record its precise location.

Back on more or less level ground, Beth began to explain, "So, when human bones are subjected to fire, I'm not talking cremation temperatures, more like temperatures of a house fire, they dehydrate, crack and shatter. But in our case, we're not talking about a house fire, are we?"

"No, and I know from listening to you that the great Indian fort of the Choctaw warriors was eventually burned by de Soto's men. That type of a fire would be much as what you are saying is a house fire, no?"

"Exactly, hence those jars of bone fragments and those others are excellent artifacts. We'll of course need lab work, but I have a feeling."

"I too feel it, Beth, my friend."

January 3, 2020
West of Tensaw, Alabama
Parking lot of Fort Mims Tourism Center
3:15 p.m.

"Thank you so much for your time, Ranger Heath," Beth Travers-Demaret said, respectfully.

She'd recently begun using her hyphenated, maiden name when back in Clark County. It helped. The park ranger was probably at least seventy years of age, she noted and silently wondered as to why he was still working. Without her asking, she'd deduced that the ranger was a local product.

Bones of the Black Warrior

"Just doing my job, mam," the state-employed park ranger replied as he touched the rim of his campaign-styled, dark green hat. "Besides, I'm real interested-like to see your tomahawk," The two stood at the rear bumper of her Tahoe, as the ranger had requested they talk outside in the parking lot instead of inside the visitor center. To answer Beth's question, he'd alluded that he preferred to be in a private setting.

Over the past six months, Beth had become an expert on a long-ago battle that had taken place at the southern tip of her family property. Plus, she had the results of the many lab tests of her findings from last June. However, her research had, for the most part, produced a huge question. Solving the mystery was the main reason for meeting the park ranger.

All of her physical lab work and carbon dating was 300 years off and aroused her suspicions that she had not discovered the long-lost site of the Battle of Mabila. First, there weren't enough bones. Repeated trips to the tip of the property had yielded nothing close to the tremendous number of dead Choctaw. In fact, her European bone count was, again, far off. She had roughly 100 examples and of that a third were adult females and another third were children of both sexes. In her phone conversation earlier in the week with Ranger Heath, she'd kept her cards close to the vest and wanted to hear the state employee utter the words.

"The tomahawk is here in the back of the Tahoe," Beth said as she swung the double doors open to reveal the rusted blade laid out on a beach towel. "We gave it a date of plus or minus twenty-five years at 1800. I texted with a primitive weapon expert his opinion and he said the design reminded him of English army production around 1790 for use in America and beyond. He thinks it's War of 1812 era."

Agent Heath leaned in and looked carefully for a full minute but didn't touch the tomahawk. "Hmm, I'd tend to agree with that fella. You gave me the GPS coordinates when we talked on the phone and that's exactly right on the money for Fort Mims. I'll even go you one better than your weapons expert and say it was definitely used smackdab in 1813. Sure, it's British manufacture, I'm positive. They supplied 'em to the Creek Indians to kill white settlers. Not to go all gruesome on you, but you can even see the top half of the blade has a tiny, slight bend, like it hit something really hard."

"Like another human's skull?" volunteered Beth, in a tone denoting she wasn't the squeamish type.

"Yes, 'zactly. Burnt Hawk's bloodthirsty warriors killed 550 whites, 'bout which about 150 were soldiers, rest were civilians. 300 women and children and roughly another 100 white male farmers. They were all from around the area here. They rightly feared the Creeks would rise up and went to Mims a-seeking shelter. Gracious me, it was a *terrible* slaughter."

"Just awful. Such a terrible cruel tragedy. But, let me add a thank you as well. I was hesitant to say anything about the fort's location, but now that you did…" Beth resolutely stated before she let her sentence trail off.

Ranger Heath then explained why they were not inside the welcome center building. He said this fort was, of course, a replica as the original had been burned by the Creek Indian attackers on August 30, 1813. But more than that, the state's always slim budget forced this compromise, a half of a mile south of the actual massacre location. Those reasons were first, ease of access as the replica was just yards off State Highway 98, and second, the actual location was north of the confluence of the Alabama and Tombigbee, meaning a bridge would have been needed to be built, plus the site was on private land with no accessibility by car. It would have been financially impossible for the State Department of Archives to erect the facility at the actual location. Just wasn't feasible. So, in the end, Mr. Heath didn't want any tourists in the building to overhear that his facility was somewhat of a historical fraud.

Beth gave a knowing nod as his explanation made perfect sense. Her and Vicki's dig from the past few months was most definitely not Mabila. Instead of it being the site where the largest massacre of Native Americans *by white Europeans* occurred, they'd ventured under the soil into the exact opposite. Fort Mims had been the largest-ever massacre *of whites* by Native Americans in North America.

The park ranger again thanked her for bringing the tomahawk by and for keeping the state's local tourism draw a secret. He left and Beth buckled into her seat. As she did, she took her cell phone out and in the notes section, pulled up the real Fort Mims GPS coordinates: 31.10 north, 87.30 west. That mystery had been solved and it brought sadness to think of all the lives lost, killed 207 years ago, now definitely confirmed, on her family's property.

The stillness and utter silence inside the car gave her a moment of reflection. The ranger's description of the little children being butchered caused Beth to harken back to the 1963 Sixteenth Street Black church bombing and the devastating emotional effect she'd experienced. Placing her hand upon the gear shift lever, she couldn't help but wonder, had the wholesale carnage from 1540, which literally left behind thousands of human bones, also be located on her tract of land?

Same day
Friday, 4:05 p.m.
Gravel parking area behind Alabimo

Beth was surprised to see the light silver VW Jetta next to her normal parking spot. That was Vicki's car and the trunk was open. As she put the Tahoe in park, she saw her New Orleans friend coming down the walk from the back porch. Vicki spoke in an excited tone before Beth could even ask what she was doing there? They had not made arrangements for a meeting this weekend.

"Beth, I'm so sorry for showing up in the blue like this, but I had to. I received news from Madre Cuevas today, read it, packed a bag and got in my car. I'm ashamed to admit that I was so excited, I exceeded the speed limit the entire way."

"Well, that'll be our secret." Beth had never said a word, but secretly loved hearing Vicki's little innocent struggles with her second language, especially since her *own* Spanish wasn't worth a flip. "No, I'm glad you're here. Close your trunk and let's go into the kitchen. It's 5 o'clock somewhere."

"I have some news, my friend, great news to tell you," Vicki was giddy with excitement as she bounded up the flagstone walkway.

Once settled at the table with two glasses of wine, Vicki then proceeded to relay her exciting news. Her mother, back in 2018, had not wanted to mislead or confuse Beth and had intentionally skipped one small section in her translation of the old diary in Salamanca. There were a series of sentences which contained strange words that, to her, possibly had no modern equivalent, nor could she solve by research. In the time since, she'd been trying to obtain assistance to decode them to pass her findings on to her daughter. Just two days ago she finally heard back from a de Soto scholar at the University of Extremadura in Baladoz, Spain, which also held rare, original journals from the conquistadors' expeditions to the New World.

Vicki set the stage for her dramatic reveal.

"Okay, so she was able to have the strange words translated and just so I don't foul this up, I'm going to read from my madre's email. I printed it out." Vicki retrieved the folded paper and read, "This is 1562 and Vasco is in America and meets Cantea, the Indian girl, I mean Native American. Here, this is the part where before she'd gotten confused. Early on, Vasco had once used the term brother, then stopped, but at least we know there was a brother. So, this is where the university professor rescues us and it turns out, it wasn't so much a history about de Soto as it was Biblical history. Vasco's diary mentions another man and he begins using a Hebrew term in the Bible, 'Ya'akov.' That translates to Greek, 'Iakobos' which then later in Latin is 'Iacomus' which, stay away with me, becomes in French as 'Gemmes' and then translates to English as James."

"James?" Beth asked quizzically. "That doesn't sound like Vasco, unless he's feeding whatever future reader of his diary a lot of bull."

"Ok, you're with me. I didn't even go into part of Mother's email where she thought that this part of Vasco's was intentionally misleading. Like you, I thought James was a false lead and, by the way, there is no Spanish equivalent for that name. However, follow this; it appears in old Latin as 'Iacomus,' which gets familiarized as 'Iaco' in Spanish and over the course of time, that somehow turns into 'Tiago' and then later, the professor said around the year 1500, it becomes the name we all know today, Diego."

"Diego, common old Diego huh, really?"

"And my Madre went beyond expectations here. In no time she figured out these other names and events, such as Iaco had traveled to Mexico; that was pure deception. She and my Padre traveled back to a little village in Extremadura named, Jerez de Los Caballeros. They visited with the parish priest's secretary and were given many volumes of old birth records, going back hundreds of years. She wrote to me and said actually my Padre found it. He discovered Vasco was born there in 1524 and had a twin brother, Diego!"

"My God, Vicki, tell me please you aren't kidding. This is wonderful! Diego is who Vasco was talking about. Oh, oh, wait. Have you ever noticed? Of course you have, behind the house, they are so big you can see their tops, two gigantic and ancient cypress trees right by the family cemetery. Vicki, that's *the mound.* Diego was the skull we found after the big rain on the other side of it. We now have a name for our European skull; he is Diego Etchevarria!"

Beth extended her wine glass to toast her friend, they both rose up from their respective kitchen chairs and did so. All of a sudden, Vicki sat down and stared at the tabletop. "Beth, we have more than a man's name and his skull. Do you recall, when we first met and how I told you on the jet flight from Madrid to Atlanta, back in 2008?"

"Gosh, Vicki, we must've talked for hours on that flight, but I can tell from the look on your face that you remember. Spit it out."

"Well, I revealed my training as a geneticist, also of my keen interest in people's physical appearance and how at the tennis match, my sister looked like the American, with her blonde hair and you…"

"Oh yeah, now I remember that. Later on, I told you my brother's fair, blonde and green eyed, right?"

"Yes, and now we must think this all the way through, where are the wives of their deceased husbands generally buried? We know; right next to them. That's why, at this moment now, I need you to get your laptop, open the file and find the results of those teeth we studied from the skull you found in the creek and the skull from the mound. Me? I'm going upstairs for my DNA kit. We're going to draw some of your blood."

"Draw my blood? Why?" Beth paused and thought about a sip, "right now?"

"Yes now. We shall see if you're the direct line of descendants from Diego Etchevarria, a son of the Old World and Cantea, his Indian wife, a daughter of the New."

"Oh my, this is…first I need to sit down," Beth said to herself, now alone in the kitchen. "Wait, I need a pen. I have to write all this down in the family journal. They'll never believe it, but I'm writing it down anyway."

January 10, 2020
North of Oak Hill
Alabama State Highway 21 south

Heading down to Alabimo for the weekend, Beth saw an incoming call on the screen of her 2016 Tahoe. Recognizing the 504 prefix area code, she knew it was Vicki. "Hola, Doctora Cuevas. Como esta?"

"A nice attempt, yes, but your Alabama accent doesn't work in Castilian. Just kidding, my friend. I had to call as soon as the lab results came back." Vicki then proceeded to inform Beth of the results of her blood work against the previous findings from the European and Native American skulls. Trying to keep the jargon to a minimum, although she had thrown in one string, "polymerase chain reaction confirmation by the amelogenin marker," and quickly apologized.

"Can you give me an idea, your opinion, of my sample tests versus the artifacts?"

"I'm seventy-five percent certain that you, Beth, share ancestry with both skulls. While that may sound promising, I could run my own blood work and likely find a thirty-three chance with the European skull and even a one or two percent commonality with the Native."

"I'm sure glad I have a friend in the business that speaks straight and not about poly chain reactions," Beth teased as she briefly floored the big V-8 engine to pass a creeping tractor on the two lanes. "Is there another test we could try? Something to give us a higher percentage?"

"Hmm, you know, I thought you might suggest that. What we really need is a true base. A sample of both teeth and long bones from a relative of yours that possessed the strong mixture of European and Native traits."

"In the family journal, there's a passage from the 1850s and I guess he'd be my triple-great-grandfather. His name was Ward Travers, and the journal says, although he tried to keep it hidden, the secret of his being born to Native American parents came out."

"I will keep my mouth closed at this point, but..." Vicki let her words trail off.

"Wait? Exhume Grandpappy Ward and test his DNA? No, no way Jose, her voice rising in volume. "We'll just stand pat and be satisfied with seventy-five percent."

"I am very happy you did not make me ask that, Beth. From where did you obtain all this wisdom?" laughed Vicki. The subject of testing any of the Travers' old bones never came up again.

Bones of the Black Warrior

May 4, 2020
Mobile International Airport
Delta Airlines waiting area

"You know Vicki, we've talked about this idiotic Covid farce before, hey but there's a silver lining here. We're saving a little money because of the hysterics." Beth bent down, the thought of money making her aware of her purse down at her feet, picked it up and placed it in her lap.

"You're right, Beth. All of this is so silly, wearing a flimsy, drug store paper mask and standing six feet apart. They take us for fools, no?"

"Like a microbe will stay exactly here," Beth pointed to an empty seat two down, "but not be transported by the breeze another inch away," as she touched her own leg. "Silly, utter silliness."

"The silver lining is that?"

"Sorry, I left you without finishing my thought. No, with both Tulane and Poly cancellations of in-person grad ceremonies, we can get over to Europe before the height of the tourist season."

"I follow you now. The prices, they are lower for flights and rooms right now," nodded Vicki.

The clerk at the ticket counter made an announcement that paused their conversation, but it did not pertain to their flight to Atlanta. When they resumed talking, they were off the Covid subject, which to both of the learned women was an insult to their intelligence. Beth had been tempted to rail again and complain about the Collegiate Tennis Athletic Association canceling all member schools' 2020 tennis season but decided to save Vicki her vitriol on the ridiculous politics of Covid.

Instead, Beth thought this was the perfect time to reveal to Vicki her big news about work. On her recommendation last week, the Alabama Polytech athletic director promoted Isabella Diaz from Assistant Women's Tennis Coach to Head Coach. Beth had initially told him this would be a good time for her to hang up the racquet and the whistle, but he convinced her to stay on as Isabella's assistant coach for one last year. With glee, she added that unless Brad Pitt or George Clooney proposed marriage, when she left Poly, her intentions were to open Alabimo as a bed and breakfast.

Vicki replied she was thrilled to hear that news, as Beth deserved to slow down running around a tennis court at forty-four, offered her congratulations and announced she'd be buying a bottle of champagne tonight for a mini celebration. Vicki laughed, quickly corrected herself and stated tonight, when in Spain, they'd celebrate with Cava, not French champagne.

With heartfelt thanks, Beth then moved the conversation back to their whole reason for being here at the airport. The two considered themselves a team and while there was no real opponent, they wanted to beat their common enemy, the mystery of de Soto's gold. As they already owed Madre Cuevas too much for her diligent and dogged earlier research, they could not impose on her any further. They would take it from here themselves. A grad assistant at the University of Wisconsin, who'd assisted Beth back in 2018 with her research, had requested to be Facebook friends, to which she accepted. Recently, he'd been doing more research on Spanish explorers in the American South and made a tantalizing post there this past April.

He'd been examining the papers of the Pedro Marquez journey in 1561. The student admitted his research was incomplete because the online material referring to the historical documents was not fully available and only half-translated into English. His last throwaway sentence had been the inspiration for their trip today. The post from Madison said the only way to test his suspicions would be to personally study at the library in Salamanca and also be fluent in Spanish. Beth felt inspired, not only for academic reasons, but if this Badget State kid's speculation was true; it might possibly be the final tool to find de Soto's purse. After all, the grad scholar had laid it out on his Facebook page, when he stated if he had the resources, he could discover a cache of Spanish doubloons, hidden for 480 years, once the personal property of Hernando de Soto.

Before Vicki had agreed to accompany Beth to Spain, she'd asked for her Alabama friend to completely present her case as to why this trip was necessary. Beth complied, of course, over the phone ten days ago. Vicki, who'd been nicknamed a Doubting Thomasina, long ago by some of her American college friends was seeking reassurance. "Beth, tell me now, again face-in-face, *all* the reasons we're making this journey?"

Smiling sweetly, Beth took her friend's hand in hers and agreed. Enthusiastically, she recited them.

Bones of the Black Warrior

"First the U of W student plainly states in the chronicles taken by Pedro Marquez' personal secretary, that Vasco Etchevarria made a side trip north of Mobile Bay. Second, Vasco's personal diary mentions it, so credible source number two. Next, the Travers' family journal has entries of Spanish gold on the property and fourth, Vasco's diary intentionally tries to mislead readers, he wants it all to himself. Alan, in Wisconsin, just disclosed when Vasco wrote the gold came back from America in 1544, it went to support the church in his hometown, Church of San Mateo. Alan posted that's outright deception; there's no church by that name in Jerez de la Caballeros. Next, everybody knows people can't keep a secret, if someone had already found it, they'd surely brag. Then, we both know de Soto had to have been extremely wealthy. Why, his portion from the Peru conquest in modern dollars would be thirty-plus million. And I saved the best for last, I've been holding out on you with this tidbit, the name of the grad student in Wisconsin?"

"Yes, I remember, Alan."

"Well, his full name is Alan Etchebarren. You heard me right. Etchebarren is the Americanized version of Vasco and Diego's last name."

"Interesting, yes, and important, why?"

"Odds are the Travers' aren't the only family with an old treasure tale. I think someone in his ancestry planted a seed in Alan Etchebarren's head and *he's* trying to discover lost gold. I've looked through the old family diary plenty of times, but never do any of my ancestors mention finding gold. But back to my Wisconsin contact; his problem is, like a lot of his generation, he keeps posting every little aspect of his life on Facebook."

"We must hurry," Vicki said in all seriousness.

Chapter 39
Treasure and Bones

May 11, 2020
Behind Alabimo
6:45 a.m.

The two women walked carefully through the gravel parking lot behind the Travers' old family home, not really having a destination in mind. Both Beth and Vicki nursed a mug of coffee and enjoyed remnants of a brilliant sunrise. This time of year, if one wanted to walk outdoors and not return home soaking with sweat, it had to be really early or late. Not wanting the morning dew to dampen their shoes, they stopped at the rocky drive's edge.

Vicki asked Beth if she made arrangements for the closest big cypress to be taken down professionally. The giant was dead and in pitiful shape due to the lightning from six years prior. All of the bark was gone. The large and medium-sized limbs, more water-logged with each rain, had grown too heavy to support and fallen off. Beth replied it was ironic for her friend to mention the tree as she'd only called a tree removal service the day before. It had become dangerous to walk under the dead giant. Then she changed the subject.

"Vicki, you don't know how much I appreciate you. All you do. I have no idea what I would have done in Spain without my friend. And it's everything, not just your handling of all the language problems for me."

"Think nothing of it, besides that's what friends are for," Vicki said before gingerly sipping.

"I'm sorry in a way. I was excited. You were excited all the way over, then when we researched in Salamanca and in Jerez de la Caballeros, too. It all went away."

"Up to a point, yes. Then, caboose! I believe your saying is chasing the golden goose?"

"Kaboom! A wild goose chase," Beth corrected without correcting. "Of all the reasons and leads we chased, the one I never doubted was de Soto himself. Did you?"

"No never. Everyone knows his being in Peru with Francisco Pizzaro made him wealthy. De Soto was a rich man."

"Keyword there being *was* and good ole Vasco never gave up. He tried to mislead everyone but got lazy. The San Mateo church is only three miles north of Caballeros and San Miguel."

"Not so good at the sneakiness, no?"

"Well, you made the big discoveries, Vicki. All those long hours studying those old microfiche records. Gosh, I was worried your eyeballs were going to give out on you. You did it girl, I am so tempted to go on Facebook and message Alan Etchebarren with the news."

"In Salamanca we learned that King Carlos grew disillusioned with the New World. There was great expense funding the expeditions, the fleet, the mines in South America only to lose so many ships to pirates and storms."

"You also saw that tiny footnote that took us to the fact that King Charles implemented a new, ambitious man in charge of the silver mines in Andalusia and gold from the Cantabrian Mountains in Castile."

"Don't forget the easy picnicking. Before, the valuables that had been readily taken from the Aztecs and Incas, were all gone. Wealth was more difficult to obtain."

"Easy pickings, yes. Couldn't just waltz in, hold a ruler hostage and have rooms filled up with gold for a ransom, anymore. That and like you said, pirates and hurricanes, less expense and risk to mine in your own backyard," Beth said.

"Carlos had all the power. The crown had an agreement with de Soto, not his heirs or widow, so when Hernando died in the New World, he just didn't pay."

"And then, Vicki, you hit the jackpot or lack of a jackpot is a better description when we went to Jerez de la Caballeros. It took us nearly two full days, but you went through all the Church of St. Michael's financial records from 1537 to what?"

"De Soto's money ran out quickly. By 1544, just two years after his death on the Mississippi River. The historians saw the royal records stating the Crown would pay X amount to de Soto, for his assistance to Pizarro in

Peru. And evidently, they assumed Carlos *actually* paid that amount. The one everyone believes would be equal to the 37 million in today's dollars. But he simply did not do it."

"And of all the things, everything you read and researched, going back to Vasco's and his writings confirm that in 1539 the great de Soto was more or less broke. The men, ships and materials the king offered were about one-third of what Hernando believed he needed, so he made up the other two-thirds out of his own pocket. Well, that ended up breaking him."

"He assumed he'd be paying himself back with more gold and silver taken from the New World. His greed, because he'd financed the two-thirds majority of his expedition, was plainly written by his secretary, that he'd keep a corresponding share, rather than give anything over one-third to King Carlos."

"Greed, one of the seven deadly," offered Beth as she raised her now empty cup in mock salute. "Well partner, we won't find any gold treasure, because there's none to find."

"I know sometimes my English, well, some words escape, but I just want to make this statement. I believe we did find treasure. You and I, my friend. We did something together; we learned many things and created many treasured memories in our shared experiences."

"Vicki, your English is muy fabuloso. That was a beautiful thing to say, my friend."

May 25, 2021
Family plot behind Alabimo
5:05 p.m.

"Darry, I took the liberty of taking a spray can out here and marking the four corners to my brother's resting place," Beth said somberly. "We had a choice of putting him next to Mama or Daddy, and his widow chose that one, next to Mama. I let her pick, but if I had, I'd have gone right opposite."

"Not a problem. Good idea so we don't have any mix up," Darry Johnson, II said as he placed a foot on the step up on his backhoe to climb into the driver's seat.

Bones of the Black Warrior

(Henrietta Gray and Jackson George Johnson had been married in 1968. George, since Henrietta already had a career, moved to Atlanta. Henrietta took advantage of a new government program for business loan guarantees directed toward minorities. On a good hunch, she purchased land near a new development called Lenox Square. There, in a relatively undeveloped section on Peachtree Road, northeast of Atlanta, in an area called Buckhead, her loan provided her the opportunity to build a sixty-room motel. Two years later, a son was born, and they agreed he'd been named for her first love and in his deceased brother's honor, Darry the second.)

At this point in life, Darry, at fifty-one years old, relished being able to wear jeans, boots and a T-shirt on a Tuesday. Too many seven-day work weeks in a full suit, working at the family's up-class motel. But now, he had a son, Cleo, who handled the day-to-day motel duties. Henrietta and George had prospered so in the fifty years of ownership and frugal living, they had left Darry a considerable inheritance. Wanting to have a country escape from the big city, he'd bought a ramshackle, overgrown small farm in the southern tip of Clark County, Alabama; the old Johnson Farm where his father and namesake had been raised. Not wanting strangers for neighbors, Anthony and Beth bought the property from George Johnson when he inherited the land after Lutilly's death in 2005. George certainly didn't want it; his promise to never return remained still intact.

(Jackson George Johnson never spoke about that day from March 1957. Frank McClain had set him to be the patsy. Frank knew about Joe, his violent streak, Tilly's con job on him, and if the VA ever let him come home, he'd kill her. Frank sent young Jackson over at the right time, called Tilly's old woman neighbor, also at the right time, and allowed the teen's eventual arrest and second-degree murder trial. The Johnsons were just lucky this time. The hung jury saved Jackson. An acquittal made no difference to the Klan; they just never got Jackson before he left Clark County. Another mouth that never opened was Doug Travers. He felt his younger brother had his life-sentence already and Frank's death-sentence-cancer was justice also being served)

Darry had refurbished and vastly improved the property value over the past four years. Now with occasional leisure time, he had all the toys on his farm; a bass boat, a four-wheeler, four-wheel drive pickup, a Harley-Davidson Road King motorcycle, a mini tractor and this backhoe. Beth had befriended Darry and occasionally called in favors at Alabimo Bed and Breakfast. In return, she looked after his place when he returned to Buckhead. She'd offered him cash compensation for excavating a grave for Anthony Travers Demaret who died of a heart attack four days ago in L.A. Typically, Darry refused anything.

"You know the correct, legal depth, right Darry? Oh, here's a bottle of water I brought out for you. Not even June and we hit 94 earlier today," Beth said, as she stood upon the eleven-foot-wide stump of the removed cypress mammoth. Warily, she stepped down and approached Darry, now seated. He nodded, took the plastic bottle, thanked his neighbor and cranked the diesel engine. He gave a quick salute, Beth couldn't manage a response and walked back to the big house. The digging event was something too sad to witness.

Darry worked the levers, and the iron teeth of his bright yellow machine took their first bite of soil. Darry Johnson II had no idea that a gigantic case of the 'what ifs' spanning 481 years had just occurred. If Beth had chosen the spot for Anthony's grave. If Beth had not walked away, stood there and watched the backhoe bucket dig down about three feet. Just those two odd and slight differences would have changed so many things for Beth's next entry into the old family journal.

Beth's grandfather, Doug Travers, and his old Army surplus metal detector had one fortunate stroke of luck, back on a cold January day in 1958. Just fiddling around really, he'd had a loud metallic hit emanating from the mound behind the guest house. Almost embarrassed that anyone might catch him digging, he nonetheless did. A short while later revealed a very worn leather pouch with fifty silver Spanish undated coins. This momentous discovery happened while he'd been reading the journal's record of the 1893 bank failures. Lost family money and lessons therein were fresh in his mind.

All too familiar with the term and actuality of the word 'scuttlebutt' from his days in the service, Doug quietly found three empty soup cans in the trash, reused them as vessels for his silver coins and moved them to the opposite side of the two cypress trees that for so long had anchored the family cemetery. He told no one, not even the family journal. The coins had value, that he knew, just not exactly how much. But should ever the day come, an unforeseen, unthinkable emergency; the Travers family would have these coins as insurance against calamity. Then, before he'd silently promised to record his discovery of the Spanish silver in the journal, he'd been tragically killed.

Beth never knew that if Darry's shovel was a mere five feet towards the house, her quest to solve Alabimo's treasure mystery, not of de Soto gold, but of his cavalry captain's soup-canned silver, would have been solved. If the backhoe's digging had continued down further, another foot or so, to reveal an aged, extraordinarily long femur, radius and ulna - those of an abnormally tall Native American - the famous Tuscaloosa: The Black Warrior, were right there.

No longer was Beth, the last of the Travers' line, enticed to search for treasure; in her opinion, she and Vickie had proven it never existed beyond one single coin. Fate dealt a second cruel hand when she also missed the long-sought bones of the greatest of all Choctaw chiefs and finally solved the riddle of the location of the historical battle between Tuscaloosa and de Soto.

As one ancient cypress died and was removed, the other remained. A witness to the saga of conquistadors, Indians, wars, freed slaves, good harvests and bad, two centuries of Travers'; the long silent bones of Choctaw, Creek, French, African-Americans, Americans and notable forgotten events at latitude 31 north, longitude 87 west, who continued to live on in the present and the past.

ABOUT THE AUTHOR

Fifth-generation Mississippian and recently retired banker, White was a long-ago history major when there wasn't as much material to memorize, is an Alabama grad, that also attended Ole Miss. Married with three children, six grandchildren, three stepchildren and six step-grandkids, he enjoys going to the gym and sometimes even excercises. When not writing, White keeps busy reading Southern History and discovering little-known minutiae therein. "Bones of The Black Warrior" is his fourth book.

THANK YOU FOR READING!

If you enjoyed this book, we would appreciate your customer review on your book seller's website or on Goodreads.

Also, we would like for you to know that you can find more great books like this one at www.CreativeTexts.com

Doug White

www.ingramcontent.com/pod-product-compliance
Lightning Source LLC
Chambersburg PA
CBHW070639100726
47907CB00007B/2043